GRACE IN DEEP WATERS

BOOK 3

CHRISTINE DILLON

www.storytellerchristine.com

Grace in Deep Waters

Copyright © 2019 by Christine Dillon

This book is a work of fiction. Names, characters, any resemblance to persons, living or dead, or events is purely coincidental. The characters and incidents are the product of the author's imagination and used fictitiously. Locales and public names are sometimes used for atmospheric purposes.

Cover Design: Lankshear Design.

ISBN: 978-0-6485890-0-6

For my parents—thankfully you are nothing like William and Blanche. Thank you for your model of how to follow Jesus, your love, and your decades of prayer. I am blessed to be your daughter.

As missionaries, part of the cost for you was boarding school for us children. Thank you to the many other parents who looked after me at Chefoo School and Faith Academy. My heavenly Father taught me much through each of you.

And in memory of my grandfather, Robert Reginald McCredie (1910-1995). Potter and master craftsman. I thought of you often as I wrote the scenes in the workshop with Reg. I wish I'd had the courage to ask you to teach me woodwork.

NOTES TO READERS

* This book is unashamedly Christian. All books are written from a worldview, be it secular, communist or New Age. If you're not a Christian the views expressed by the characters might appear strange BUT it's a great opportunity because it allows you to see things from a new perspective. Are the character's views consistent and does their worldview make sense of the challenges in their lives?

* Christian authors are told not to put miracles in their stories. This seems like peculiar advice since God is a God of miracles. One of the reasons for this advice is that people don't want to raise the false expectation that God will always work miracles. Sometimes he chooses not to. Any miracles in this book are based on real life examples.

* This is an Australian story and thus may contain unfamiliar spelling, grammar, punctuation and word usage.

* Some of this book is set on Lord Howe Island. I apologise for any errors and for any times the needs of the story trumped the real place.

PROLOGUE

11 November 1944
Sydney, Australia

*T*he radio dominated the room. All gleaming wood and intriguing metal dials.

William zeroed in on it, ignoring all the people, desks, and type-writers crammed into his father's office. This was the first time he'd ever been allowed here, although Ian, his older brother, was always welcome.

William reverently stroked one finger across the radio's wooden case.

"Careful son," his father said.

"He won't hurt it, Mr Macdonald." William could hear a smile in the lady's voice. His face warmed and he looked around at the people eating and drinking out of tall glasses. The kind lady offered him the plate of crackers. William looked towards his father, who nodded. He took a cracker and thanked the lady. Mum always insisted he show good manners.

"Nearly time," said someone at the back of the room. His father pulled out his fob watch and then came forward to switch on the radio. It crackled to life.

"One hundred thousand people packed into Flemington race track today. Good sports and good sorts." The marching music in the background and the way the radio announcer emphasised the words sent reverberations into William's stomach. "The bookmakers' area is seething with punters."

Yesterday he hadn't known what all these words meant, but last night his father had explained what would happen today and had given him strict instructions about how to behave. Being too noisy or behaving like a hooligan would get him sent home.

"Bookmaker." William whispered the word to himself. Dad wasn't a betting man. Said it was a game for mugs but he allowed something called a sweepstake at the office and he'd promised both boys a ticket—against their mother's protests. Dad picked him up, sat him on the edge of one of the desks, and handed him a slip of paper with the number four and one word written on it.

It was a strange word and William didn't know if he could pronounce it correctly, but he knew it must be the name of a horse. S-i-r-i-u-s. He looked over Ian's shoulder and read his horse's name —Peter. Dad said the first three horses would win money—a whole shilling for the winner. William could hardly imagine it. He never won anything. Ian might have been only two years older, but he was bigger and faster and smarter. He always came out on top, and Dad was always there to clap enthusiastically.

"And the ladies," the radio announcer said. "A sea of blue and green, red and pink. Whoops!" The announcer's voice rose. "There goes someone's hat."

Who cared about ladies and their hats? William swung his legs and clipped the side of the desk. His father glared at him over his glasses, and William froze. He mustn't mess up his first visit to Dad's office.

People said his father was a successful man. He supposed Dad was, since he was boss of this office and had a big car and house, but William wished they saw him more. Dad almost always arrived home after William and Ian had eaten. By the time his father finished dinner, William was in bed and only Ian got the chance to talk to him. The weekends weren't much good either for kicking a ball around or getting help with his train set, because Dad spent all his time attending Ian's sports matches, instructing the gardener, or reading the newspaper.

Mum said they were lucky to have Dad home at all. Half the boys at school had fathers away in Europe, fighting.

"They're coming out now. Twenty-three of the nation's finest horses. Look at the sheen on their coats. Look at the way they prance and fight the bit. They know what's coming—Australia's greatest race."

William couldn't control a tiny wriggle. The announcer sounded so excited, and all the adults were motionless, staring at the radio like they didn't want to miss a single word.

"Two miles of speed and glory. Two miles of agony and ecstasy. Two miles to prove who's champion."

The announcer reeled off information about each horse. William glanced down at the paper cradled in his hand. He was only interested in …"Number four—"

William sat up straight.

"Sirius, ridden by Darby Munro and owned by Reg Turnbull, our very own Chairman of the Victorian Racing Club. Three to one favourite." William's stomach fluttered. The numbers meant nothing, but favourite sounded promising. If only his horse would win.

"Ladies and gentlemen, the 1944 Melbourne Cup is about to begin. May our boys be home from the front to watch the next one." The announcer's voice went sombre for a moment. Dad said the tide of the war had turned, and Hitler would soon be running for cover. Course he would. How could he stand up against the great British Empire and the Americans?

A gunshot sounded, and William jumped in his seat.

"They're off!" The microphone squealed. "A great start to the 1944 Cup."

William had seen last year's race on a newsreel, and he could picture the horses all bunched together.

"Clayton has settled down near the fence."

He didn't care about Clayton. Where was Sirius?

"As they pass the two furlongs post for the first time, Clayton is out front by two or three lengths. In second place is Judith Louise, and Sirius in third place."

Sirius had a chance. William clenched his fist around the slip of paper. *Come on, Sirius.*

"As they come to the third furlong, Sirius is moving up." The commentator's voice sped up. "He's looking in control."

Come on, Sirius.

"Two furlongs from home, and Sirius is still in the lead."

Could he do it? Could he win?

"Sirius now a length and a half in front. Cellini in second and Peter coming up on the outside."

Not Peter. Any horse but Peter.

The commentator's voice rose in a crescendo. "Peter on the outside has thrown out a challenge. He's surging forward."

William squeezed his eyes shut, clenched his jaw, and willed Sirius on. *Go, go.*

"Peter is closing the gap. He's closing the gap."

William wanted to vomit.

"Sirius is being ridden for dear life. Can he hold his lead?"

Come on. Come on. William pounded his fists on his knees. *You have to win.*

"And it's Sirius by a head," the commentator finished, his words breathless. "Peter in second and Cellini third."

William pumped his fist in the air and flashed a smile at his brother. Finally. A win. He jumped off the desk and waved his paper. "Sirius won! He won!"

A whole shilling. What could he do with a whole shilling? Maybe buy the model aeroplane he'd been staring at for weeks in the shop window. Or maybe he'd keep the money and treasure it. He bounced up and down. Today he'd beaten Ian for the first time, and he didn't intend it to be the last. Dad often told them "no one remembers who is second."

Well, Sirius would be remembered, and maybe, just maybe, his father would notice him at last.

CHAPTER 1

Late 1990s
Sydney, Australia

illiam had buried his youngest daughter three days ago.

He hadn't technically done the burying, but she was buried nonetheless, and now it was 9:59 on Sunday morning. William rolled his shoulders and took a breath to relax himself. His church leaders had urged him to take the month off, assuring him everyone would understand.

Everyone might understand, but William couldn't do it. Sit in the house and stare at the wall? Never. He'd go crazy. Much better to be in his normal environment, here at church. Doing what he loved and what people loved him to do.

The music swung into the bridge to announce his entrance. William braced himself. As he heard the last notes, he strode from behind the curtain and across the stage. The lights blinded him for the first few seconds.

Out there were his people. His congregation. Every week he

provided them with the spiritual food they longed for. Every week he went home pumped up, having sent them home happy, replete with the words he'd digested and regurgitated for them.

William scanned the people in front of him. Years ago, his mentor had taught him to concentrate on a small selection of representative people. Make them feel he was speaking especially for them. It was a technique he'd perfected, one of the secrets of his success. And he was successful. Victory Church had been dying when he'd started here, and now look at it. Thousands of members. Sure, some left each year, but this church wasn't about those who couldn't fit in. There were plenty of other places for those kinds of people. This was a church for winners. People like William.

A winner? Really? What about Blanche?

He mentally squelched the questions before they could bloom into doubt. Blanche would be back home soon. They'd had a ding-dong all-guns-blazing fight, but she'd understand he'd been under pressure. Blanche knew his foibles—she'd been married to him long enough. She'd come around in time. She always did—not that she disagreed with him often. In fact, she'd only become argumentative the last few weeks. That was Esther's influence, but Esther wouldn't be influencing anyone any more.

William shivered. Esther was another thing he didn't want to think about. Time to pull himself together. Do what he did best.

"This is the seventh of our sermons on heroes of the faith." Noah and Abraham. Joseph and Moses. Joshua and Gideon. This morning it was David's turn.

"The Philistines came out to fight against the Israelites. They occupied one hill and the Israelites another, with a valley in between the two armies." He gave a quick summary to give the context. A few years ago he'd done training with a professional storyteller and learned people preferred hearing stories over a dry Bible reading. Telling stories meant he could skip the tongue-twisting names and jazz things up a little. Those biblical authors had written for a different audience. A different culture in more primitive times. Nowadays he needed to keep the stories short and snappy.

"The Philistines sent out their champion, Goliath. He was three metres tall and wore bronze armour weighing nearly sixty kilos." William hefted an imaginary spear. "His spearhead alone weighed seven kilos."

The men in the congregation loved these details. They sat up taller as though they were shouldering their own armour.

"Goliath stood and shouted, 'Choose a man and have him come down to me. If he is able to fight and kill me, we will be your subjects, but if I overcome him, you will become our subjects.'"

William used his voice to project the Israelites' fear, the Philistines' bravado. The congregation gazed at him with rapt expressions, and the teenager in the front row shivered. Good. He was in top form, despite the dramas of the last few days. Another person in the third row jerked back as the imaginary stone flew through the air and landed in the centre of Goliath's forehead. Exactly the kind of reaction he was after. He should have been an actor.

William had practiced his story ten times the day before. It kept his mind off other things like the emptiness of the house without Blanche and wondering when she'd be home. If Blanche stayed away more than a week or two, the elders were going to start asking questions. Awkward questions. He'd already had to evade several curious church members who wanted to know why they hadn't seen Blanche for a few weeks. It was none of their business, and he had managed to palm them off with the excuse of a sick relative. Not a lie. Specifics would lead to questions about why he wasn't with his wife. Maybe he should send flowers to her. Women usually appreciated flowers when they were upset.

"'So David triumphed over Goliath with a sling and a stone.

CHRISTINE DILLON

Without a sword in his hand, he struck down the Philistine and killed him.'"

William had memorised the line because the rhythm was perfect. Sometimes even he couldn't improve on those biblical writers. He paraphrased the next part. "Then David ran over and stood above Goliath. He took Goliath's own sword and hacked off his head." Hacked sounded so much better than cut. "When the Philistines saw their hero was dead, they turned and ran. And so Israel conquered the Philistines."

The story had already taken a quarter of his sermon time. This week he hadn't been able to concentrate to prepare his normal quality of content. Instead, he'd focused on polishing what he had and working out a memorable title and section headings. All the content in the world wasn't much help if he bored people to death.

"Do you have giant-sized issues in your life? Issues that seem insurmountable? Issues well beyond your own ability to deal with?" Rhetorical questions, relevant to people's everyday lives, were one of his favourite ways to start. They snared people's interest from the first line. Pertinent questions, plus humour, plus stories, equalled a perfect formula for success. It was something he was drilling into Nick, his protégé.

"Know your enemy." William enunciated his first point. He listed off possible enemies—sickness, difficult people or work challenges. His listeners nodded. He avoided mentioning cancer. Would anyone notice? If only Esther had shown more faith. Her prayers had been half-hearted from the start.

But yours weren't.

Where had this pesky thought come from? There had to be some explanation for why Esther hadn't been healed.

All over the auditorium, people were maintaining eye contact as he launched into his second point, "Know your God." This was a point he made so often, he had to work hard to make it sound new. After all, he couldn't say "God is powerful" every week.

Nick frowned from the front row. William would have to speak to him after the service. He and Nick were as close as a father and son, but Nick couldn't appear to disagree with William. Not in public. Disunity among staff members destroyed churches. Ripped them apart. That was one reason Esther had had to leave. Her doubts threatened everything he'd built.

A shiver of sadness slithered through him. If only she had dealt with her giants and come home.

As usual, the congregation were eating out of his hand by the end of the final point, "Nail your giant." He had them repeat the phrase several times. The final shout would probably have registered on the Richter scale. Thirty minutes of speaking, and he felt like he'd completed an Ironman race.

The musical postlude swelled, and William sat down on the preacher's chair and mopped his brow with his handkerchief. That had gone well. He bowed his head to pray and his coat rustled. He'd absentmindedly slipped the envelope he'd found on his church desk this morning into the inner pocket. It had been more than twenty years since he'd seen his mother's handwriting. She'd stopped writing to him after he'd marked half a dozen of her letters 'return to sender'. Why would she be writing to him now? Considering its timing, the letter wouldn't say anything he wanted to hear. He should toss it and be done with it.

But what if it was from Esther? A pressure rose in his throat, and he covered his mouth lest it erupt. They'd exchanged hard words recently, but she'd always been tractable. It wouldn't be like her to hold a grudge. He'd open the letter in a heartbeat if it was from Esther, but that wasn't likely. The letter was probably a lecture from his mother, and he wasn't in the mood for lectures. He pushed the envelope deeper into his pocket.

He'd put it in a safe place and read it when he was in the right mood.

Whenever that would be.

CHAPTER 2

A magpie carolled outside Blanche's bedroom window. She groaned, turned over, and squinted in the sunlight.

She'd never felt less like birdsong and sunshine. It had only been four days. Four days since thirty years of loving had been reduced to a pile of ashes.

The days before the funeral had been full of frantic activity. Now it was too quiet. Eerie. Hushed. Like there'd been a city-wide blackout.

Blanche stretched, feeling the welcome pull along her back and down her legs. Last night she'd collapsed, exhausted. Exhausted from trying to hold herself together. Exhausted from planning a funeral. Exhausted from pain and grief and despair. And joy. Esther had died well.

It was living with her death which was proving hard.

A great bubble of grief pushed up Blanche's throat and squeezed her heart, but tears no longer came. The well was cried dry. She ached in every joint and muscle like someone had beaten her with a meat tenderiser. She had given everything she had these last few weeks. If only she didn't have to get out of bed. Ever again.

What was there to get up for? Blanche had nothing. No job, no goals, no purpose. What did a mother do when her daughter died?

The kettle whistled in the kitchen. Her mother-in-law was up. Blanche might not want to get out of bed, but she couldn't stay here and drown in her memories. She needed activity. Everything might feel pointless without Esther, but they still needed food and a clean house, and Naomi was too old to carry any more burdens.

Blanche rolled out of bed, feeling every stiff muscle and joint. She took the dressing gown down from behind the door and trudged out to the kitchen.

"Morning," Naomi said, the lines on her face even deeper today. "I won't ask you how you slept."

Blanche nodded as tears filled her eyes. So the well wasn't dry after all. She turned her face away. How were they going to get through this?

"Rachel's about to head off to work."

Blanche sniffed, a habit she hated in others. "I envy her. I have no idea what's next for me."

Naomi handed her the marmalade. "Why don't we start with something to eat?"

They busied themselves with bowls and spoons, teacups and toast. The minutiae of daily life.

"Let's eat on the verandah," Naomi said.

Blanche nodded, relieved not to have to decide.

Rachel came rushing into the kitchen in her work overalls and cotton shirt. She grunted a greeting but avoided looking at them as she headed to the fridge.

"Slow down a little, can't you?" Blanche snapped.

Rachel glanced over her shoulder, eyes wide, and no wonder. Blanche had always been a mother who ran from any potential conflict.

"Sorry," Blanche rushed to say. "I don't know what got into me. I know you're in a hurry to get to work."

"No, I'm sorry," Rachel said. "I shouldn't have barged in here before you were finished."

Blanche smiled a tremulous smile of truce. All three of them had been irritable the last few days. Too many nights of broken sleep and mountain ranges of unresolved grief made them overly tense and self-conscious with each other. They kept apologising unnecessarily and starting sentences that trailed off into nothing.

Better to remove herself completely from the situation before she burst into tears and made matters worse. Again. Blanche picked up the tray and followed Naomi outside. Who cared if the neighbours spotted them in their dressing gowns? She had no energy to present her usual perfection to the world.

They sat in the sun together, the only sounds the crunching of toast and quiet chewing. Ordinary sounds, on this unordinary day. Ordinary sounds to cover her inability to say anything worth saying. Her mind was one vast, aching hole. She didn't want to talk about Esther. Yet not talking about her didn't seem right either, as though Esther's loss hadn't been important. Was this what the rest of life would be like, a silence pregnant with pain?

Everything she used to spend her time and energy on seemed pointless. Running around for William. Looking right and saying the right thing at the right time for the right people—for what? The death of a daughter? She couldn't do any of it again—and that's if such a role even existed for her any more. Her fight with William was weeks back, but there'd been no word. No word as Esther lay dying. No word after she'd sent the funeral details. No word since.

She suddenly realised Naomi was speaking. How much had she missed while she'd been wallowing in her own thoughts?

"We did everything wrong when Ian died," Naomi said, her voice paper-thin. "We never mentioned him—we curled in on ourselves, nursing our pain." Naomi stared off into the distance. "My depression, Norman's rage, and our joint neglect of William were the results of allowing grief to grow and twist in on itself."

"But how do you avoid grief getting twisted?" Blanche asked, her breath catching in her throat. "How does anyone get through something like this?"

"Step by step." Naomi leaned across the table and took Blanche's hand in her arthritic ones. "When Ian died—and then Norman—I had nobody to lean on. No family, no close friends, and I didn't know the difference Jesus could make."

"Jesus," Blanche whispered. "How does he help? How does he help me get through today?"

"He makes all the difference in the world. Somehow we have to help each other look at him." Naomi's voice cracked.

"I'm not sure I know how."

"That's why we're in this together. Grief wants to tell us we're alone, but we're not. We're a group of people who loved Esther and were impacted by her life."

Blanche teared up again.

Naomi patted Blanche's hand. "There are going to be a lot of tears over the next few months, but we mustn't fear them. They're healthy." Naomi's bottom lip trembled. "We must talk about Esther and what she meant to us."

"It hurts to even hear her name."

Naomi took a lace handkerchief out of her sleeve and blew her nose. "Eventually we'll stop wincing."

Blanche shifted in her seat. "Wincing. That describes exactly what it feels like. Like I don't want to hear her name or think about her, but I can't bear not to—"

"I know dear. I feel it too."

Blanche wrapped her arms around her middle. "I'm suddenly thrown into a foreign country where I can't speak the language and have no idea what's going on." She closed her eyes. "And William—" She stumbled over his name. "—must be in a worse state than I am."

Even saying William's name made her fume. She'd been distraught when he never came to say his goodbyes to Esther, because she knew he'd eventually regret it. But his no-show for the funeral had really made her blood boil. Hot enough to scald if he'd come within range. Which he hadn't. What possible excuse could a father give for not turning up to his daughter's funeral?

Of course they'd had their differences recently, but honestly. She clenched her fists. He and Esther had been close, and she and William had loved each other too. She presumed he must still love her, but his stubbornness was unbelievably irritating.

Naomi shook her head. "If I could do it again ..." She looked out to the garden and let out a breath. "Putting William in boarding school seemed the right thing to do." She corrected herself. "Well, the easiest thing, at any rate." She gave Blanche a wry smile. "It was hard enough to deal with Norman and me falling apart. I couldn't deal with a child's grief as well." She looked down at her lap. "It's my biggest regret. We were poor parents, and I'm sorry for it."

Blanche pulled her chair over to sit next to Naomi. "I have regrets too." Too many to think of now and mostly entangled with the mess of her anger and feelings about William. She took Naomi's hand again. "You've been a wonderful grandmother, and you're a wonderful mother-in-law."

Naomi hugged her. "You are such a gift to me."

Blanche leaned her head on Naomi's shoulder. There were a lot of lost years to make up for. "It's strange, isn't it? We've had such a mixture of joy and pain, sunshine and rain."

"I've often wondered if true joy needs pain to be fully appreciated," Naomi said. "Somehow the contrast between sun and rain makes us appreciate both more."

"That's what I feel about Esther. Even her death and funeral combined sunshine with the rain."

If only Esther had had anything but cancer. William was almost allergic to the word.

Cancer. Blanche turned the word over in her mind to see what power it still held over her and was surprised to no longer feel the dread and terror it had once provoked. Cancer had sliced its way through their lives, separating father and daughter yet drawing mother and daughter together.

Cancer refined Esther to pure gold.

Blanche wiped her eyes.

Cancer had changed her too. It had given her courage. She smiled to herself. Ironic that she needed courage to stand up to her own husband. She let out a sigh. Perhaps it had come too late, though. If she'd been brave years ago, how different their lives might have been.

"And we can't begrudge Esther what she's experiencing now."

Blanche's skin tingled. "Being with Jesus forever. Such a contrast to the last weeks of her life."

"Why don't we pray together first." Naomi put her breakfast dishes on top of Blanche's. "And then what would you say to cleaning the kitchen and doing the vacuuming? Housework has been a little neglected of late."

Blanche laughed. "It would be a relief. I feel aimless, but I don't want to tackle anything major."

"A clean house will make both of us feel we're achieving something," Naomi said.

"Yes, and we can do a bit at a time and leave bigger tasks to deal with another day."

They held hands and bowed their heads to commit the day to the Lord.

How had she survived all those years without Naomi's support —no, without any real support at all? If only she had dared to stand against William earlier and work at the relationship with her mother-in-law. Her old fear of putting her head above the parapet had prevented her doing what was both right and wise. This fear of provoking anger had kept her silent. Silent when William had vilified his mother. Silent when Rachel had run away. Silent when William had pushed Esther out of the house.

She'd let fear bind her. What might life be like if she walked free?

CHAPTER 3

*B*lanche hung the mop up on its hook and ran a critical eye over the damp bathroom floor. Having this simple task to do had gotten her out of bed this morning.

She put her hands on her lower back and arched backwards. Naomi must be ready for a break too. The look of concentration on Naomi's face earlier had signalled she'd been pleading in prayer for their family while she dusted. Blanche had tried to follow Naomi's example, but had been distracted. Instead of praying she'd caught herself wondering when she should go home. Or if.

She walked down the hall and poked her head into the living room. "Naomi, are you ready for a cup of tea?"

"I certainly am."

Blanche soon had the tea ready, and they sat down at the kitchen table.

"I've spent a lot of time praying for William," Naomi said. "Have you heard anything from him?"

Blanche shook her head. "Nothing and I don't know what's next for us." The only way she knew William was alive was from listening to his weekly radio programme, and that was little comfort. His voice was the same as ever. Shouldn't it have betrayed something? Did she—did Esther—mean so little to him? "I don't know if I should visit or if writing would be better. Writing feels odd." Tears sprang into her eyes, and she dabbed them with the back of her hand. "I don't even know if I'm welcome at home."

"Do you think it would help you to talk about what happened?"

Blanche's stomach cramped. "I appreciate you waiting this long to ask me. You must have been curious."

Blanche went over to the sink. She'd be able to talk more easily if her hands were occupied. Naomi got to her feet and reached into the drawer for a new tea towel.

"The week before Esther died, she dictated a note to William, begging him to visit her." Blanche scrubbed the plate in her hand too vigorously. It was hard to travel back to that horrible day. Hard to relive how William had behaved. Up to that day, their marriage had been easy. Not because it was the good marriage she'd believed it to be, but because she'd never dared to say anything to disturb the glassy smooth water on the surface of their relationship.

Naomi opened her mouth. "Do you—"

But Blanche raised her hand. "Naomi, please don't interrupt or I won't be able to get through this." She gripped the dishwashing brush and forced her memory back.

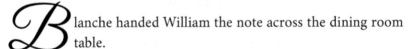

lanche handed William the note across the dining room table.

William took it from her hand and scanned it. "This is your writing, not Esther's." His words were cold.

"Esther is in palliative care." Blanche couldn't help speaking slower and louder than normal, like she was explaining things to someone who couldn't grasp simple facts. "She no longer has the energy to write. The doctors think she may have as little as a week left." It was an effort to get the words out. Each sentence she spoke was like the clang of a death knell. *Lord, help me not to break down. Not now.*

"She was fine a few weeks ago."

She wanted to shake him but stayed patient. "Sometimes the end comes swiftly. The cancer has spread into her lungs." She gulped. "And her liver, and her brain. Esther wants to say goodbye properly."

"None of this would have happened if she'd been less half-hearted about asking for healing."

"I don't agree," Blanche said, heart thudding and knees trembling.

William's head snapped up. "What do you mean, you don't agree?"

Normally his belligerent tone would shut her down, taking her back to docile agreeability, but not today. Today was more than time for a new start.

Blanche kept her voice low and even. "I've been full of questions lately and now I find I no longer believe things I once did."

William pushed out his chair and came to loom over her.

She wanted to push her chair back and run screaming out the front door.

"Are you suggesting I've taught things which are unbiblical?"

Her knees trembled, but she was not going to be cowed into silence. She slid out of her chair and went around to grip the back of it. She concentrated on the light she knew was behind the shadow.

"W-William." *Lord, help me not to tremble.* "Whatever I say, you'll be angry."

"Don't I have the right to be angry about this?" He stuck out his chin. "I never thought Esther's rebellion, her lack of submission, would be contagious."

She'd known he'd use that word. He knew she would fold when

submission was thrown at her. He always made things sound like he was in the right and everyone else in the wrong. "Go and see her, William. She has such peace and joy, and she's facing death with courage."

"If I go, we'll only clash."

Help me, Lord. "She's concerned if you don't go you'll regret it for the rest of your life."

"I'm concerned if I went, I'd regret it more." William pounded his thigh. "We'd become angry with each other."

"Esther has no intention of quarrelling." Normally, Blanche would have backed down and fled into the kitchen by this stage in a discussion. Today she stayed, not ducking her head below the parapet as she habitually did, but holding her ground.

"Esther has stirred up this family far too often in the last eighteen months."

Blanche wanted to weep in pity for this man she had once loved so much, this man who was blind to the fact that he, not Esther, had caused the fractures in their family. "Can't we be a family who remain friends even if we disagree with each other?" She cracked a wobbly smile.

William turned and looked daggers at her. "What are you implying?" He narrowed his eyes into tiny slits. "Do you think I force people to agree with me?"

Blanche took a deep breath. "Yes, dear, I think you do."

There was a lowering silence, an icy calm before the blast.

William smoothed down his already perfect hair. "I cannot believe I heard correctly. Where is your loyalty?" he said, voice harsh. "You're my wife. You're supposed to support me."

He was too clever to use the 'submission' word again, but she could feel it tattooed into her skin all the same. She clutched the back of the chair. If only she could escape. "I do support you, but that doesn't mean I agree with you on everything. I've kept silent for far too long."

GRACE IN DEEP WATERS

William's neck flushed a deep red.

"I'll not be home much this week," Blanche said. "I want to spend every minute with Esther."

"I have a busy week—with planning meetings, preparation, radio programmes. I need you here." William jabbed his finger onto the table top. "With me."

She wanted to punch him on the nose. How dare he place Esther so low on his priority list? She took one calming breath, then another, willing herself to remain in control.

"I cannot believe I heard you say that." She coughed as her saliva went down the wrong way. "Most fathers would cancel everything to spend time with their dying daughter." *Lord, don't let me think about Esther dying right now. Don't let me cry.*

"I'm not most fathers. I have a radio programme influencing tens of thousands and soon going to be heard overseas."

Her chest tightened with pity. "Your daughters are more important."

William's whole face flushed, and a vein throbbed in his temple. "I only have one daughter."

"You can say that as often as you like, but it doesn't make it true." She took a step away from him. Parts of her, long unused, were gaining strength as she trusted Jesus, and it was becoming easier to speak. "It's no more true than what you said about your mother." Blanche took a deep breath and lifted her head. "I love your mother, and wish I was more like her."

William narrowed the gap between them once again. His face was the same deep red as her father's had been after a hard Saturday night at the pub. The Saturdays that had made her childhood a misery of fear and shame.

"How dare you go behind my back to see my mother."

Surely William wouldn't strike her. Still, Blanche couldn't help stepping backwards again. "I met her in Esther's room at the hospital."

"So Esther has joined you in this rebellion." He shook his head. "I might have known."

William might get angry, but it was mostly manipulative bluster. It had worked successfully for years, but speaking the truth was proving liberating.

"When you asked Esther to leave here, she went to your mother. Naomi has been the parent we failed to be." She swallowed. "Even Rachel ran to your mother after she left."

The red line surged up his neck again, and he thumped the table with his clenched fist. Had she been wrong about the physical threat? "I told you long ago, never, ever to mention Rachel to me again."

Blanche looked around the room, elegant and genteel. Such a contrast to their conversation. The silence between them stretched out and gave her time to summon her courage. "Rachel is my daughter, and I love her."

Mentioning Rachel was like raising the dead, but it was the right thing to do. Her past silence had been a kind of lie too, but from now on, she'd champion truth. "Rachel has spent twenty-five years in a spiritual wilderness." Blanche hiccupped as William turned to stare out the window, his jaw clenched. "I don't know if … she'll ever be whole again. But if she is, it will be because of the grace she's experienced through your mother and Esther."

William stalked off into the lounge room, and Blanche cleared the table. She was exhausted. *Thank you, Lord, for giving me courage when I asked for it.* She stacked the dishwasher and took her time to wash the few pots and pans before collecting her handbag and keys.

William was sitting in his usual seat in the lounge, motionless. She didn't look at him as she headed for the front door.

"Where do you think you're going?" he said, each word spaced out for emphasis.

Blanche half-turned towards him and paused with her hand on

the door handle. "I told you. To Esther. You're going to have to fend for yourself."

"If you walk out that door, I won't permit you to come back."

His words struck Blanche like a fist. Unbelievable. He was reusing the same ploy he'd used with Esther. She gripped the handle. "Are you saying I must choose between you and Esther?"

"Yes, me or Esther." His tone was truculent. Maintaining his position. Determined to be right. "If you leave, you can't come back."

Had she once loved this man? Pity squeezed her heart. The pity of someone looking on broken splendour. The pity reserved for those who've had everything and lost it through their own careless actions. Her knees trembled, and a dizziness filled her head. The old Blanche would have given in at once. So much easier.

But she remembered the shame of going along with William when Rachel ran away. She remembered Esther. And she remembered three young men standing before Nebuchadnezzar and making a harder choice than hers. She straightened her spine. "You are beyond belief. There's no need to say such a thing. I'll make sure you get your meals."

William repeated bullishly. "Me, or Esther."

"The choice is obvious," Blanche said. "I'm going to Esther. It's what Jesus would want."

"O h, Blanche," Naomi said, tears running down her face. "I'm ashamed of my son. Ashamed of how he treated you and the girls." She reached for a tissue from the box on the kitchen bench and blew her nose. "He was such a sweet little boy, but I withdrew from him when he needed me most. I'm so sorry."

Blanche wiped her hands on the hand towel and put her arms around her mother-in-law. "We've all been part of the problem, but at least you stood up to him." And William had responded by shutting his mother out of his life.

"William surrounds himself with adoring fans and ignores any criticism. That's not good for anyone." Blanche stood back and held Naomi at arm's length. "And I was part of the problem. I never dared to question him either."

"If it's any consolation, you've done the right thing," Naomi said.

"Yes, I think I have. It was a total miracle. I was as wobbly as jelly inside, and I've never prayed so hard."

Naomi looked directly into Blanche's eyes. "I'm proud of you. Proud to call you my daughter-in-law. My Ruth."

Blanche choked up. Ruth. That Naomi should liken her to that faithful daughter-in-law. "Would you be willing to let me call you Mum? I've wanted to ask for a while."

"Willing? I'd be absolutely delighted."

Blanche enveloped Naomi in a hug. "Mum." She savoured the word. Her mother had died so long ago. "We need to pray for God's mercy on William. He needs Jesus so badly."

"We will, dear, we will. Together. It will mean a lot to me to have someone else praying for him with me."

Blanche knew Naomi had been praying for William, year after year. They'd seen God answer prayer for three out of their four family members, but they'd need an Exodus-size miracle for William to change. He was as stubborn as Pharaoh.

"Do you think I should go and visit?" Blanche asked. "Or should I go home? I worry that might send the message that all is okay between us. He'd expect things to be back like they were, but I can't do that. I've changed too much."

"Do you want to go home?"

"Yes—and no. Not yet." Somehow she had to get clear in her own mind.

"Then wait," Naomi said, smoothing down her skirt. "Write to William. Tell him you're sorting Esther's stuff. It's a normal thing to do after someone's died. It will give you more time to grieve and pray."

Blanche nodded. She did need to go through Esther's things, but she would also use the time to think about when—and how—she would return. There had to be changes, but she was clueless as to how to go about expressing her views, or even what her terms were.

CHAPTER 4

*B*lanche walked out to the back shed, lifted the latch, and spotted the boxes. Ten of them, neatly stacked. Esther's possessions. It didn't seem much to represent thirty years of life. Of course, there was still her bedroom inside, but Blanche wasn't anywhere near ready to tackle that. If she cleared out Esther's bedroom, she'd no longer be able to pretend that Esther might walk in at any time and throw her arms around her.

Blanche stepped into the shed. Dust motes danced in a sunbeam. Did Esther now dance like that in her Saviour's presence? Blanche wiped the tear that ran down her cheek. How was she going to get through this task? The problem was that there was nothing else on her agenda. The house sparkled, the cupboards groaned with food, and she wasn't in the mood for crafts or window shopping. Although maybe William would contact her if she maxed out the credit cards. She sneezed as dust tickled her nose. His anger, bad as it was, might be better than silence.

She bent her knees as Esther—ever the good physiotherapist—had taught her and picked up the first box. She'd do the sorting in the formal dining room. They weren't going to be having guests for a while, and the room had plenty of space to make piles of things to keep, give away, or throw out.

Blanche went back and forth, transporting the boxes into the house. It was a mindless task, but it exercised her body and might help her sleep. Not that sleep was restful. The past few nights she kept dreaming she was wandering from room to room in her home, searching for Esther or William. She'd wake with her pillow drenched with tears. She wasn't the only one struggling to sleep. She'd heard Naomi and Rachel weeping during her trips to the bathroom.

Blanche stretched her back and stared at the boxes. Each was neatly labelled with blue marker on white paper. Esther must have done it when she'd moved here.

Blanche pulled a chair out of the way and used a box cutter on the well-taped top of a box labelled, 'Childhood books/trinkets'. On top was a plastic bag filled with soft objects. Blanche laid the bag aside to look at later. The top book was *The Poky Little Puppy*. How many times had Esther clapped her hands and demanded, "Again, Mummy. Again"?

Blanche swallowed the lump in her throat as she flipped through the pages. The story was as familiar as if she'd read it yesterday, not decades ago. Blanche squeezed her eyes shut. She could still imagine the warm, wriggling weight of the child on her lap.

Half the box was filled with Esther's favourite Enid Blyton books. *The Naughtiest Girl*, *The Magic Faraway Tree* and *The Island of Adventure* and its sequels. Blanche used to have to prise Esther out of her bedroom where she was curled up on her bed, immersed in another world.

Had Esther kept these books for dreamed-for children? Macdonald grandchildren now seemed an impossible dream. Blanche gnawed her lip. She mustn't cry or she'd never get the job done.

She stacked the books back in the box and wrote 'Rachel' on the label. She was the family member most likely to want them, as several had been her books before they'd been Esther's.

Blanche picked up the plastic bag she'd laid aside and felt inside. Clothing. She pulled the items out and teared up before they were fully visible. Four baby dresses Blanche had smocked with bunnies, elephants, and flowers.

She clasped the dresses to her chest and sobbed. Losing a child after so many years of living and loving tore her heart into shreds. Ragged shreds that would probably never be able to be sewed together again.

She smoothed the wrinkles out of the tiny dresses. Why was she doing this to herself?

Mentally shaking herself, she scanned the labels on the other boxes. Box six was physiotherapy textbooks. Esther's boss, Sue, would know if any of the books were still current.

Blanche tidied up the two boxes she'd dealt with and put them in different corners of the room. She glanced at her watch. Naomi usually went on a gentle walk about now. Maybe Blanche should go with her. Tomorrow she'd continue her task.

The next morning, Blanche got started right after her prayer time with Naomi. Praying used to be something she did perfunctorily, but now she found it both restoring and soothing. It was something that filled the time stretching out to the hazy horizon.

She still hadn't heard from William. Not one word in nearly three weeks. Would he even answer her letter?

The first box she looked at was labelled 'diaries'. She rubbed her eyes. She was no way ready to face those. Esther had been writing a diary since she was sixteen. She'd said it helped her to process her thoughts and emotions.

Blanche pushed the box aside and pulled another labelled 'Documents' towards her. She opened it and found a folder right at the top. The first item was a cutting of Esther's birth announcement in the Sydney Morning Herald. The crisp type couldn't possibly convey the excitement and wonder that had gripped her and William. Ten years of waiting. Ten years of fervent prayers. She remembered the reverence and delight with which she'd kissed each of Esther's tiny fingers and toes.

Next was Esther's old passport with stamps for Fiji, England, and France. Then her physiotherapy degree—the entry to a job she'd loved. How she'd had to fight her father on that one. He'd wanted her to study something with more status. Blanche smiled. That was the first time Esther had prevailed against William.

The next item was her baptism certificate, from when she was fourteen. Signed by William. Blanche blew her nose with a lace handkerchief. She'd been proud at Esther's first baptism, but the more recent baptism had been even better. And William had missed it. *Oh Lord, have mercy. Help him to understand your grace. Please do the impossible for us.*

The rest of the box was filled with swimming and athletics medals and an occasional trophy. Esther had never been an outstanding athlete, but she was a good all-rounder. Blanche had usually been Esther's sole cheerleader because William had always had some conflicting appointment or other. Now it was too late. Why hadn't he come to the funeral? She hugged her arms around her waist. Could she forgive him? The one day she'd wanted—needed—him beside her, and where had he been?

He hadn't missed his radio show. Not once. How could that be more important than saying goodbye to Esther?

Sorting Esther's ten boxes took all week, with an average of two crying bouts per box. Each item linked to a story like a single rabbit hole that connected to a whole warren of interconnecting passages, underground and unseen.

Naomi had been right. Sorting not only gave Blanche something to do but allowed her to grieve and remember. Each memory was something precious to be cherished.

As she went through the boxes, an idea sprouted, and she laid aside the items that had triggered it. The baby dresses, the badges from Brownies, and the list of favourite verses she'd found tucked away in Esther's well-worn Bible. Blanche alternated between tears and praise. How blessed she was to have had one such daughter. Now she had to get to know the other.

CHAPTER 5

illiam yawned. The sleeping pills he'd needed the past few weeks made his head foggy. He stretched, and his toes encroached on the cold side of the bed. He recoiled and groaned. Blanche hadn't warmed her side of the bed since their fight.

She'd written a letter to him the morning after Esther died, asking him to call her about Esther's funeral. He'd sent a note instead, leaving the arrangements to her and Esther's church. He'd vacillated between whether to go to the funeral or not. Which was best for his reputation?

Home used to be his retreat. Blanche would be waiting with her soothing presence, anticipating his every need. No deadlines or demands. Nothing in the house out of order. He liked order. Everything in its place, where it should be. Everything of the highest quality.

Why had Blanche changed? It was Esther's fault, and Blanche was too naive to see what was happening. He'd send her flowers today and a brief 'Missing you' note. That ought to do the trick. No woman could resist feeling needed.

The dressing table was covered in dust again. He'd never realised how much work it took to keep the house in order. He'd closed off most of the rooms and lived in the bedroom, the lounge, and kitchen. Even his study was neglected. The house was no longer a home, it was a hotel—a second-rate hotel with house-keeping to match.

He dressed and went down to the kitchen where he opened various cupboards. He clicked his tongue in frustration. He'd forgotten to buy cereal. Again.

He'd go out. Find a place where no one knew him and hide out for a while with the newspaper and a hearty breakfast. He scrambled into his clothes, jumped in the car, and drove fifteen minutes to a café he'd often passed but never entered.

He chose a seat with his back to the other customers and ordered bacon and scrambled eggs. He hadn't allowed himself bacon in years, but if there was a time for an extra pick-me-up, it was now. Then he settled down with his paper.

He was reading an editorial when he heard a voice behind him.

"Did you hear what happened to the pastor of that Victory church place? You know, the one always advertising those big events and conferences?"

"Run off with the secretary, has he?"

The first man guffawed. "Nope. He's one of those 'believe in Jesus and you'll never have any more problems' types."

William clenched his jaw. Ignorant pagans.

"My sister-in-law is one of those crazies," the second voice said.

"He might have to rethink."

There was a pause long enough for William to picture the second man leaning forward, mouth open. Women weren't the only ones who loved juicy gossip.

"His daughter recently died of cancer." There was a soft snicker.

William's jaw ached, and he laid down the paper. His eyes flicked side to side. There was no escape.

"Oh? That'll cause a shake-up."

"I heard they tried all sorts of prayers and hocus-pocus at the beginning, but it didn't do any good."

Tension gripped his lower back. There'd been nothing wrong with the way they'd anointed Esther with oil or combined fasting with prayer.

"Not surprising, since you know I don't believe God exists."

If only God would send a thunderbolt on the man's head. That would rattle him. William picked up his paper and ploughed on with the editorial.

A few minutes later, the men finished their meal, paid their bill, and left. William followed as soon as it was safe. He wouldn't let their comments get under his skin. They weren't worth it.

"Reverend Macdonald, live in two minutes," Steve, the programme manager, said.

William took a drink of warm water. He'd spent the last quarter of an hour warming up his voice as a flautist would warm her instrument. His voice was one of his greatest assets, and he kept it in top form. No clearing his throat. No cold water. No alcohol.

He placed his headphones carefully on his head so he didn't mess his hair. He chuckled at himself. Did it matter on radio? But it did matter to him. He'd seen others saunter in wearing T-shirts and shorts, but he'd never do it. Clothes mattered.

"One minute, Reverend Macdonald."

The formality was a sign of respect. His shows used to be pre-recorded, but they'd switched to live soon after he'd started. He usually started with a short talk full of soundbites and followed it with an interview or open Q and A. Christian authors, sports stars, politicians, scientists—anyone who would draw a crowd. They were interspersed with local musicians, and sometimes, big names in Christian music from overseas.

The lead-in music swelled to its climax. They'd had three hundred competition entries for the privilege of introducing his show. The recording light flashed red, orange, green.

"Good evening and welcome to *Hour of Victory* for this Wednesday." Every word clear and warm. He'd practiced the phrase over and over, searching for the perfect cadence, pitch, and emphasis. Not too showy, but not too flat. He pictured the audience all over Australia, sitting in their living rooms and hanging on to his every word. This was what he was made for.

He did his introductory chat and then glanced down at his programme notes. Next was the guest interview—Justin Harvey. The name drew a blank, which William didn't like, but it would be all right. He was good at ad-libbing. Normally he'd have contacted the guest personally and at least flicked through their book before the interview, but he hadn't even looked at the cover. Somehow time had slipped away from him over the past week.

A musical interlude played next, with a song from an Australian band. He grimaced and made a mental note to scold the producer later about the choice. The interviewee took his seat in a sound reducing chair. William's assistants worked in polished routine and by halfway through the song everything was ready. William reached across, shook the guest's hand, and mouthed "welcome" at him.

The countdown to recording started, and William squared his shoulders.

"This evening we welcome Justin Harvey to *Hour of Victory*. Thank you for joining us." He paused to allow his listeners to absorb his guest's name. "Justin has written four books in the medical field, but today we are talking about his latest book, a memoir."

He glanced up at Justin. "Justin, you're a medical researcher. This memoir is quite different from the other things you've written, and I understand it came out of a significant life-changing event."

Justin laughed. "Most of my life is too boring to write about. I mean, I've been in medical research for twenty-five years. Only scientists have read my other books, but this memoir is written for a wider audience."

William leaned forward. "What area of medical research? You haven't found a cure for baldness, have you?" He grinned at his own joke.

"Cancer research. Specifically, pancreatic cancer."

A tight band constricted William's chest. Not cancer. Anything but cancer.

"And what was your life-changing event?" His skin prickled.

Justin chuckled. "Pancreatic cancer."

William's palms broke out in a sweat. Cancer. He thought he'd been clear he would not do cancer-related interviews. Quite clear. Someone had slipped up and heads were going to roll. This topic pursued him like a slavering Doberman, eager to fasten its teeth into his flesh.

His stomach cramped and his mind blanked. Justin looked across at him, eyebrows raised. One second of silence was an eternity on radio, and this silence stretched longer. William had never frozen before. *Quick, quick, quick.* What could he ask?

"Bit odd, a pancreatic cancer researcher getting pancreatic cancer," Justin said with a grin.

William's hands shook. Justin had rescued the day.

"Yes," William said. "Sort of ironic." His voice worked but the balls he'd been juggling were scattered over the floor. He'd always been proud of his ability to think on his feet.

"Pancreatic cancer isn't as common as lung cancer or

melanoma, but it's a killer," Justin said. "It's common to die within a few months of diagnosis."

Was William going to be able to gather his thoughts? A question would form, then roll away. Out of mind.

"I was lucky." Justin's words filled the air. "Both my father and grandfather died from pancreatic cancer, so I've been routinely scanned for research purposes. It's rare to catch pancreatic cancer early, but I'm happy to be an exception."

"Can you tell us a little more?" William's usual melted chocolate voice sounded like a saw cutting through knotty wood. He took a quiet sip of warm water.

"By the time pancreatic cancer shows symptoms, it is usually too late."

Symptoms. There was something he could hold on to. "What are the symptoms?"

It wasn't elegantly worded but at least it was a question. He could see the radio team outside the soundproof glass having a whispered consultation. Steve scribbled on a piece of paper. William turned away and forced himself to concentrate.

"... unexplained weight loss, jaundice, bloating, changed bowel habits."

Not subjects needing to be discussed in detail on air.

Steve plastered a piece of paper against the studio window. The printed words said, ANNOUNCE AN AD BREAK.

They were attempting to rescue the situation and allow William to gather his thoughts. Beads of sweat gathered on his forehead. What if his thoughts were gone for good?

"Before we continue interviewing Justin Harvey about his memoir—" William glanced at the book in his hand for the first time. "—*My Journey: A cancer researcher's battle with cancer,* we'll go to a message from our sponsors."

Steve put on the longest ad possible.

William mopped his brow and looked at the floor.

The producer came through the door and drew him aside. "Can you carry on?"

William nodded. Everyone on the other side of the glass avoided looking at him.

"Look, we've never needed to give you questions, but I've written a few down, just in case." Steve looked apologetic.

William flushed and his stomach tensed as he scanned the list. He'd stick to the script, get through this, and come back with a better show next time. One slip in ten years wouldn't lose him a job. That would be too ridiculous. Not with the ratings the show garnered and the advertising dollars rolling in.

The producer left the studio, and William taped the questions to the desk so they wouldn't crackle. He took a deep breath. He'd soon be back in his stride. The ad ended, and William's cue counted down.

"What were your first thoughts when you heard your diagnosis?" he asked.

Justin answered smoothly and the tension in William's back loosened off. Years of practice was rescuing the day. It was hard to keep a pro down, and Justin was a surprisingly good interviewee for someone stuck behind a microscope all day.

William's eyes moved down the page to his next question. "What difference did it make being a Christian when you were diagnosed?"

Justin angled his head to one side. "I'm not sure it made much of a difference right at the moment of diagnosis. There was too much emotion. Shock. Denial. All the usual things. The big difference happened as I began to process. I was able to remind myself I was in God's hands." He paused for exactly the right length of time. "It was a huge comfort. To know God is with me whether I live or die."

Normally William would have jumped in and challenged this too-easy acceptance of death, but he didn't seem to be his normal self. What if he challenged his guest and froze again? What if freezing once made it more likely to happen again? He didn't dare find out.

Justin kept talking. "Another difference was I had a real sense of peace. It wasn't a lack of feelings, like my earlier denial, but a strong sense that God had things under control."

Blanche's letter said Esther had been at peace. It seemed wrong. She should have been fighting the cancer to the end. Claiming God's promises. Not submitting to death.

"Some people say God will always heal those who ask with faith," Justin said. "I don't think it's that simple."

Behind the glass, the production team were studiously looking away. William let out an inaudible sigh. If this botch-up job of an interview had been booked and run three weeks ago, he would have delighted in debating Justin's views, but today, he couldn't do it. He asked a few more questions and wound up the interview.

Once Justin had gone, William exited the studio. He ignored the production team scuttling out of his way, marched straight into Steve's office, and closed the door behind him.

"I thought I made it absolutely clear I wouldn't interview people who'd had cancer," William said.

"You did," Steve said. "I checked and Dr Harvey was booked in while I was on holiday. My assistant listed him as a medical researcher and I didn't check further. I apologise."

William nodded. He'd have to accept the apology. He'd always had a good working relationship with his producer, and there was no need to say anything further. He turned to leave the office.

"Your show is one of the best we broadcast, and we want it to stay that way."

William could hear the 'but' in Steve's voice. Steve wouldn't dare to say much about what happened today, not after he'd benefitted from ten years of the programme's success. He half turned back towards Steve.

"You've had a tough time lately. Why don't you take a few weeks off?"

Not this advice again. No one seemed to understand. He didn't want time off. Time off gave him time to think. Time off terrified him. He preferred to be doing the things that gave him a rush.

"A week, maybe two—" Steve shrugged. "We can see how it goes and how you feel after a break."

"I'm feeling fine." He wasn't going to mention his recent sleep problems. It was none of Steve's business.

"I expected you to ask for time off."

He'd have preferred no one at the station knew about Esther, but his contract stipulated that the producer be told about anything which could possibly affect performance. Not that he'd expected his performance to be affected, but he knew how fast gossip travelled around the church community. It had been better for Steve to hear about Esther from him directly, but he'd asked Steve to keep things quiet.

"I prefer to keep myself occupied."

Steve rubbed his ear. "Look, anyone whose daughter has just died won't be at the top of their game. It's normal."

William clenched his teeth. He'd never been normal. Never been weak. This had been his show from the beginning. His brainchild, his name and reputation, his hard work. This show wouldn't be the same without him. How dare they do this to him?

"I made enquiries about someone to stand in for you a few weeks back. I'll follow those up."

William broke out in a cold sweat. Already the plotting had begun. Everything had been normal this morning, and now he was being swept out the door like a stray dog.

The problem was he couldn't think of any way to convince Steve to change his mind. He'd have to give in gracefully and pretend he needed the time off.

An icy shard of fear poked his gut. He was known for his decisiveness, but it appeared to have temporarily disappeared over the horizon.

He shook himself. No matter. He had more than enough to keep himself busy at Victory. He'd go home and get a good night's sleep, although even that seemed more and more elusive.

CHAPTER 6

$\mathcal{T}$he following Saturday, Blanche invited Esther's Bible study group to visit. They caught up over morning tea, then Blanche ushered them into the dining room where she'd pushed the chairs out towards the edges of the room and placed an assortment of bags on them. Naomi sat, but Rachel, Gina, and Joy stood.

"Thanks for coming, and sorry it took so long to invite you around." Blanche clicked the end of the pen in her hand.

"We didn't expect invitations anytime soon," Gina said with a gentle smile.

Joy leaned over and touched Blanche's arm. "It takes time to adjust. I couldn't handle visitors for two months after my husband died. Not even family."

"As far as I'm concerned, you and Gina are family." Blanche's voice wobbled. "You were Esther's best friends, and you were there for her when she needed you."

Unlike William. But thinking about him would set her crying, and crying wasn't how she wanted to spend the day.

"Mum suggested that sorting Esther's belongings would help

me. She was right." Blanche swallowed and gestured towards the bags on the dining room chairs. "It was emotionally draining, but going through Esther's things gave me an idea. I'm not sure what you'll think of it—or even if you have time to help me." She looked down at her hands.

"Tell us what you want, Mum." Rachel touched her shoulder.

Rachel had appreciated receiving Esther's books. She didn't say much, but she had taken to doling out sudden hugs. She often talked with Naomi in the evenings, and she did more than her share of the housework. The house had never been cleaner.

"Have any of you heard of a memory quilt?"

All except Naomi shook their heads.

"It's a quilt made to celebrate a special event or anniversary, but they can also be made to commemorate someone."

Blanche picked up one of the bags from the closest chair. "I found all sorts of things in Esther's boxes we could use to make patchwork squares. Dresses I made for Esther while I was pregnant, favourite clothes, and the badges she earned at Brownies." Blanche laid out Esther's shorts, the sundress she'd worn her whole seventeenth summer, and the cooking, outdoors, and reading badges. "There are lots of ways this can be done. We can make shapes to represent different aspects of her life, like her work or interests. I also found a list of her favourite Bible verses in her diary. Those could be embroidered on different squares and scattered over the quilt."

"Blanche, are you asking us to help?" Gina asked.

"If you don't want to be involved I'll understand," Blanche said. "I know sewing isn't everyone's thing."

"I love the idea," Joy said. "But I'm not sure how useful I will be. I can sew on a button, but I've never done patchwork."

"It's not hard. I taught and supervised lots of amateurs when we made the banners at Victory."

"I'd love to be involved," Rachel said. "But I'm working. So are

Gina and Joy. You and Gran would be the ones doing the majority of the sewing."

"I'm still thinking through the details. Clear off a seat and I'll explain."

They moved the piles onto the table and sat down.

"I don't fully understand how grief works or how to do it properly, but Naomi has given me a few hints. I'd love for us to meet and pray and encourage each other." She looked around at the group, willing them to want to meet as much as she did. She needed their support, especially with her future being so uncertain. "If we had a practical project to do while we met, I think it would help. I would plan the quilt—I already have plenty of ideas. Each of us can pick parts of the project we'd like to do, and I'll help anyone who needs help."

"It's a yes from me, but fair warning, I'm going to be asking for quite a bit of help," Gina said with a laugh.

"Me too," Joy said.

"What do you think, Mum?" Blanche looked at Naomi.

"My eyes aren't what they were, but I'm willing to give it a go. What have you considered for the design?"

Blanche pulled a piece of paper out of her pocket on which she'd made a quick sketch of a basic block based on squares and triangles. "We could embroider the verses on and scatter them across the quilt—"

"—with picture or design patches in between," Rachel said. "Have you thought of an overall colour scheme?"

"I have loads of scraps from the church banners in my sewing room at home. Esther always called them our stained-glass windows."

"And we could choose the verses that most touch us and explain why we like them." Gina dabbed a tear from her eye. "I like your idea. I miss our times together, and this will be beautiful."

Blanche relaxed. She hadn't realised how much this meant to her.

It didn't take long for everyone to agree to the best time to meet each week.

Blanche reached over and pulled a shoebox towards her. "I've already written all Esther's favourite verses on the material. Why don't we all choose one or two which most speak to us?"

Rachel held out her hand.

"No. I'm getting ahead of myself," Blanche said. "First, everyone needs to wash their hands so the material doesn't get dirty. While you're out of the room, I'll lay the choices out on the table."

They were back before she'd finished the task, chattering like a flock of sparrows. Each woman peered at the rectangles of white cloth. Blanche had tried to keep the writing a similar size, but she'd only been able to fit the first phrase of some verses on the small squares of fabric.

"Mum, I've found one I like. Could I also do one of the verses from my baptism?" Rachel asked.

Blanche nodded, throat constricted. The baptisms had been a special day. This was what she'd hoped would happen, everyone contributing their own ideas.

Blanche held up a rectangle. "I've got a completed verse here to show you, and when you're ready, I'll demonstrate the stitch for you."

They all looked at what she'd done and threaded their needles with dark thread. Then Blanche showed them how to do a perfectly tensioned stem stitch. Too tight, and it pulled the fabric. Too loose, and the shape of the letter didn't show properly.

She only had to glance at Naomi and Rachel's first few stitches to confirm they knew what they were doing. Joy and Gina needed a little more coaching. "The key thing is to have your thread below the line of stitches to avoid everything getting tangled."

Soon the only sound was the ticking of the clock and the occasional intake of breath as someone stabbed a finger.

Blanche looked at all the bent heads. Rachel's tongue protruded from the corner of her mouth as Esther's used to. Blanche paused to collect herself. "Are you able to share why you chose the particular verse you're working on?"

Gina put her cloth down on her lap. "I chose the verse as a reminder to myself. 'Don't be anxious about anything ... rejoice always.' I need to work at trusting God with the little stresses and use my energy to tell others about Jesus like Esther did."

"I watched Esther deteriorate day by day," Rachel said. "When I asked her how she coped she'd laugh and say, 'I'm only proving I'm a jar of clay. Maybe now people will better see the power of God shining through the cracks.' My verse says, 'treasure in jars of clay to show this all-surpassing power is from God.'"

"My verse used to comfort me in prison in China. Esther also mentioned how it comforted her on her worst nights," Joy said. "'I am the light of the world. Whoever follows me will never walk in darkness.'"

Blanche finished her final stitch. She'd leave this easier work to the beginners. She had an idea. Esther had loved hiking in the Australian bush. Blanche could make a series of panels with different embroidered wildflowers—flannel flowers, bright yellow wattle, and red grevilleas. Orangey-yellow banksia too—perhaps she could add gold thread to get the right colour. The others might have favourite flowers too. And a huge red waratah, symbolising not only Esther's love of the bush but her home state of New South Wales.

Joy frowned. "The material is wrinkling."

Blanche stood and walked over. "Make the stitches looser, then that won't happen. Let me undo the last three, and then you can keep going."

"Is there any way we could incorporate the words of *Amazing*

Grace in the quilt?" Joy asked while Blanche unpicked her stitches. "It was such a feature at the funeral."

Blanche put her head to one side. "It would make a fantastic border." She pictured it in her mind. "Perhaps if we had a solid colour round the edge about so high—" She indicated three inches with her fingers. "—the verses we sang at the funeral could start at the top left corner and go all around the quilt."

They continued sewing and chatting. There were some tears but mostly 'do you remembers' and laughter.

An excitement pulsed in Blanche's veins as she listened in. Esther would be delighted with this creativity from a circle of women whom she'd loved—and presumably still did, even as she now walked in her Saviour's presence.

If only returning home was as easy as organising this group had turned out to be. Picking up the scraps she'd use for the quilt would be a convenient excuse to check out the situation. *Lord, give me courage, courage to say what needs to be said. Help me remember not to be anxious.*

illiam muttered as a cloud of black smoke rose from the toaster. He was sick of burnt toast and over-cooked eggs. Why didn't Blanche come home? Esther hadn't owned much. 'Sorting her things' was probably an excuse to avoid him.

He pulled the toaster cord out of the wall before picking up a knife to extricate the burnt offering from the toaster slot. Getting electrocuted wouldn't improve his mood. The knife slipped across the edge of the toast, and his finger touched the hot edge of the slot. He cursed out loud. Blast Blanche. He'd never sworn before she'd up and left him, and it wasn't as if he hadn't tried to fix things. He'd sent flowers and a note, but he hadn't heard back. What did she want? A new dress? A new car?

Maybe she was waiting for him to crawl back on his hands and knees. Well, she'd wait forever for that to happen. Other men might do it, but he wouldn't. She shouldn't have left him. It was her duty to be here.

A pile of dirty dishes was stacked in the sink, spilling across the draining board. There were toast crumbs spread across the counter and they crunched underfoot. How could a man pastor a church if his home was a mess? He'd love to hire a cleaner, but then the news about Blanche being away would leak out. The church members and community would love it—more grist for the gossip mills.

It was his day off. Not that it was going to do him much good. Even with daily laps in their pool he hadn't slept well in weeks. Yesterday he'd managed to offend one of the mainstays of the church by not greeting her in the way she expected. Telling her he hadn't noticed her hadn't helped. Silly old trout. He'd have to buy her off, or she might refuse to organise the refreshment rosters. More flowers, he supposed. He wasn't a baker like Blanche. Her shortbread would melt the Rock of Gibraltar.

He walked out of the kitchen. The whole house needed a vacuum and if he didn't do something about the bathroom soon, the health inspectors would come calling. *Day off.* He snorted. It would take him all day to get the house liveable. He looked around him. Best get on with it. If he hurried, he might get time for a swim. At least the pool was useable. The garden looked the same as it always did, because there was no need for the gardener to discover Blanche wasn't here.

Esther had always had a soft spot for the gardener. She'd spent hours traipsing behind him. Made sense. She didn't have a grandfather, and he was a pleasant old man with time for kids.

Esther.

Why couldn't he keep her out of his head? If he couldn't get any peace in this house, he'd have to move. The house was too full of memories. He'd inherited money from his father when he'd turned twenty-five, and they'd moved here when they'd started at Victory. This historical house on the elegant North Shore matched his job. Big houses that smelled of old money. He'd let Blanche have a free hand with the decorating, and she'd done a brilliant job. She'd been born with more taste in her little finger than most people had in their entire body. Blanche. How had everything gone so wrong?

William went to the cupboard under the stairs to get the

vacuum cleaner. It took him ten minutes to untangle the cord. That would teach him to wind it up properly this time.

Sweat trickled down his back. What a stupid way to spend his day. So different to his days off in the past. Blanche knew he needed a long leisurely morning with a late brunch, everything laid out like a Woman's Weekly photograph. Then a swim. By the time he was out of the shower his clothes would be laid out, ready for him to slip into. Then a quiet afternoon doing his daily crossword and reading, a thriller by preference. He didn't even need to walk to the library. Blanche knew his taste and borrowed the right kinds of books. If necessary, she'd have ordered the latest books weeks before.

He put the vacuum away. Only the kitchen and bathroom to go. Could he get the job done before lunch and only wreck half his day? At least housework gave him something to do to fill the silence. He'd always appreciated the quiet before, but now the house was heavy with it. He'd taken to listening to music to fill the spaces and pretend the house pulsed with life. Yet even the music reminded him of things he wanted to forget. Rachel had loved singing.

Rachel.

He sprayed the kitchen counter and wiped it down. He had successfully blocked thoughts of Rachel for years until Blanche told him their daughter was back. What had she been doing? Rachel could have been and done anything she wanted, but running away at fifteen had blown her chances of having any kind of future. He was grateful for small mercies, though. At least she hadn't come home and embarrassed him.

It was weird thinking of both Rachel and Blanche living with his mother. What a mismatched group of women. Good luck to them. They were certain to get on each other's nerves, which might be a good thing. Especially if it forced Blanche to come home.

He scrubbed a stubborn spot in the sink and stood back to

admire his handiwork. He didn't do it as well as Blanche—there were still smears in the sink—but he wasn't willing to spend any more time on the task. There was still the bathroom to do. Pity he'd left the worst task to last. Blanche liked cleaning bathrooms. Said it was satisfying, but he couldn't see it. Housework seemed pointless. Do it once, and it needed doing again a week later. Not nearly as satisfying as preaching. Although come to think of it, people were like cleaning. They needed the same lessons again and again. Slow learners, most of them.

By the time he'd finished the bathroom he'd sprayed himself with water, spilled the cleaning liquid, banged his head, and stubbed his toe. Why was he even doing this? Surely there must be cleaners who would do the job without prying into his private business.

William stretched his aching back. As he snatched the dirty towels off the rails to take to the laundry, the doorbell rang. He jumped and swore again. Who would come to visit him? The gates kept most uninvited guests away.

He caught a glimpse of himself in the mirror. His shirt had big sweaty circles, and his hair stuck out like an Olympian's wreath. There were two dirt streaks on his cheek. He leaned in and wet the corner of the dirty towel. Maybe if he took his time the visitor would go away.

The doorbell rang again as he scrubbed his cheek. What a pain. He'd have to answer it. Either the person knew his routine or it was a lucky coincidence. He tossed the towels towards the laundry basket and headed down the stairs to the front door.

The doorbell rang again.

"Hang on," he muttered under his breath. He stomped the last few steps, unlocked the door, and tugged at the door handle. It stuck. He grunted and gave another tug. The door flew open, striking him on the shin. He muttered another curse under his breath.

Blanche stood on the doorstep wearing a linen dress, without a hair out of place. A basket was hooked over one arm, and she looked good enough to eat.

"I knew you'd be home today," she said. "I didn't want to use my key and come straight in. I've brought lunch."

CHAPTER 8

*B*lanche had never seen William looking all dishevelled and ordinary. His cheek was damp and there was dirt on his chin.

"I've brought lunch," she said again to cover the moment. "Can I come in?"

He opened the door wider and his cheeks flushed. "Things are a bit of a mess."

"I understand." She stepped into the hallway. Goodness, this was awkward. There was dust on the top of the sideboard, a pile of newspapers near his armchair, and the room had the mustiness of being shut up too often. William had never been competent in the home. Not that he'd ever needed to be.

She went to the kitchen and placed her basket on the counter. He followed her. She busied herself unstacking the basket to mask the ongoing silence stretching between them. Theirs had never been a relationship full of conversation. William talked to colleagues and to Nick or Esther. He came home to be quiet and read his paper or swim laps. They'd been quite content to jog along with their own activities and only occasionally come into each other's orbits. The problem was they now jogged out of step and there was a wall between them. A wall that was widening every day.

"William, I wanted to look in my sewing room for materials for a quilt I'm making."

"Go ahead," he said. "You don't need to ask permission."

She opened her eyes wide. Too easy. She'd expected a challenge or his usual salesman's bluster. Maybe her prayers had worked and William had been doing his own thinking and processing. She left him tidying piles of paper on the kitchen bench.

The window of her sewing room hadn't been opened in far too long, but the room was exactly how she'd left it. Everything precisely in its place. She went straight to the chest of drawers where she kept her fabrics and kneeled down to open the bottom drawer. There were enough scraps from the church banners to make several quilts. She ran her hand over the beautiful jewel-like colours. Esther had loved them.

Esther. The room was full of memories. Her wedding dress still hung in the wardrobe, shrouded in its protective cover. There was something pathetic about an unused wedding dress. It represented hours of work and multiple layers of broken hopes and dreams. Who would want to wear it now? Even if they did, how could she bear to sell it?

Esther. It was in this room that the cancer had first made its presence known, although they hadn't seen the pinprick of pain for the insidious life-strangler it turned out to be. Here they'd worked together in rare contentment. Well, Blanche had been content. Esther had nearly required tying to the chair. Sewing wasn't her thing. Strange their interests had been so divergent. Esther loved sport, yet had a mother who couldn't bear sweating. Esther loved camping, whereas Blanche was a total homebody who wanted a hotel if she went anywhere.

She had a memory flash of Esther twirling in her wedding dress.

She gasped and put her hands to her chest. When would this get easier?

Minutes passed. She'd better stop hiding out in this room and get on with lunch. She'd come to talk to her husband—if he'd talk. She wanted to know what he was thinking, to discover if he was working through the grief process and to find out if he was considering the other issues Esther's cancer had pushed to the surface. If he hadn't made significant progress, how could she come home?

She padded across the plush carpet in her usual high heels, went out the door, and closed it quietly behind her. Where was William? She looked both directions in the corridor. Most of the bedroom doors were closed. She'd love to go to her room, but what if William caught her? Her face warmed. He might misunderstand. Then things between them would be even worse.

She slipped off her shoes and headed for Esther's room. It was cool and dark and musty. The tears came before she had even gotten past the door, and she leaned against the wall. Most of Esther's things were gone, but the room was populated by memories. They'd moved here when Blanche had been pregnant with Rachel. She'd dreamed of at least four children, but had to be content with one for more than ten years. There'd been a brief time of joy after Esther had arrived, but it hadn't lasted. She'd been so caught up with Esther that she hadn't understood the depth of Rachel's desperation. By the time she'd spotted it, Rachel's back was disappearing out the door.

Tears streamed down her face. *Lord, this is hard. I messed up with Rachel, and just as we were working through the past we lost Esther. More grief.*

She sniffed. It was better than wiping her nose on her sleeve. She'd left the tissues in the kitchen.

The kitchen. She'd better get back there before William came searching for her. A quick trip to the bathroom would restore some semblance of normality. She wasn't wearing makeup, which made it easier to fix. Lately she hadn't wanted to. What would William think of her new look? He'd always paid more attention to her appearance rather than what she thought or valued.

As she approached the top of the stairs, William came up looking pleased with himself. "Just finished cleaning the kitchen. I'll grab a quick shower."

A shower would keep him out of her hair while she laid out their lunch. She still didn't know how she was going to tackle their much-needed conversation. Sitting with an outsider would make things easier, but William would veto counselling. He'd always protected his privacy. She'd learned more about him in a few conversations with Naomi than she'd learned in nearly four decades of marriage.

She busied herself preparing the salad to have with the quiche and fresh bread. It had been difficult to know what to bring. This was not the time for candles, flowers, or chocolate. She was trying to think of this as a meal between two friends who were dealing with the death of a child. A meal when she had to keep her cool and speak rationally. If only she didn't feel so stupid compared to him.

William came downstairs fifteen minutes later, freshly scrubbed and looking ruggedly handsome in his favourite jeans and shirt. She caught a whiff of his cologne as he passed her. Uh oh.

They took their seats but she couldn't relax, not with all the long weeks of unresolved anger and lack of communication between them.

"How have you been?" William dropped his fork and its contents onto the table cloth, leaving a slight stain.

He flushed, and his confusion gave her a brief moment to consider whether she'd go with politeness or the truth. Truth. "It's been tough. I've cried more tears than I thought possible."

He went rigid when she mentioned tears. He'd never been good with anyone showing or mentioning emotion. The silence stretched out between them. So it would be up to her.

"Between the tears, I've focused on being thankful for all I learned from Esther—thankful she lived well, and died even better."

His Adam's apple bobbed.

If only she could clam up and leave, but that wouldn't resolve anything. Esther had shown her what courage was. Despite all the unpleasantness of treatment and her almost total dependence on others at the end, Esther had worked at honouring Jesus in every word and action.

"I find it difficult to sleep," Blanche said. It wasn't a question, but surely it opened the way for him to respond in kind.

He shifted in his seat. "Sleep has been a challenge."

"What are you doing about it?"

"Lots of swimming and sleeping pills," he said.

"I find talking helps. It stops me bottling everything up inside." She looked across at William. "I'm concerned you don't have anyone to talk to."

"I'm fine."

He avoided looking at her. So this was going to be hard work. She clasped her hands together under the table. *Give me courage, Lord. Help me to honour you.*

"Knowing how I've been, I doubt you're fine. Our daughter died."

"I don't want to talk about it," he snapped.

Help, Lord. "I can't live in a world where my daughter, my precious, precious daughter, is not talked about every day."

"And I don't want to live in a world where I can never escape the fact."

She exhaled. "Then we have a problem. I refuse to stay silent about Esther like I did about Rachel. Staying silent nearly destroyed me."

"I don't know anyone called Rachel," he said.

A hot tide surged in her veins. "You can deny Rachel's existence all you want, but it doesn't change the fact she's alive and well and living with your mother."

"I've told you repeatedly not to mention my mother to me."

She wanted to shake him for being so unbelievably childish. "And I was wrong to listen." She took a mouthful of water. "Your mother has been nothing but kind and generous to me. I'm angry you kept us apart." It felt good to say the things she'd dammed up inside for so many years. "I'm angry you persuaded me to keep quiet about Rachel, and I'm angry that you're determined to make Esther die a second time." Blanche stumbled over the last phrase.

William didn't say anything.

"Esther is more full of life than you or I can imagine, and I'm going to remember her every day."

Last time she'd spoken like this, William had used his superior height and bulk to intimidate her. Perhaps this time he sensed it would be a waste of effort. His skin looked grey and less taut, as though these last months had beaten him up more than he let on. Pity engulfed her.

"One of the things I've been learning is how to grieve," she said gently.

"I'm not a child. I don't need lessons on the subject."

She ignored his attempt at terminating the topic. She wasn't going to leave until she'd had her say. "Maybe you don't, but I did. I never grieved properly for Rachel, and all my emotions were curdling inside and eating into my heart."

He grunted.

"Your mother has taught me a lot."

"She's hardly a model for how to grieve." Sarcasm dripped off his tongue. "She shut her bedroom door for three years."

She'd have to ask Naomi for more details. "She acknowledges she did a terrible job of grieving your brother and your father."

"I don't want to talk about my brother."

Blanche sighed. "You're going to have to talk about him one day, and the sooner the better by the sound of things."

He turned his head away from her. "It's a long time ago."

"I don't think it matters how long ago the death was. If it's buried, it does damage. I'm having to go back and grieve for Rachel."

"She's not dead."

Well, admitting Rachel existed was progress. "Any loss has to be grieved. I've learned stuffing emotions down and burying them isn't healthy."

He shifted in his seat. "Just because it works for you doesn't mean I need it."

Would William ever stop running? "The way I'm doing things this time is better, and cheaper than going to counselling."

William snorted. "Nick's going to counselling. I told him to save his money."

She was curious, but she wasn't going to follow any rabbit trails. There were more important things to talk about.

"When are you coming home?" William's tone was casual, but there was a tic above his eye.

The man was predictable. If other methods didn't work, he would switch the topic.

"I've been praying a lot about when and whether to come home. I'm not willing to return until you're willing to discuss the issues needing to be discussed."

"Your place is here." He jabbed the table with his forefinger. "You not being here is a bad example for the other women in the church. If they discover we're living apart, what's to stop other women leaving their husbands whenever they hit a tough spot?"

She hated it when he preached at her.

"We need to show the congregation marriage is important—it's for life, and you don't walk out when the going gets a little rocky. I can't keep covering up for you at church if you're away any longer."

Guilt flooded through her. She'd expected him to play the

submission card, but it didn't make it any easier and it was only part of the story. "You're not covering up for me. You're covering up for yourself. I don't mind if people know I'm struggling after Esther's death. It's normal. I'm much more concerned that you think you're not struggling."

He speared her with his gaze. "So you want me to crack up?"

"I want you to be human. I want you to acknowledge that having a daughter die is a big deal." She took a deep breath. "And I want you to acknowledge you let her down. What kind of man doesn't say goodbye to his daughter?" Her breath burst out of her. "What kind of man doesn't attend his own daughter's funeral?"

Trembling, she reached for her glass and took a big mouthful of water.

William took a grape as though he hadn't a care in the world. "It sounds like you're the one with the anger issue."

Oh, how he loved to do this. "Too right I've got an anger issue. I'm angry that my husband cares more about his reputation than his own family." She dabbed her lips with her serviette. "You rejected your mother, you rejected Rachel, and you topped it off by rejecting Esther. You're the pastor of a church. You should be forgiving people, not cutting them out of your life. What you do is not normal."

"Have you finished?" His words were cool, but there was a flicker in the corner of his eye.

She drew a ragged breath. "Yes, thank you. I've said enough." Pushing out her chair, she stood and gathered her basket. "And the answer is no. I'm not coming home at this stage. Whether or not you think you have issues, I have plenty."

She turned towards the front door. "I'll leave the leftovers for you." And the dishes. She didn't say it. Vindictiveness was not her style.

It was twenty steps to the door. Behind her was only silence.

She let herself out.

CHAPTER 9

illiam had never needed an alarm in the past, but he should have set one the day after Blanche's visit. He'd tossed and turned until the early hours of the morning before falling into a broken sleep. Now he'd have to hurry. There was only thirty minutes until his weekly appointment with Nick.

He leapt out of bed and tripped over the clothes he'd thrown on the floor last night. Kicking them aside, he rummaged in his wardrobe for clean clothes and rushed into the shower. He made it to the church car park with moments to spare. He hesitated outside the door and then strolled in with breezy greetings all round. The office staff got nervous if he wasn't on top of things. Being the pastor of a church like Victory was like being in politics—plenty of hand shaking and promises. With pastors' promises, of course, being more reliable than politicians'.

He was seated with a folder of reports on his lap, looking relaxed and in control when Kylie, his assistant, ushered Nick in. William nodded to him but didn't lift his head from the papers he was reading until Kylie had returned with the cappuccinos she'd made.

"Offerings are up eight per cent this month." He tapped the report. "Good work, Nick. The new focus is working."

"Great." Nick's flat tone didn't match his word choice.

William narrowed his eyes. What was the matter with him? "Were you hoping for better results?"

Nick seemed startled. "No, the results are fine." He sipped his cappuccino.

"So the problem is …?"

"I haven't been sleeping well." Nick rubbed his eyebrow. "I've been struggling for weeks, and yesterday the counsellor probed deeper."

Counsellor? So he was still going, despite William's warnings. William's peers had always viewed going to a counsellor as the top of the slippery slope towards the madhouse, but Nick believed it was no different than a car having its annual service. Nick might not be so casual if word got out one of Victory's pastors was having counselling.

"He said the death of someone close to us can trigger memories of someone else who died." Nick looked at the toe of his shoe. "I've been dreaming of Dad nearly every night. Something I haven't done in years."

William's head jerked up. Funny, he'd been dreaming as well, scene after jumbled scene. Last night he'd dreamed about the policemen arriving on the doorstep the day Ian drowned. His childhood self had assumed his parents would finally pay him some attention. But no. Mother withdrew into her room, Father withdrew into work, and William got shunted off to board at The King's School.

His father had always been impressed by Ian's high achievements, so William determined to pour every ounce of energy towards the goal of all-round excellence. That year, and all the remaining years of high school, he topped every subject but one.

His father dutifully came to the annual prize-giving and clapped like all the other parents, but William had known. His father didn't even see him.

Nick cleared his throat and William jumped. What had he missed?

"The counsellor asked heaps of questions about my father and his death. I guess I never had time to grieve before. The minute Dad died there were people telling me I was now the man of the house." Nick cracked his knuckles. "I was only a teenager, and I took everything they said as gospel truth. I felt I had to protect and provide for my mother and younger brothers."

Too much self-examination was a bad idea. It had sabotaged many of William's theological classmates' careers. He was one of the few still going from strength to strength. Discipline. Most people lacked discipline. "Nothing wrong with being responsible," William said.

"No, but I shouldered too much myself. No one showed me how to lean on God. I did my duty and buried my resentment. Resentment against my loss of freedom." Nick stared out the window. "I think that might be why I shied away from Esther when she needed me most."

William winced inwardly as if someone had jabbed an open wound. Maybe that's what all this was about. Nick was being sentimental and guilt-ridden about his broken engagement. If Esther were still alive and well, he wouldn't have been so keen to get back together with her.

"What's happening at Victory youth?" William asked. "Any situations we need to discuss?"

They spent the next half hour discussing their work. He didn't tell Nick about his break from *Hour of Victory*. It was none of Nick's business. None of anyone's business. If he didn't make a big deal of it, it might pass unnoticed.

"William, I've been meaning to ask about your Goliath sermon."

Now what was on Nick's mind? He particularly remembered that Nick had frowned during it. Was it about something he'd said? William sat up straighter. Perhaps Nick merely wanted to dig deeper. He was a conscientious young man.

"I wanted to know why you focused on the big problems in our lives." Nick's voice shook a little, and he fiddled with his pen. "When I read the passage, it seemed to focus on the reason why David stood up to Goliath. Because Goliath was setting himself up in defiance against God—"

William forced himself to concentrate. "I don't know what you're trying to say."

"I think I'm questioning whether I got the main point in the past. It seems to me the application is more about God's glory. David was enabled to kill Goliath because he understood that Goliath was challenging God's glory." Nick paused. "I've been thinking … about whether I give God glory and if I really care more about God's glory than my own."

Good grief, Nick was annoying today. What had made him so ridiculously introspective? It wasn't a characteristic William had noticed before. He'd spent the last years preparing Nick as his successor, and now he was cracking up. Maybe he'd been mistaken about Nick all along.

illiam watched Nick leave, then sat down to continue his sermon preparation. He'd barely reread what he'd already written down when Kylie poked her head around the door. "Steve from *Hour of Victory* has called to ask if he can drop in."

Now what? Maybe Steve couldn't find anyone to stand in for him for two weeks and was coming to eat humble pie.

"Sure, tell him to come—and Kylie, two glasses of Perrier water and lemon to start with, and a piece of the carrot cake Mrs Jones brought." Never let it be said he wasn't ready to hold out the hand of peace.

Steve arrived and accepted the glass of Perrier and the cake but refused any coffee. "I've just dropped in on my way past. I had a sudden idea which might be totally absurd."

William's heart gave a mighty leap. He'd always loved new projects. He gestured to one of the two armchairs in his study and took the other. Steve put down his water and finished a mouthful of cake. "Last week my daughter returned from a holiday on Lord Howe Island. She loved it, but when she went to church they mentioned they hadn't had a minister for ages."

William raised an eyebrow. Where was Steve going with this?

"No one wants to stay out there, and so they use two-month interims. My daughter promised she'd ask at my radio station. I immediately thought of you."

William held up his palm. "I don't think it would suit me at all." Not way out in the middle of nowhere.

"I wouldn't say no right away. A change is good when you've had a bereavement. It's a beautiful place." Steve grinned. "You and your wife could laze on the beach."

William's stomach turned to jelly, picturing Blanche lounging on the beach. He mentally shook himself. She wouldn't consider it, not in her current mood. "I thought you said it was a church job."

"My daughter says it's only one service, leading a Bible study, and making a few pastoral visits. More like a holiday for someone like you, and they'd really appreciate having someone of your calibre." Steve stood, reached into his pocket, and took out a card. "My daughter gave me the contact details. At least think about it."

"Sure, I'll think about it." William took the card and tucked it into his wallet. He didn't promise to do any more.

It didn't sound like his kind of holiday, but it might solve several of his immediate problems. If he went so far out of the way, everyone would assume Blanche had accompanied him. That would give him another two months' breathing space.

CHAPTER 10

*B*lanche had finished the weekly shopping and arrived home, glad to rest her feet. She twirled the rings on her fourth finger. Was her marriage over? It was a question she had never expected to ask, not since William had first swept her off her feet. She'd been a nearly eighteen-year-old mismatched for extra work experience at his advertising agency because she'd mentioned she liked art. His confidence had been a stark contrast to her shyness. William told her later he'd lost three contracts in a week because he'd been so distracted. He was lucky not to lose his job. They were engaged nine months later.

Her attraction to him may have been fuelled by the escape he offered. It had certainly helped that William was handsome, confident, and adored her. She'd been naively certain of the adoration but wasn't sure anymore. Lately she'd realised her skills in hospitality, strong sense of style, and good manners were perfect for a man like William, someone who demanded his wife orbit around his career and needs. Even her innate shyness had worked to his advantage—she wasn't likely to upstage him.

She hadn't noticed these things before. Was it because she had enjoyed her position and the security of being Mrs Macdonald? Life wasn't perfect, but she could ignore many of its imperfections from the security of her home. She'd even stomached Rachel's departure—Blanche reached up to touch her flushed cheek. She'd been blind. Lulled into delusion by the cotton wool comfort of their lives. Esther's cancer had woken her up. She'd been angry at God, but Esther, Naomi, and Joy had helped her see even cancer could be part of God's wider plans. Maybe what she and William were going through could also be used by God for their good. Oh, she hoped so.

Lord, thank you for not giving up on us. Thank you for your grace and mercy. Please let William experience it too.

Blanche looked over at the table. There was already a stack of embroidered verses ready to be matched with their surrounds. She now had most of the fabric needed to move on to the next steps. The ladies would be coming tomorrow, and she'd teach them how to appliqué each verse onto a border.

If only William had such a support group. Or even one man to encourage him. *Lord, give him what he needs rather than what he feels comfortable with.*

She twirled her rings again and then looked at them more closely. Was the stone loose? She'd better go and have it checked. If it was only cleaning, she'd leave it, what with how things were between her and William, but a loose stone was another matter. There was a jeweller two doors down from the quilting shop. She could do two things at once.

---

*B*lanche rubbed her newly naked finger as she left the jeweller and headed for the quilting shop.

The owner, Naida, had introduced herself last time and greeted her like family. Blanche had spent a lot of time here lately, buying fabrics and other things for the memory quilt. The first of the wild-flower embroideries was complete, and she was ready to buy more fabric now she knew what she was missing. She'd also brought samples of the other fabric scraps, as she needed more light-coloured fabric to offset the brighter colours.

"Would it be okay for me to lay out my fabric on this table?"

"That's what it's for," Naida said. "Let me know if you need any help."

Naida was twenty years younger than Blanche but had streaks of silver through the dark strands of her hair. She was busy typing something on the computer.

Blanche searched for fabric to frame and back the quilt. She'd deliberately chosen the wrong colour once, years ago, but she wouldn't this time. This time she was pleasing herself, not aiming to hide. Nor to lose the school sewing prize. Nor to keep her head below the parapet.

Blanche took a deep breath and moved towards the counter.

"Could you wait one minute?" Naida took a piece of paper out of the printer. "I've been trying all day to get this notice up. I must do it, or I'll never get any help."

"Help?"

"The shop is getting too much to manage on my own," Naida said. "I need a part-time assistant—someone who knows quilting."

Blanche's stomach fluttered. "How many hours are you wanting?"

Naida laughed nervously. "Initially, three per day but we'd figure it out as we went along."

"Would you take someone older?" What was she doing, asking questions? It wasn't as if Blanche wanted a job. William and his work had always been her full-time job. She'd never earned a wage and was clueless about being an employee. She'd probably be a disaster.

"Are you interested?"

Blanche blushed. "I don't know if I'd be suitable."

Naida put her head to one side. "I'm looking for someone who might even be able to teach a few students. Do you think you could teach?"

Blanche perked up. "Teaching's one thing I can do. I've managed quilting projects with up to forty volunteers, most of whom didn't know one end of a needle from the other."

"How about I give you my card? Have a think about it and call me back."

"I am at a bit of a loose end at the moment." Blanche touched her empty ring finger. "I'll go and talk with my family and—" Did she dare to say anything more, like Esther would have? She swallowed. "—and pray about it."

Naida blinked. Was she offended?

"Are you a Christian?" Naida asked.

"Yes." Blanche said, suddenly shy. She had no practice talking to new acquaintances about her faith.

"You might turn out to be the answer to my prayers." Naida put the notice in a drawer. "I'm going to wait. Could you contact me within, say, three days if you want to talk further?"

Blanche nodded. "Yes, although I'm petrified at the thought."

"Don't be nervous. I think we might turn out to be a good team."

Blanche took the proffered card and stammered a goodbye. On shaky legs, she headed for her car. Was she seriously thinking about taking a job? At her age? Naomi and Rachel might think she'd lost it. William would be horrified.

She opened the car door and got in. William could say what he wanted. If things continued as they were, she'd need a job.

CHAPTER 11

*T*he doorbell rang, and Blanche opened the door. Gina and Joy stood outside, holding up their embroidered patches.

"We've finished our verses," Gina said.

They'd done well. After their initial lack of confidence, they'd managed three verses each. Blanche's own embroidery was powering on to completion—she had nothing else to do except a little gardening and housework.

Blanche took them through to the dining room, where she'd laid her completed embroideries out on the table.

Gina leaned forward to look. "The flowers are gorgeous, Blanche. You have a real gift."

Blanche gave them a moment to look more closely and get out their own contributions. Then she handed out cardboard pattern templates and demonstrated how to add the coloured borders around each embroidered patch. Everyone chose a coloured fabric, ensuring the distribution of each colour was even. Soon the snipping of shears and the whirr of two machines were the backdrop for quiet conversation.

Once the others had finished their tasks Blanche handed them some blank paper. "It's time to get creative. We want squares to represent different aspects of Esther's life. Her work, her interests, the stages of life, or even her character. Just draw something—but stick to simple shapes, please, because they'll be cut out of cloth." She opened a box and reached inside. "I've also got Esther's Brownie and Girl Guide badges and a selection of her favourite clothes. Start by doodling and let's see what you come up with."

They each picked up various items. "Here's her physio uniform," Gina said. "Perhaps we could use the name badge and the hospital logo as part of the work square."

"Should we put all the badges on one square or scatter them over the quilt?" Joy held up a small pile.

"Scatter them," Rachel said. "Maybe with some of the buttons to add texture."

Blanche smiled with the pride of a woman watching a well-oiled team and turned back to her sewing machine. These Saturdays were already the highlight of her week, an oasis that refreshed her for the emotional desert either side of it.

"Blanche, would you like me to go and press all the seams flat?" Naomi asked.

Bless her. She and Naomi had talked through the tasks needing to be done before the others arrived. Naomi's eyes had deteriorated, but she still wanted to be involved. The ironing board was already set up in the corner of the room.

This afternoon was the deadline to phone the quilting shop. She'd vacillated between yes and no since she'd been offered the chance. What did she want? It was an unfamiliar question. Since her marriage, the question had been how could she support William to do what he wanted, or how to be the best mother. But even those questions hadn't come up often. Mostly her choices were related to small things like what to wear, or cook, or what ministry to support.

The ministries had changed over the years as the size of the church increased. From music and munchies or tots and toddlers in the early years towards an increasingly remote figurehead role.

By the end of an hour, everyone had another task they could work on at home. They gathered on the back verandah with a pot of tea and freshly made scones.

"I never expected to enjoy doing sewing," Joy said. "In China we only sewed to mend clothing."

"It wasn't something my family did either," Gina said. "I've loved this project though. It's made me think more about Esther." She cleared her throat. "Which has kind of helped, you know?"

"I'm not sure if it's helped me or made everything worse," Rachel said. "Hearing you all talk about her—there were a lot of missing years."

Blanche must remember to give Rachel all of Esther's diaries.

Blanche cleared her throat. "Thank you for working on the memory quilt with me. It's been a key part of my grieving process." She clasped her hands in her lap. "And thank you for not asking about why I'm still living here. I can't put off making several decisions, and I need your advice and prayers."

She'd always been a private person and had never made real friends within Victory, not with the constant pressure of always controlling her appearance, speech, and actions. That not only prevented her maturing but also prevented her becoming part of the church community.

"When Esther ended up in palliative care, my husband gave me an ultimatum, an ultimatum I couldn't follow. It was time to make a stand and follow my conscience." She blushed. "Something I'd often failed to do. The way I grew up, you got in trouble if you stood out. I guess I carried my fears into my marriage."

"What's changed you?" Joy asked.

"Do you remember the story you told about Shadrach, Meshach, and Abednego?"

GRACE IN DEEP WATERS

Joy nodded. "I experienced a strong urge to share their story that day, but I had no idea why. It's encouraging to know it was for you."

Blanche crossed her ankles. "I kept thinking about how they'd had courage in a far more difficult situation than mine."

Rachel caught her eye and smiled.

"It's been even harder after Esther's death. I have no idea where I'm at in terms of my relationship with William. I don't want to park my brain and conscience to one side or bury issues."

"What do you want?" Naomi asked.

"Maybe a marriage that's more of a partnership." Blanche fanned her warm face. "I've told William we have to sort things out before I move home, but I fear we're going to drift apart rather than resolve anything."

Joy clasped her hands as though she was praying.

Blanche sighed. "All my life I've been told to submit to my father, my husband, and any church leaders, but I don't know how submission works in the current situation. I don't know who I am or what I'm supposed to do." She looked around the group. "And now it's complicated by the fact I've had a tentative job offer and I need to let the lady know this afternoon."

Naomi's eyebrows rose. "Who's made you a job offer?"

"The lady at the quilting store is looking for part-time help. Sales and teaching a class or two."

"Mum, you'd be fantastic. Look how you've taught all of us these past weeks."

Her heart warmed at Rachel's wholehearted support. "It's not really about whether I can do the job. It's more about whether I should. Your father would probably be upset about it."

Rachel snorted. "He needs to learn not to take you for granted."

The words found a home in Blanche's stomach. How she wanted William to respect her. She lingered with the feeling for a moment, then swallowed the metallic taste of shame. No. She

75

wasn't an immature child intent on revenge. She was a woman who wanted to honour God more than anything.

"I don't think taking the job or not is the real issue." Blanche wrung her hands. "I'm confused about the biblical meaning of submission." The word itself twisted her gut. "In my mind, submission is only negative. I don't know. Are there any biblical stories of married women which might help me?"

There was a long, drawn-out silence.

"That's not an easy question, because Scripture doesn't necessarily tell us much about their marriages," Joy said. "Wives are commanded to submit to their husbands as to the Lord, but what do you think, ladies? What Bible characters can we think of who submitted to the Lord?"

"What about Mary?" Gina said, wrinkling her brow. "She submitted to the Lord with regards to accepting God's plan for her to be the mother of the Saviour, and Joseph did too when he believed what God told him about the baby and married Mary."

"I was looking for examples more like my situation. Maybe I need to widen the net." Blanche closed her eyes. "So for them, submission was a combination of trusting God to look after them and a rock-solid belief God had things under control." She gave a wry grin. "Not easy when they must have known no one would believe them."

"I can only think of negative examples," Naomi said.

"Maybe they could help, because they'll tell us what submission isn't," Joy said.

"Negative examples are easier," Rachel said. "Eve passing the fruit to Adam and expecting him to follow her lead. And Sarah's plan to gain a son through suggesting that Abraham sleep with Hagar."

Blanche raised her eyebrows. It was good to know Rachel had been reading her Bible.

"Rachel lying to her husband, and Leah buying time with Jacob so she could score off her sister." Gina laughed.

Blanche had known talking to the group would help. She'd been mulling over this topic for days and getting nowhere, but now things were dropping into place. "Each of these people rushed ahead of God and went their own way."

"I think you're onto something," Naomi said. "The Ephesians passage that gets quoted at women all the time is often used to bludgeon and manipulate women, but the passage talks about submitting out of reverence for God."

"Do you think there is a proviso like there is with the submission to rulers and authorities?" Gina asked.

Blanche leaned forward. "What do you mean?"

"Well, we're told to submit to the government because God has allowed them to rule, but it's always with the proviso that, if we're asked to do something against God, God's rule trumps all else."

That made sense. William had tried to manipulate her with the whole submission thing during their arguments, but she'd gone with her conscience in the end. As she'd put God's ways above her own fears, she'd experienced both peace and the courage to go forward.

"Thanks for helping me think through this. It's something I've been confused about for a long time." Her mother seemed to think submission included putting up with her husband beating her every Saturday evening. Bile rose in Blanche's throat.

"But isn't it the same for all of us, Mum?" Rachel said. "I mean, I'm new to all this and having to grieve and everything. It's often hard to drag myself out of bed, but I'm trying to follow Jesus one day at a time, trusting he'll sort out tomorrow when it comes."

Blanche reached over and laid her hand on Rachel's arm. "Thanks, honey. You've helped me make up my mind about the interview. I'll go in, and if she still wants to hire me then I can go part-time—at least until my situation changes. Then I'll better contribute to this household."

Naomi smiled. "You contribute. Don't get a job because you feel obligated."

Naomi was the best of mothers-in-law. "If I take the job, it's because I think I'd enjoy it."

They spent the next twenty minutes praying for Blanche's situation and how they'd each submit to God in whatever situation he placed them.

The minute they were gone, she'd ring Naida at the quilting shop and talk about the job. Her insides quivered. It had been years since she'd felt this bubbling excitement.

CHAPTER 12

*W*illiam parked in his garage before strolling back to the letterbox. He reached into the box for the pile of mail and headed back to the house.

He poured an orange juice, seated himself in his favourite reclining chair, and used the lever to elevate his feet. That was better. Then he sorted through the pile. Bills and fundraiser pleas, as he'd expected. Right at the bottom was a letter with an unfamiliar postmark. He peered at it. Lord Howe Island.

His skin prickled. He'd written on a whim, a gamble, because he felt ready for something new. He hadn't expected a reply, because he was all too familiar with the denomination—they'd have rejected the Apostle Paul if he didn't fulfil every one of their conditions.

The letter was handwritten in a clear script.

Dear Reverend Macdonald,

Thank you for your application.

The classic start for a rejection letter. William sighed and scrunched the letter up to lob it towards the bin. One phrase caught his eye.

NORMALLY WE WOULD NOT ACCEPT ...

It didn't sound like a rejection. Perhaps he'd been too hasty. He smoothed the letter out on his knee.

... SOMEONE FROM ANOTHER DENOMINATION, BUT WE HAVE BEEN MORE THAN A YEAR WITHOUT ANY ASSISTANCE. ALL OUR LEADERS ARE READY FOR A BREAK. WE HAVE PRAYED ABOUT YOUR APPLICATION. ALTHOUGH WE RECOGNISE OUR CHURCH WILL BE COMPLETELY DIFFERENT TO WHAT YOU'RE USED TO, WE'D LIKE TO INVITE YOU TO COME IF YOU'RE STILL AVAILABLE.

William flipped the page. There was a clear list of ministerial duties. Nothing different from what Steve had mentioned. He'd have so little to do he'd have to take a pile of books or learn to fish.

What was he thinking? He didn't intend to go through with this harebrained scheme. Or did he? He hadn't mentioned it to his elders. He tensed at the thought, then relaxed. There was nothing to worry about. The elders would veto this scheme outright.

The third page of the letter contained details of the accommodation. Just as he thought, a primitive 1950s-style beach cottage. He shuddered. It probably came complete with unreliable hot water. No way.

He leaned back in the recliner.

The photographs from the book he'd looked at in the library

GRACE IN DEEP WATERS

drifted through his mind. White sands, aquamarine seas, dramatic mountains covered in rainforest. People paid serious money to holiday on Lord Howe Island.

He hadn't had a quiet holiday since before Ian died. Before that, they'd had an annual beach holiday. One memorable year, his parents joined William and Ian in building a huge sandcastle. At least, it had seemed huge to William's five-year-old eyes.

He rubbed his eyes and forced his concentration back to the final lines of the letter.

IT WOULD BE GREATLY APPRECIATED IF YOU COULD CONTACT US IMMEDIATELY BY RETURN POST OR PHONE US ON THE NUMBER BELOW TO LET US KNOW IF YOU'RE COMING.

IN CHRIST,

REG PETERS (CHURCH SECRETARY, TREASURER)

Reg's job titles said it all really. He was likely all the leaders rolled into one. This job was the equivalent of a one-horse town, a complete dead end for someone like him. Yet his heart felt a curious tug towards the place.

He snapped the recliner back to upright and shook his head to clear it. He'd always despised sentiment.

By the time he'd walked back into the kitchen and rinsed his glass, he'd made up his mind. He'd talk to Archie, his head elder, and sound him out on the idea. He'd soon uproot this ridiculous notion from William's heart.

*A*rchie was a lawyer, so they arranged to meet for lunch in the city.

Once they were seated and eating their bruschetta starter, William asked polite questions about Archie's work. What he really wanted to ask was so out of character he struggled to introduce the subject.

His stomach fluttered like at the end of every school term when he'd stood at attention in front of his father as his report card was read. One year had been particularly tense.

His father purred through the first five pages of his school report. William held his breath. His father turned the next page and the purring stopped. Throttled. William still remembered gulping. He had no hope in science.

His father flicked the paper. "What's this?" He looked up, his gaze sharp as a skewer.

"One of the other boys is a genius," William stammered. "His dad is a physics professor at Sydney University." Short of cheating or murder, William was doomed to second.

"Well, you know what I always say."

William bit back a sigh. "Yes, Dad, I know. People only remember the gold medallists." His father was obsessed with the upcoming London Olympics. Saw them as a wonderful source of life principles to ram down William's throat.

Nick claimed Esther's death had triggered other memories. Was that what was happening to him? He'd assumed his memories were securely locked up in the drawers of his mind. Obviously not.

Their main courses arrived, and Archie glanced at his watch. William would have to get on with his purpose for the meeting.

"Have you ever wanted to do something crazy?" William shifted in his seat. "You know, something out of character?"

Archie's fork stopped in mid-air. "Like buy a Lamborghini or shave your head?" He chuckled, as if amused by his own joke.

"Nothing so expensive or shocking." William touched his still-thick hair.

"What's on your mind?"

"Well, the *Hour of Victory* programme manager dropped by with a suggestion. He thought that with the recent happenings in my life, I should have a change of pace."

"Go on," Archie said, cutting another piece of his medium-rare steak.

William related what he'd done and the arrival of the response letter. "—and they'd love me to come and help them out, but I think the whole idea is …"

"Yes, I can see why you think the idea is harebrained." Archie peered over his glasses. "But it also kind of makes sense." He wiped the thick linen napkin across his lips. "The elders have been talking—"

William's stomach cramped, and he raised his head to look at Archie.

"—and putting ourselves in your situation. Many companies would have given compassionate leave for someone who has been through …" He paused. "… what you've been through."

William focused on his next mouthful of steak, his chewing loud in his ears. He appreciated Archie's tact. It was probably the reason he hadn't enquired about Blanche. Her seat in the front row had been empty for several weeks, and church members were asking questions, but William had managed to put them off by telling them she was sorting out Esther's affairs. But he couldn't keep using the same excuse. It wasn't as if Esther had a complicated estate.

"Part of our job as elders is to protect the pastor."

William nodded.

"We know you wouldn't appreciate twiddling your thumbs on a cruise. You're a man of action."

Which was what made this idea seem absurd. Lord Howe Island wouldn't provide much in the way of action.

"But we do think a break or change would keep you at the top of your game for the next ten years."

Ten years. He liked that. He intended to leave at the perfect time. The time he orchestrated.

Archie raised his hand to attract the waiter's attention.

"This interim job sounds like a win-win. It might not be anything like what you're used to, but with such a small congregation, you'll get plenty of time for yourself and Blanche."

William kept silent. Two months to either work things out with Blanche or for him to work out what to tell the elders. No one need know Blanche wasn't with him. He'd write to her. Send photos and tell amusing stories. Remind her why she'd married him. A bit of distance might work in their favour.

The church wouldn't keep on a man separated from his wife. Not even him. Despite all he'd done for them. The elders wouldn't risk damaging the church's reputation.

"I'll talk to the other elders tonight and get back to you in the morning. I don't think there will be any problem. You've both given us your everything. You've more than earned the time off." Archie laughed. "Elders are supposed to teach. It's time we all took a turn."

Good. One of his reservations about going was that someone might come in and steal his congregation. With no single leader in charge, the church would be desperate for his return. Charismatic leaders were a danger he could do without.

illiam spoke with Archie the next morning, then picked up the letter from Reg and punched in the phone number he'd given. The phone rang and rang. William sighed. Was he sorry or not Reg wasn't there? His doubts about the wisdom of this decision puzzled him. He was usually Mr Decisive.

84

He was about to hang the phone up when a breathless voice said, "Reg speaking."

William gripped the handset, his palm sweaty. He'd felt like this back when he'd applied for his first job. It had been years since he'd had to apply for anything. His book deals and even the radio programme had all come about without him seeking them. "William Macdonald, ringing in response to your letter."

"Good to hear from you, William. Give me a second while I catch my breath. I've run in from my shed."

Was Reg retired then? Strange. He sounded younger.

"Are you going to come and help us out then?" The voice had a gentle, lilting quality, an unhurried country voice without the harshness of city stress. The nervous tension in William's abdomen uncoiled.

"I am available, but there's one problem—" He needed to phrase this carefully. "My wife is unable to come."

"Oh?"

"We've had a death in the family, and she's at my mother's, sorting things out."

There was silence at the other end of the phone. Reg cleared his throat. "I'm sorry to hear that. Are you sure you don't need to stay with her?"

"She's got things in hand, and it's easier without me in the way." He gave a self-deprecating laugh.

"Well, that brings me to another question."

Despite the leisurely voice, this man didn't sound the kind to be easily fooled. What if he asked a question requiring a direct answer rather than a mere sidestep?

"Are you a cook?"

William's neck tightened. Good grief. Was there an unwritten rule the interim minister had to offer hospitality to all and sundry?

William gave a small cough. "Not really. Burnt toast is my specialty."

"My wife has done the cooking for several interim pastors before, and she's willing to do it again. If you take care of your breakfasts and lunches, she'll look after your evening meals."

William's shoulders relaxed. "That sounds wonderful. Your letter mentioned the need to order supplies from Sydney?"

"We'll do it, as long as you're happy with her home-made muesli and toast."

Happy? He'd be relieved to not have to think about mundane things. This was sounding better and better.

William found himself agreeing to leave in two days for an island he knew little about. Reg had tentatively pre-booked the plane ticket and would now confirm it.

"If you turn up at Sydney Airport with your driver's license, the ticket will be there."

William hung up the phone and stared at his bookcase. Two days and he'd be on a plane, flying somewhere he'd never planned to go. A speck in the Pacific Ocean. That probably meant it was hot. Or was it? Could it be prone to cyclones? He'd better check.

He had to tug the 'L' encyclopedia out of the bookcase in the hall and blow the dust off the top. It probably hadn't been opened since Esther left school twelve years ago. Something to send to the charity shop when he returned. Assuming they'd accept something so out-of-date.

He opened the large volume. The spine creaked in protest and the pages crackled as he turned them. "L-I," he murmured. "L-O. L-O-R." There it was. A small crescent shaped island in the Tasman Sea between Australia and New Zealand, 600 km directly east of Port Macquarie on the mainland.

Tasman Sea. He'd assumed it would be considered part of the Pacific. He looked at the map. The island was ten kilometres long and never more than two kilometres wide. What was he doing? Marooning himself on a pimple on the southern fringe of the Pacific.

Mount Gower, he read, was the tallest mountain at 875 metres. The entire southern part of the island was covered in subtropical forest.

He continued to skim the salient points. Settled from 1834 ... A birdwatchers' paradise. He scanned for the essentials. Good, the island was part of New South Wales and therefore used Australian currency.

He ran his finger over the chart with average temperatures. It was much cooler than he'd expected. He'd have to pack some warm clothes. Somehow, he'd assumed the temperature would be more like the Great Barrier Reef, but it was considerably further south.

Back in his office he wrote a long 'to do' list. Bills—water, electricity, and gas. Gardener. Tell Blanche. Contact details to the office. Then he left a blank space before listing the clothes and books he'd need.

Two days. The tension ran up his spine. Would two days be enough time to get everything ready?

He went into his bedroom and began to lay clothes on the bed. Two suits, two sets of pyjamas, underwear, shirts, and a coat.

He clicked his tongue. He mustn't forget a decent raincoat. Or a comb.

It had been more than forty years since he'd had to pack for himself. Packing was another of Blanche's jobs. How often had he thanked her? Maybe that was part of her problem, not wanting to be taken for granted. He jotted, 'send flowers to Blanche' on his list. He'd give her his address and phone number with the card, in case she wanted to contact him.

He added notepaper, envelopes, and stamps to the pile of things. He could write a good letter. That might help the situation with Blanche. Hopefully she was getting herself sorted out and would soon see reason.

CHAPTER 13

"*B*lanche, did you get the job?" Gina asked before she was fully through the door the following Saturday.

Blanche couldn't contain her grin. "I did. Fifteen hours a week, starting on Monday."

"Congratulations!"

Blanche dropped her thimble. "I've been klutzy all week. The nerves are getting to me."

"You'll be fine. Wait until we're all here and you can tell us all about it."

Gina was such a dear. How had Blanche managed to miss her qualities in the past? She'd let William's views on Esther's friends cloud her judgment. Her world had revolved around the wrong central point. That must never happen again. *Oh Lord, please let there be a new start for William. Help him to seek you.*

Everyone had brought several draft designs. Joy's square focused on Esther's love for music. Gina had been to the library and traced a horse outline on hers, and Rachel's stethoscope had come from a medical textbook.

"I'm going to stick to ironing the seams," Naomi said. "Embroidery is beyond me nowadays."

Blanche showed them how to trace out their designs, pin on the material, and get the right balance of objects before she headed back to the sewing machine to work on the main framing of each block. At this rate, they might be able to begin on the words of *Amazing Grace* next week. It would take planning and patience to measure all the words so they were distributed evenly around the quilt's border.

Later, when they all took a break, Joy asked. "Blanche, was your job interview as scary as you'd thought it would be?"

"It wasn't hard at all," Blanche said. She still couldn't believe she had a job. "Naida asked me to bring in photos of my quilts, and she recognised one of them."

"Where from?" Gina asked.

"The church banner that won the Easter Show four years ago. She must have seen it on display." Blanche looked away to hide the small smile of pride she couldn't keep off her face. "Anyway, she didn't really ask me any questions after that."

"Was the winning banner the one with all the biblical flora and fauna?" Gina asked. "I loved that one."

"That's the one." Blanche allowed herself a bigger smile. "Then I told her about this quilt, and she got excited about it. Said she thought others would be interested in the idea of memory quilts and might even want to learn how to make one themselves." Blanche looked around the group. "Would you be willing for our quilt to be displayed as an advertisement for a class?"

"It's not a problem with me," Gina said. "Does it bother anyone?"

They all shook their heads.

"It was going to have to go somewhere," Rachel said. "It may as well help you with your job. Esther would be pleased."

The doorbell rang, and Rachel got up. They heard her muffled voice talking to someone at the front door.

"Mum, delivery for you," Rachel called.

Blanche got up and went out into the hall to see Rachel carrying a large purple orchid.

"They're probably from him." Rachel wrinkled her nose. "Trying to buy your favour."

Blanche opened the card. William's writing was still capable of giving her palpitations. Before they were married he used to write eloquent love letters. Their rarity had made them even more precious.

THESE COME WITH MANY THANKS FOR ALL YOU'VE DONE FOR ME OVER THE YEARS.

She covered her mouth with her hand. It was lovely to be thanked—she'd often wondered if William even noticed all she did. If only she could believe the words. She'd become cynical, and when would William learn to deal with issues rather than sending gifts? She turned the card over.

I'M TAKING TWO MONTHS LEAVE. AN INTERIM POST ON LORD HOWE ISLAND. THE DUTIES WILL BE LIGHT, SO THERE WILL BE PLENTY OF TIME TO TAKE THE REST THAT EVERYONE SEEMS TO THINK WOULD BE OF BENEFIT.

Lord Howe Island! He must be mad. How was her city-bred husband going to cope on a tiny island with few people and even fewer amenities? The only things on the island would be sand, salt, and seagulls, none of which he had the slightest interest in.

She plopped herself on the nearest chair. This was unexpected, but it did give her more space. More space to work out what she should do next. She gave a wobbly laugh and looked down at the card again.

WRITE.

Was that a plea or a command? She'd be more inclined to do it if he'd softened it with a please.

Her whole body felt lighter. Two months would give her more time to pray now that the first knife thrusts of grief were over. Two months would allow her to settle into work and see if such a lifestyle suited her.

But was two months long enough for the miracle she prayed for? She'd wait and see. William didn't see the need to change. A transformed William might be a miracle too hard even for the creator of the universe.

CHAPTER 14

*T*he plane droned over the Pacific. William returned to reading his book. There was nothing to look at but sea and more sea.

When the intercom finally crackled with the announcement they were descending, William checked the window. Nothing was visible yet, but the island was so small he'd miss it if he read another page of his book. Only 350 permanent residents. Victory had more teens attending youth group. Would he go out of his mind with boredom?

An excited chatter burst out from the other side of the plane. Zooming towards the airstrip, William only had time to glimpse the mountains carpeted in rainforest and the breathtaking blue-green of the lagoon. At least the beauty lived up to the glossy advertisements.

There were no normal procedures, merely a stroll across the hot tarmac to a building about the size of a bus station, where it only took a few minutes to collect his luggage. This truly was in the sticks.

The scrawny sparrow of a man checking all the strangers

walking through the door must be Reg. A smile cracked his weath-ered face and he walked forward, hand outstretched. "You must be William. Welcome to Lord Howe."

Obviously this place was less formal than William was used to. He could kiss Reverend Doctor goodbye.

"I've borrowed a car to take your things. Most of us walk or ride bikes."

Bikes! William stifled an eye roll.

"But I'll take you for a mini tour while we've got wheels, eh?"

William looked around and pretended enthusiasm. The main street—if you could call it that—was a ramshackle assortment of ten or twelve businesses. He'd never visited a place with which it took so little time to familiarise himself. A map would be a waste of paper.

"Here we are," Reg said as they pulled into a driveway with an old gate propped open with a rock. "Ivy has filled the fridge and cupboards with breakfast things. We're through the gate over there." Reg pointed towards a fence to the left. "We'll expect you at six for dinner, and I'd love to pray with you afterwards. I always like to start an interim ministry by giving things into God's hands."

William blinked. He couldn't object—it wouldn't look good. Reg helped William unload the car, then handed him a keyring with a single key. "I doubt the door is locked. We don't usually bother, but it's there if you want it." He laughed.

"I'll be fine," William said. "Thanks for—" He gestured around. He couldn't say "thanks for everything". He wasn't sure he felt thankful. All he knew was he wanted Reg to go and leave him alone.

"Cheerio, then." Reg reversed his borrowed car out.

A tree near the front door dropped scented flowers onto the green lawn. William manhandled his suitcase up the two steps onto the verandah. He pushed the front door and went into the shady coolness. The house smelled a little musty, but all the windows

CHRISTINE DILLON

were open and there were fresh flowers in the middle of the dining room table. When had he last stepped into a house like this? It was adequate, he supposed, but a far cry from his daily life.

Unpacking took him twenty minutes. He shook out his clothes before hanging them. His suit shirts would need ironing, but he'd search for the iron and board later. Ironing was one household task he'd mastered before his marriage. Looking smart was an essential both for a marketer and a preacher.

Reaching deep into the pocket of the suitcase, he heard a rustle and pulled out a letter—the one his mother had sent after Esther's funeral. Strange. He didn't remember packing it. He shoved it back into the pocket and pushed the suitcase under the bed.

There was nothing for him to do inside. How was he going to fill his time until six? Perhaps he could visit the church and practice his sermon.

He opened his briefcase and took out his sermon folder. He'd brought a selection of his recent sermons. He had no plans to spend his time preparing new material. The congregation wouldn't know they were getting rehashed sermons.

With the folder under his arm, he picked up the key from the dining table. The residents here might not lock their doors, but he'd brought his brand-new laptop. As he turned the key, he heard a noise in the bushes. His neck hairs prickled. Were there animals on the island? Or snakes? He'd have to ask.

He hurried over to the church building. The door was unlocked. In fact, there didn't seem to be a lock. That didn't bode well for the quality of the equipment inside.

He was right. Simple wooden pews marched in pairs either side of the central aisle. The platform was only raised six inches. The audio equipment consisted of two microphones on stands and a single speaker. He exhaled noisily. Thankfully, he'd trained his voice for a huge auditorium. He needn't be limited by their equipment.

He walked up the front, placed his folder on the lectern, and stood, looking out at an imaginary congregation. The sides of the folder hanging over the edge poked into his fingers. He took his hands away again. It didn't feel right. Too cramped. No matter. Preaching didn't require a custom-made lectern. He opened his mouth for the first line of his sermon. He'd have to say a few words of thanks for allowing him to come and pad it with fluff about being glad to be here. *Blah, blah, blah.*

His voice echoed in the room. *Gracious.* Terrible acoustics. He'd have to pull his voice way back and slow down. Trying it again, he preached the first minute of his sermon. This felt better. His sermon would wake this sleepy place up. After two months it was likely he'd leave the church bigger than when he started. These places tended to plod on from week to week, rather like the dying church he'd inherited. It hadn't taken him long to turn it around. Rebranding had been one of the first factors. Gave it a name to be proud of. Victory—who could fail to be stirred by such a name?

Odd that the pulpit was way off to one side. He wriggled the heavy piece of furniture. It wasn't attached to the floor. He half pushed it and half dragged it to the centre of the room, where it should be. Much better. Preaching was what the church was about, so why had they put the pulpit in such an out-of-the-way position?

He found a broom and swept away the dust marks from where he'd moved the pulpit. Sweeping only took him a few minutes, and there was still an hour to dinner. What was he going to do in this place?

He went out the main entrance of the church, strolled around the garden, and poked into the shed. Gardening tools, a couple of deck chairs, and a kayak. He'd have to ask about a pool or a gym. They'd probably tell him to go to the beach. He shuddered. He liked swimming but never in open water. Rivers and oceans reminded him of Ian. Even golden boys weren't immune from drowning.

There was a loud creak. A young boy was swinging on the gate between the church and Reg's place.

William was about to reprimand the boy but changed his mind. It wasn't his gate, and it looked like the boy and the gate had come to an understanding long ago.

The boy grinned at him. His skin was a mass of freckles and his eyes sparkled. "Are you the new minister?" he called.

William walked towards him. "I guess I am for the next two months. Who are you?"

"I'm Davy." He pointed his thumb over his shoulder. "I live there."

"With the—"

He nodded. "They're my Gramps and Grams."

William raised his eyebrows. He'd have to ask Reg for details.

"I heard you in the church. You sounded funny talking to yourself."

Was this kid going to be a pest who'd hang around all day and comment on everything he did? He decided to take control of the conversation. "What year are you in at school?"

Davy straightened and puffed out his chest. "I'm in Year Two and the fastest runner in the school. Were you a fast runner?"

He thought back to a race down the street with some of the neighbourhood kids when they were about Davy's size. He'd been winning, hadn't he? Or had it been his best friend, Timmy? Neither of them had a chance after Ian decided to join in. Smarter, faster, better. He made a face. "I was better at debating."

"What's debating?"

"A sort of speaking competition. You have to argue your case."

Davy frowned. "Didn't you do any running or swimming?"

"Of course." William grinned in what he hoped was a friendly way. "I still swim a few times a week. Is there a public swimming pool on the island?"

Davy raised an eyebrow. "Why do we need a pool when we've

got the sea?" He pointed towards the water. "You can see fish while you swim."

William didn't plan to swim in the ocean anytime soon. "What about a gym? Does the island have a gym?"

"What's a gym?"

William shrugged. "It's not important. Just something we have in Sydney. A place where you can use all sorts of machines to get exercise."

Davy cocked his head to one side. "Why would you need machines to help you exercise?"

"It must seem strange to you. Have you been to Sydney?"

Davy shook his head. "I've never been anywhere but here."

Davy's whole life was 350 people plus tourists.

Poor kid. He had no idea what he was missing. Davy clearly had potential, but he'd never use it if he remained here.

CHAPTER 15

*B*lanche was early. Would it look better if she turned up with time to spare, or would that put Naida out? Perhaps she'd better sit in the car and pray. Or try to pray. She was sweating, and she never sweated. She took her handkerchief out of her handbag and dabbed the beads of perspiration on her forehead.

The clock ticked on ten minutes. She opened the car door. As she pulled out the keys she dropped them on the floor of the car and had to fumble for them. She hadn't been this nervous since the first time William asked her out.

By paying careful attention, she made it to the store without tripping over or walking in front of another car.

Naida looked up as she went in. "Good morning, Blanche. Good to see you nice and early. I'll show you where to put your things, then I'll start as I hope we can continue."

What could Naida mean?

Naida indicated the door at the back. There was a space crammed with rolls of fabric, a lock-up cupboard for their bags, and a tiny bathroom, which Blanche used. She peered into the mirror above the sink, ran her hands over her hair, and reapplied her lipstick. Then went back into the main part of the shop.

"I've never had an employee before," Naida said. "Now that I know you're a Christian, I'd love us to start each morning with prayer. Would that be okay?"

Blanche nodded. She didn't trust herself to speak. This job was a gift from God, and to have a Christian boss as well was almost overwhelming.

Naida bowed her head and prayed without hesitation. "Dear heavenly Father, thank you for blessing this business so I need extra help. Thank you for sending Blanche to join me at exactly the right time."

Blanche blew her nose. It was humbling to be the answer to someone's prayers.

"Thank you for the gifts and talents you've given her. Please use us for your glory right here in our shop," Naida continued. "Send people to us in whose lives you're already working. In your name, Amen."

Was she expected to pray? Blanche glanced at Naida, who still had her eyes shut. Blanche took a deep breath. "Heavenly Father, thank you for giving me this job." It was less than six months since she'd first prayed in public, and now she was praying with someone who was almost a stranger. Amazing. "You know I've never worked in a shop or anywhere much at all. Help us to work as a team in a way that honours you. Help me to learn quickly. In Jesus' name, Amen."

They both looked up at the same time and grinned sheepishly at each other. Kind of weird, but nice.

Blanche pointed at the cash register. "I've never used one of those. You'd better teach me before the first customer arrives." She laughed nervously. "I'm not sure my bungling would honour Jesus."

Naida laughed. "Humour too. I am blessed."

Blanche blinked. No one had ever said she had a sense of humour.

They'd just finished the how-to session on the register when the first customer bought a pile of fabric and thread. Naida hovered in the background while Blanche managed the cash register for the first time, albeit slowly, and said goodbye to the customer. A glow of satisfaction warmed her heart.

"Soon it will be second nature. Now let's get you familiar with the stock and how to order."

Fabric had been Blanche's constant companion since high school. It had always been a pleasure to feel, smell, and work with beautiful fabric. She soon grasped what Naida was telling her. It didn't seem right to receive pay for working in such a place. She took a deep breath. Subtle fabric scents, the smell of heaven.

Naida constantly tidied the counters, rearranging and stacking. "Classes are where I want you to focus. They'll generate more customers, especially beginner classes. Speaking of which, when do you think your quilt will be finished and ready for display?"

"Soon," Blanche said. "Would you like me to bring in the embroidered wildflower panels first?"

Naida raised an eyebrow. "Why not? In fact, you could assemble the quilt on the central table. There is nothing like an actual project happening to bring in the customers." Naida glanced at the clock. "Do you think you can manage on your own while I have lunch?"

Blanche gulped. "Pray I don't get asked anything too complicated."

"If you do, have a good chat and delay them until I come back."

Blanche laughed. "Chatting I can do."

Naida had said lunchtime was busier. She was right. Blanche had five customers, but they were all clear on what they wanted, so she didn't have to solve any difficult problems. They all expressed surprise at seeing her, asked about Naida, and welcomed her to the job. They also patiently waited their turn in line and talked animatedly with the other customers.

"Do you quilt?" one lady asked Blanche.

She shared about the projects she'd been involved with and the memory quilt.

"I've never heard of those," one middle-aged woman said.

"Us oldies have heard about them," another said.

"If I come back next week, could you tell me more?"

"Naida asked me to bring my memory quilt in as soon as I can," Blanche said. Should she tell them about the class? "Naida hopes people will see the quilt and want to do a class."

"Will you have a sign-up sheet here next week? I'm Mary. You can sign me up."

"I'm not sure how fast we'll get things going. It's only my first day."

Naida came back in the door.

"Naida, we like your new assistant," the middle-aged woman called across the shop. "She's already convinced us to sign up for the new class."

"Looks like I'll have to promote Blanche soon."

The women laughed and headed back to work. Watching them leave triggered a thought in Blanche's mind. "Naida, when do you run the classes?"

Naida considered a moment. "We've always done them in the mornings, but then we only get retirees. Evenings might work, but it makes for a long day."

"Have you considered running lunchtime classes?"

"For workers, you mean?" Naida rubbed her ear. "But normally classes run for two to three hours."

"The memory quilt group I've been running is only an hour."

"One hour. What can you get done in an hour?"

Had she overstepped the mark by suggesting something new on the first day? The last hour had raised her confidence. "It's a different mentality. You don't come expecting to finish a project. It's more of a regular catch up for inspiration and to stay on track. They do most of their sewing at home."

Naida nibbled her lip. "You know, it might work. We could do an experiment and run the memory quilt class two ways. One morning class from ten to twelve, and one lunchtime class from twelve to one."

Blanche nodded. "Yes, see what's most effective."

Naida grinned. "If only I'd found you earlier. I've been missing out and haven't even realised it."

CHAPTER 16

*B*lanche pulled the desk drawer open and selected two pieces of writing paper. Blue with a gold edging. Paper that was a pleasure to write on.

Naomi had urged her to write, and William had almost commanded it. Well, Blanche would do it, but on her own terms. She'd write like she was writing to a friend. There'd been so many lies, so many things unsaid. She might not have the courage to say them all, but she was determined to write them.

Dear William,

By now you will be on Lord Howe Island. I wonder what you are making of it.

You asked me to write, and Mum thinks it's a good idea. I'm not so sure, but I'm not willing to give up on our marriage. I made promises and I intend to keep them, with the Lord's help.

Who was this new woman? Maybe she should have been writing letters all these years. When she wrote, she wasn't intimidated by William's facial expressions or the way he stepped into her personal space. Too often, his shadow had overawed her and reduced her to a quivering mouse.

I'M GOING TO WRITE ABOUT WHO I AM NOW AND WITHOUT CENSORING ANYONE OUT OF IT. I DON'T REGRET A SINGLE MINUTE OF LIVING HERE. IF I WERE TO SEE YOU TODAY, I MIGHT PUMMEL MY FISTS ON YOUR CHEST BECAUSE YOU KEPT ME AWAY FROM YOUR MOTHER. SHE ADMITS SHE WAS A DIFFERENT WOMAN WHEN YOU KNEW HER, BUT JESUS HAS CHANGED HER. BEING HERE IS AN OASIS. SEEING HER OFTEN IS ONE OF MY NON-NEGOTIABLES. I'M ANNOYED—

No. Annoyed wasn't strong enough. She crossed it out and continued.

I'M ANGRY YOU DEPRIVED ME OF SOMEONE WHO COULD HAVE BEEN MY SUPPORT ALL THESE YEARS. AND I'M ANGRY AT MYSELF FOR LISTENING TO YOU. I SHOULD HAVE BEEN FRIENDS WITH YOUR MOTHER. WHAT A DIFFERENCE THAT COULD HAVE MADE IN MY LIFE.

NOW I HAVE HER SUPPORT AND THE SUPPORT OF ESTHER'S FRIENDS, I'VE DISCOVERED HOW LONELY I'VE BEEN ALL THESE YEARS. I LIVED ON A PEDESTAL, NEVER BEING PART OF THE PEOPLE I WAS SUPPOSED TO BE SERVING. BEING SEPARATE SPARED ME PAIN, BUT IT HAS ALSO REMOVED ME FROM THE JOY AND SATISFACTION THAT COMES FROM GETTING MY HANDS DIRTY.

AND RACHEL. IT HASN'T BEEN EASY, BECAUSE I WASN'T THERE

FOR HER FOR TOO LONG. SHE'S WORKING AT A JOB SHE LOVES. IT
MAY NOT BE FANCY, BUT IT'S GOOD FOR HER. SHE COMES HOME
FROM THE PLANT NURSERY WITH A GLOW IN HER EYES AND A SONG
IN HER HEART. SHE SAYS BEING WITH PLANTS ALL DAY IS CALMING.
SHE'S BEEN PROMOTED TO CHIEF DESIGNER AND DOES ALL THE
MAIN DISPLAYS.

HER WORKPLACE IS ANOTHER FAMILY. DIRK, HER BOSS, IS
ONLY ABLE TO MANAGE PART-TIME WORK AFTER HIS HEART
ATTACK, BUT THE SON, PETE, UNDERSTANDS THE VIBE OF THE
PLACE. SHE VISITS DIRK AND HIS WIFE AT LEAST ONCE A WEEK.
HER OTHER GOOD FRIEND THERE IS JOSH. HOW CAN I DESCRIBE
HIM? HE IS FULL OF CHILDLIKE WISDOM. HE IS THE KIND OF
PERSON RACHEL NEEDS AROUND HER. SOMEONE IN WHOM THERE
IS NO FALSEHOOD. HE LOVES HER LIKE AN OLDER SISTER.

Had she written enough to intrigue William? To make him see
what he was missing out on? She'd avoided mentioning the most
obvious thing about Josh, the thing that made everyone he met
judge him. She'd heard people express the belief that one day all
Down syndrome foetuses would be aborted. She shuddered. Who
would want to live in such a world? Josh's Down syndrome was the
gift that made him the special person he was.

She tapped her pen on the desk. They must invite Josh over.
Maybe they could all go out for a picnic. He'd like that. Did he get
asked out by people other than his direct family? What a narrow
existence he must have had before Dirk employed him. Bless
the man.

Writing in this way was freeing. Blanche Macdonald, uncen-
sored. She'd kept a tight rein on everything she said for most of her
life, and it hadn't led anywhere worthwhile. If this was a mid-life
crisis, it was nothing to be afraid of.

I'VE FINISHED SORTING ESTHER'S THINGS. IT WAS TOUGH, AS IT
STIRRED UP SO MANY MEMORIES, BUT IT ALLOWED ME TO GRIEVE
PROPERLY. I BELIEVE GOD GAVE ME THE IDEA TO MAKE A QUILT IN
MEMORY OF ESTHER.

I'M WORKING ON IT WITH MUM, RACHEL, JOY, AND GINA. I
HOPE YOU'LL SEE IT WHEN IT'S FINISHED.

I'D ALWAYS KEPT MYSELF AWAY FROM DYING PEOPLE AND, AS A
RESULT, MISSED OUT ON SO MUCH. I WAS A FOOL.

She'd been about to write "we were fools" and thought better of
it. Suggesting William had faults would only increase his pushback.

I HAD NEVER REALISED WHAT A GREAT PRIVILEGE IT IS TO SPEND
TIME WITH SOMEONE WHO IS DYING AND WHO KNOWS JESUS.

A tear dropped onto the page. Blanche touched it, and the word
beneath it smudged. She'd never forget their last night with Esther.
Despite Esther's pain and physical weakness, that last night was like
standing in the anteroom of heaven. Esther didn't leave crying and
complaining. She left with the triumphant shout of a child running
home, confident in her welcome.

Thank you, Jesus, for forcing me on this journey.

She reread everything she'd written. No, she wasn't going to
change it. It was time William heard her heart. She'd always with-
held it from him. Not trusted him with it. Their marriage had been
impressive from the outside, but it was all a façade, an optical illu-
sion. She'd been guilty of propping up the fake fronts as much as
William.

Blanche nibbled the end of her pen. What to write next?

THE BIG NEWS THIS WEEK IS I'VE STARTED WORK AT A QUILTING
SHOP. I NEVER EXPECTED TO GET A JOB, BUT IT WAS OFFERED TO
ME. I'VE BEEN AT A LOOSE END WITH LITTLE TO OCCUPY MY TIME.
SITTING AT HOME ALL DAY MADE ME TOO INTROSPECTIVE AND I
WANTED TO CONTRIBUTE TO THE HOUSEHOLD. I PRAYED ABOUT IT
AND TALKED IT OVER WITH THE OTHERS.

What would she do without them? They'd become a society of sisters, supporting each other in everything. William was likely soldiering on, on his own. What was it with men?

IT'S ONLY FIFTEEN HOURS A WEEK, BUT IT'S A PERFECT FIT. SOON
I'LL START TEACHING TWO CLASSES. NAIDA IS A RELAXING PERSON
TO WORK FOR. IT LOOKS LIKE MY FIRST CLASS WILL BE TEACHING
PEOPLE TO MAKE MEMORY QUILTS LIKE WE'VE MADE FOR ESTHER.

William would probably tell others that she was teaching and neglect to mention the subject. She'd always excused his pretensions as harmless, but false fronts weren't harmless. False fronts blew down in storms and hurt people. The Bible likened Judgement Day to a fire. Only materials like silver and gold would survive. Grass, wood, and stubble would burn up. What would survive from her life? From William's?

She ended the main body of the letter with general questions about Lord Howe and his situation. It took her a full five minutes to decide how to sign off. Your very own Blanche was too intimate. Sincerely was too cold and businesslike. In the end she wrote.

In Christ, Blanche.

That was true, no matter what.

Putting her head in her hand she prayed. *Lord, use something I've written to help William. You are master of the universe, so please master us. Turn our hearts towards you and towards each other.*

She'd likened their marriage to a false front. Her breath caught in her throat. When did a marriage become unsalvageable?

CHAPTER 17

*H*e should have known the church service would be a disaster. The most competent person present was the bell ringer, and that turned out to be eight-year-old Davy. The congregation might win the world record for the oldest average age. People addressed him as 'young man'.

The microphones either squealed or didn't pick up the voices. The organ wheezed, and Davy had to get on his knees and pump it by hand more than once. And the singing. Well, the singing had stumbled along with what appeared to be people singing two different songs. It might just have been two different speeds, but it sounded bad. Really bad. He congratulated himself for not plugging his ears.

There were only about twenty-five attendees, and they sat in scattered groups. The singing might have had a chance if he could have convinced everyone to sit in the first five rows. Or turn on their hearing aids. As it was, they probably couldn't hear each other, which might account for their ragged efforts.

The traditional parts of the service, the Creed and Lord's Prayer, were coherent, but William had never seen the value of reciting liturgy. Not that he could cut tradition, but he intended to do something about the singing. If he didn't, he wasn't going to last two weeks, let alone two months.

The one thing he could guarantee was that his sermon would be smooth and professional. A shame that he'd bowed to Reg's suggestion of someone else doing the Bible reading. If it was done at the same standard as everything else, the service would be better without one.

Reg got to his feet and walked to the front. He opened the Bible and found the page. "1 Samuel 17." His words were slow and clear.

William had told Reg to only read the ten verses he'd preach on. Had Reg forgotten?

There was a rustling of pages. Reg watched as the congregation found the place. It took an age. William would have to see what he could do to speed things up. Reg opened his mouth and began to read. His voice was a little rough. Not good enough to have earned him the right to read publicly at Victory. "Now the Philistines gathered their forces for war and assembled at Socoh in Judah. They pitched camp at Ephes Dammim, between Socoh and Azekah.'"

Why not skip the complicated names? Reg didn't stumble on a single one, but listening was tedious.

"'Goliath stood and shouted to the ranks of Israel, "Why do you come out and line up for battle? Am I not a Philistine, and are you not the servants of Saul? Choose a man and have him come down to me. If he is able to fight and kill me, we will become your subjects; but if I overcome him and kill him, you will become our subjects and serve us."'"

How could such a scrap of a man project the voice of a giant? Yet Reg's voice rang out. "'"This day I defy the armies of Israel! Give me a man and let us fight each other."'"

Reg had obviously prepared. William snuck a glance around the congregation. Several followed the words in their Bibles, but most sat with their eyes closed. The looks on their faces—oh, the looks on their faces. He'd never seen anything like it. Was it joy?

He'd seen adulation from his myriad of fans, yet these people paid no attention to Reg. It was the words. They lapped the words up like they were the sweetest spring water in the world.

Reg didn't hurry. Every phrase, every nuance was perfect. He must have spent hours practicing to get to that standard.

There was no shuffling of feet, no staring out the windows at the sun dancing outside, no fiddling with pens. Only rapt attention.

"'The king said, "Find out whose son this young man is." As soon as David returned from killing the Philistine, Abner took him and brought him before Saul, with David still holding the Philistine's head. "Whose son are you, young man?" Saul asked him. David said, "I am the son of your servant Jesse of Bethlehem."' This is the word of the Lord." Reg closed the Bible.

"Thanks be to God." The congregation responded in perfect unison. They sounded like they meant every word.

Something trembled deep in William's gut. For the first time in his career, he didn't want to get up and preach. How could he follow something so sincere, so full of absolute assurance? People said he was confident, but they hadn't heard Reg. Reg's confidence was as different from his as a rainforest is from a single tree.

William shivered and opened his mouth for his introduction. He'd woken before the dawn and practiced his sermon. Whispering some lines and shouting others. Polishing the pacing. Counting out the pauses. Emphasising for impact.

Yet his carefully composed lines seemed to come out as a meaningless collection of discordant notes. It wasn't his fault. It was the congregation. It was as if he spoke to a collection of corpses. They didn't laugh at his jokes or appreciate his catchy headings. They didn't hang on his every word. He tried, oh he tried, but whatever he did, failed. Three of the old dears turned off their hearing aids and settled down for a pleasant nap.

William saw Reg out of the corner of his eye. His head was down. Praying?

This motley bunch of geriatrics probably didn't even know who he was. A preacher to thousands, with a radio programme that went even further afield. Talk about giving pearls to pigs.

Why didn't they close the doors and blow the place up? It would be a mercy.

CHAPTER 18

*M*onday, day off or not, William had risen at dawn. There was so much to do at Victory he'd gotten into the habit of rising early to fit it all in. Here, though, the week stretched ahead of him with nothing but a few pastoral visits. Reg had given him a list of the names and addresses he was to call on over the next two months.

He hadn't done pastoral visits in years. That's why he had elders. They divided the task between themselves and left him to concentrate on church growth strategy, developing his leaders, and preaching. He grimaced. Yesterday had been a disaster. No praise from anyone for his sermon, only Davy's earnest assurance he'd get better with practice. Oh well, the congregation would get used to his style, and he'd survive seven more weeks.

For now, he'd better get out and explore so he'd have something to write to Blanche about. He clearly wouldn't be writing much about the church.

A bicycle was waiting down at the shed, tyres fully pumped and seat at the proper height. He hadn't been on a bike since his early twenties, except for the stationary bike in his personal gym.

He pushed the bike out into the yard and checked over his shoulder before straddling the unstable creature and pushing off. He lurched a little to one side and had to put his feet down. Take it slowly. He'd manage. They always said no one forgot a skill like cycling. He pushed off again and did a few circles of the lawn. Did he hear a giggle?

Perhaps walking would be better for today. He parked the bike and set off for the beach, footsteps crunching on the gravel. A cool breeze feathered his hair and he shivered. He should have brought a jumper.

The beach was a wide strip of pale sand, smoothed by last night's high tide. Tiny waves lapped against the shore, and the sea glimmered turquoise, the darker patches revealing the presence of coral under the surface. Several snorkelers were swimming up and down in erratic circles.

He shivered, shaded his eyes, and looked further out. Beyond the reef, the sea darkened to a deep blue fringed with the frilly froth of breaking waves. The area towards the shore looked more like a huge, protected pool. Nothing to be afraid of. Perhaps he'd search the garage for snorkelling gear. If he had something to keep his attention, he might not notice where he was swimming. He'd glimpsed a kayak and boogie boards. What else was hidden in the garage's depths?

He took off his shoes, knotted their laces, and stuffed his socks in the toes. The cool sand pumiced his feet. He couldn't remember when he'd last been to a beach. Rachel had been the beach baby. *Rachel.* Memories of her were locked in one of the drawers in his mind, one he avoided opening for years at a time.

Now Blanche was staying with his mother and Rachel, his mind slipped their way more often. Did Blanche like snorkelling, or would she prefer to sit on the beach? He didn't know. Forty plus years since they'd met, and he couldn't remember the last time he'd asked her a question about herself.

"Mr Macdonald, Mr Macdonald, wait."

He turned around. Davy skidded to a stop on a bike that had seen better days. He grabbed two sets of snorkels out of the basket attached to his bike and scampered over. "Grandpa won't let me snorkel alone."

"Aren't you going to school today?"

"It's still early. Plenty of time before school." He kicked off his shoes and moved towards the water. "Lots of the pastors let me go snorkelling with them. Early morning is best, before it gets too hot or windy." He looked back at William, face alight with expectation, and offered one of the snorkel sets.

Best to give in with good grace. He hadn't the heart to watch Davy's expressive face fall with disappointment. He'd have to go in with his running shorts. He reached out his hand and took the snorkel set.

"Cool," Davy said. "Come on, then." He grabbed William's hand to drag him towards the water.

"Wait, wait," William said. "Let me at least put my shoes down and take off my shirt."

"Don't want to miss anything." Davy stepped into the water, spat in his mask, and scooped up a handful of water to swirl it out.

William put down his things in a neat pile beside the clothes and shoes Davy had scattered in his haste. Then, checking no one was near, he spat in his mask and followed Davy into the water. He drew in a sharp breath at the cold.

Davy already had his mask on. "Come on, come on." He pranced in the water.

William dragged his mask on. At least it fit.

"Haven't you been snorkelling before?" Davy said, his head on one side.

"How did you know?"

Davy pointed. "You've got hair in your mask. The water will get in. Every bit has to be pulled out."

Davy splashed around as he waited for William to obey.

"Now you put the snorkel into your mouth like this."

It took two tries before William grasped the snorkel correctly. He took it out to ask a question. "What if water gets into the snorkel?"

"Then you do this." Davy waded out to waist deep and dived under the water, moving like an over-enthusiastic puppy. He swam to the surface and water spurted out of the end of the snorkel. His head popped up, grinning. "Did you see, did you see? I went like this." He pursed his lips and gave a big huff.

William laughed. "I think I can manage that. You're a good teacher."

Davy puffed out his skinny chest. "You'd better stick by me until you get the hang of it."

A warmth settled into William's belly. This kid with his lopsided grin and sticking-out ears was endearing. All bobbit and bounce.

"Don't put your feet down out there. There's lots of sharp things, and it's bad for the coral."

William put the snorkel in his mouth and gingerly put his face in the water. A little water leaked into the snorkel, but he expelled it and adjusted his lips and grip on the mouthpiece. He took a few breaths until he was confident, then focused on what was beneath. The sand undulated below him. A tiny pale-rose fish approached his toes. He wriggled them, and the fish darted away. He laughed and swallowed a mouthful of water. Spluttering, he lifted his head.

"You okay, Mr Macdonald?"

He nodded. Davy would be growing impatient with him.

"You can't laugh or sing underwater." Davy grinned. "At least, not with a snorkel. I tried." He indicated a nearby patch of water. "I'll stick around here until you get the hang of it." He pushed off into slightly deeper water.

Perhaps William should practice swimming up and down and breathing first. He refitted the snorkel and took a few strokes. Then a few more. No problem. He only had to remember not to turn his head to breathe. Let the snorkel do its work.

He approached the first lump of coral, a miniature mountain rising off the sand desert beneath. He'd nearly moved on when he saw the first flicker. There was life there. And there and there. He was about to shout but remembered the consequences in time. He didn't want to lose sight of what was below. He floated, motionless, and slowly scanned the rock. What he'd taken for an empty rock was covered in small fissures and folds. Tiny plants clung for dear life—fawn and brown, pink and white, red and green. A miniature universe.

A dark-blue fish swam into view, and another. William watched as they moved along the rock and out towards deeper water, where he saw layer after layer of corals. Flat and rounded, small as a cat, or large as a small whale. He raised his head and scanned for Davy. He was only a few metres away. He'd obviously decided William needed watching and took his responsibilities seriously.

William grinned. If he kept grinning, his facial muscles would be sore. He hadn't grinned this much since he was Davy's age. Confident, all-conquering smiles and the serious intellectual look had been more his style.

The further he went and the slower he moved, the more he saw. Striped fish and spotted. Solid colour and multicoloured. Round shapes and slender pencil shapes. Black and white, pink and purple, blue and canary yellow. Tiny world upon tiny world, a feast for the eyes.

The coolness of the water enveloped him, and he glided forward. This must be what it was like to be a bird. Gliding and swooping above the creatures below. Did he look so insignificant to the birds? To God? Like the Psalm, "What is man that you are mindful of him?" He'd always thought he was significant, but out here made him think again. He must be the merest ant to God.

"Mr Macdonald," Davy yelled, loud and excited.

William raised his head and trod water to work out where Davy was.

Davy waved. "Come over here. Quickly."

What had he found? William swam over while scanning the seabed.

There it was. A mottled green turtle, grazing the seaweed like a cow in a paddock. It took no notice of them hovering above it. Davy raised his thumbs, and William raised his back, catching the excitement.

A sunbeam shot down into the water, changing the colour to gold. It was like swimming in cold champagne. More pinks and purples became visible. Davy pointed towards a crevice. William swam around so he could look into the shadowed area. Two long sticks protruded and moved. Some sort of creature lay hidden in the dark.

He poked his head up and spat out his snorkel. "What is it?"

"Lobster. A small one. They get much bigger."

A whistle pierced the air, and a figure on the grassy area waved at them.

"That's Grandpa. He knows I forget the time. Gotta go." Davy started swimming for the shore. William followed, hungrier than he'd been for weeks.

CHAPTER 19

*A*fter breakfast, William opened the gate between his place and next door. He was tired of reading. Reg had a carpentry workshop somewhere, and William was curious about Davy—why was he living with his grandparents?

The air was filled with a whirring sound and an accompanying buzz. He followed the sound around the back of a large shed. The main doors were open, and Reg stood in front of a spinning lathe. He touched a tool to the wood's surface, generating a cloud of dust.

William kept quiet, not wanting to disturb Reg's concentration. Reg picked up another tool and worked for a few more minutes. Then a third and a fourth. The wood dust swirled.

William moved closer to better see the emerging shape.

Reg reached to the right, clicked off the switch, and there was a sudden silence. He looked around. "Oh, William!" He smiled broadly. "Good morning. Thanks for going snorkelling with Davy."

William chuckled. "I'm not sure I had any choice."

"Yes, Davy knows what he wants. Don't be afraid to tell him if you're busy and don't want to be bothered."

It sounded easy, but William would find it hard to refuse the

119

appeal in Davy's eyes. Ian had had a dog with eyes like that, but the dog had been sent to the pound soon after the accident.

"Do you mind me watching?"

Reg wiped his hands on a cloth. "No. As long as you don't expect me to philosophise on something too abstract."

"What are you making?"

"I'm turning the central column for the drop-leaf table over there."

William turned and looked towards the table Reg pointed at. The main section was a rectangle, but there were extra flaps on each side to allow it to transform into a much larger round table. Clever. He peered closer at the grain. "What kind of wood is it?"

"Red cedar."

The grain met in peaks and lines. William ran his hand over the surface. He didn't have anything else to do, and there was something soothing about watching Reg work.

"If you want to watch, why don't you drag the stool over near the lathe? It will be easier."

The stool would also keep him from getting in the way. The corner of William's mouth twitched. Reg had a way of gently getting things done.

Reg turned the lathe on and held a template against the wood. The nails on the template scratched marks on the surface of the wood—much faster than drawing them in one at a time. As Reg picked up each chisel-like tool, he held it up for William to see. They were all angled in different ways, with sharp or rounded edges.

The lathe whirred as Reg held the tools to scrape away the unwanted parts of the wood. "Want to have a go?"

"Me?" William's voice rose. "I'll mess up your work."

"As long as you gently touch the edge of the tool to the wood, you'll be fine."

Reg first had him practice holding and angling the tools with the machine switched off. Then he switched on the lathe and swung the guard rail into place. "Let your back hand guide the tool. The front hand only needs a light touch."

"You didn't use the guard rail thing."

Reg chuckled. "I've been doing this since I was knee-high to a grasshopper."

Grasshopper. Davy was a bit like a grasshopper. Had Reg once been like his grandson? A knife-like thrust of pain lanced through William. *Grandchildren.* They weren't something he was ever likely to have. Rachel certainly wouldn't let him meet any child of hers.

"Ready?"

He placed the chisel—or whatever it was called—on the guard rail and eased it closer to the rotating block of wood.

"Angle down a little so the gouge is more horizontal." Reg raised his voice over the roar of the machine.

William obeyed and touched the tool to spinning wood. It leapt under his hand and he changed his grip pressure. A steady flow of dust shot out.

"Well done."

A warm glow rushed through him, surprising him with its intensity.

"Would you be interested in making something while you're here?"

"I'm sure you have better things to do." William regretted his flippant rejection the moment he said the words. He hadn't come here looking to make something, but the idea seemed strangely appealing. He could write about it to Blanche. It was something new. Maybe they'd both grown too predictable.

A bicycle bell trilled.

"That'll be the postman." Reg turned to the bench to pick up another of his countless tools. "Could you go and get the mail for me while I finish this off?"

William reached Reg's box in time to see the postman dropping something into the box out the front of the church. A letter for him? It seemed unlikely at this early stage of his visit, but he would check. With Reg's small pile of letters in his hand, he walked over to his own box. There was a smooth, blue envelope, with his name in a familiar hand on the front. *Blanche.*

He shoved Blanche's letter into his back pocket to read later and took five steps towards Reg's gate. He stopped. No. He'd read it now.

He sat on a log near the front fence and skimmed through the two pages. If the letter hadn't been Blanche's writing, with its artistic, loopy letters, he would have thought it had been written by a stranger. Where had this confidence come from? His Blanche was a mouse, seldom emerging from her hole in the shadows. This Blanche was different, defiant. Not afraid to tell him she was angry. Not afraid to tell him she had a job.

What on earth had possessed her to do such a thing? Sure, they'd had a fight, but he'd expected her to come around by now. Perhaps this was a mid-life crisis. He'd thought only men had those. He chuckled grimly. She should be grateful he hadn't gone out and bought a Ferrari. Maybe he should—that would scare her.

He reread the letter. It wasn't fair. Blanche didn't even sound like she was missing him, what with all her talk about his mother and the other women. He'd always longed for a group like that but never had it. Not that it had been his fault. First his parents had ignored him, then Rachel had run away. Even Esther had turned against him. They'd always been close, and he still didn't understand what had possessed her to do such a thing. Had the cancer moved to her brain and changed her personality? It had happened to someone he knew. He'd become a raving lunatic before the end.

Esther. He still hadn't opened the letter from his mother that might or might not contain a last message from Esther. He mentally slammed the drawer in his mind shut, got to his feet, and headed back into Reg's workshop.

"Thanks, the letters can go on the table," Reg said. "If you look in the box over there, there's a photo album with lots of my projects. See if there are any that pique your interest."

William flipped through the pages. Chairs and tables, mirrors and rocking horses, photo frames and chests of drawers. The mirrors looked too difficult, and they already had plenty of tables.

"See anything you like?"

"Blanche loves craft." He'd always let her spend whatever she wanted to on her projects, but this was different. If this wouldn't win her heart, nothing would. "Could we make something suitable for that?"

"Did you do woodwork at school?"

William shook his head and grimaced. "Latin and Greek."

"Did your father make something with you at home?"

William's chest tightened. *Not likely.* Only Ian had received such marks of favour.

"In that case, a blanket box would be best. We could add a tray with sections for buttons and bits and pieces if you have time." Reg rummaged in a drawer and pulled out a tattered drawing. "A blanket box will give you the basic skills without causing too much grief."

To each of them probably, though Reg was too much of a gentleman to say so.

Reg had better not get too high an expectation. William could change a light bulb or tighten a screw, but anything more was a step too far. He was the kind of guy who missed the nail and hammered his own thumb.

His father had once made a go-kart with Ian. William had dreamed of doing something like this with his father, but he'd never dared to ask. Bile burned his throat. It would have hurt too much to be turned down.

CHAPTER 20

*B*lanche had found a stack of boxes containing old buttons in the storeroom. Naida had bought them but never found time to sort them for sale. So Blanche used spare moments in the day to sort them into colours.

"Good morning." A deep voice interrupted her sorting.

Her hands jerked, and the button container flew off the counter. It hit the floor with a crash, and buttons rolled towards dark corners like cockroaches scuttling for cover.

"I'm so sorry," Blanche stuttered. "I didn't hear you come in."

"And I'm sorry I gave you such a fright."

Blanche looked up into a pair of twinkling blue eyes. Eyes perfectly matched with his silver hair. She stepped back, and her heel crunched a button.

A stylishly dressed woman her age smiled from behind the silver-haired man. Not the smile of superiority or amusement but a smile of genuine friendliness.

"Permit us to help chase the buttons." He had a slight accent. European? Whatever it was, it had faded over many years.

A line of warmth spread up her neck. "I'll manage."

"No," the woman said, her voice cool and confident. "We startled you, and it's going to take a while to gather all your escapees. Have you got a broom?" She smiled. "Or maybe two or three?"

Blanche wiped damp palms on her work apron. Why did this have to happen while she was alone in the shop? "I think we have several brooms. I'll grab them from the back."

She almost scuttled out. *Hurry back, Naida.* What was it about the couple she found so unsettling? Maybe it was the fact of having a man in the shop at all. This business seldom saw anyone besides women.

It took an embarrassingly long time to retrieve all the buttons. The couple didn't seem the least put out, and at least the floor was clean, as it was swept first thing every morning. A dirty floor would have added to her humiliation.

"What does a quilt shop need buttons for anyway?" the man asked.

"I'll show you." Blanche had brought their completed memory quilt in that morning. It was still in the bag because she hadn't had time to remove another quilt from the display rod in the front window.

She moved the button box and laid the quilt out on the central table.

The woman gasped. "It's stunning. Who made this?"

Blanche's face heated again. She'd always found it difficult to accept praise.

"It's yours?" the woman asked.

Blanche nodded. "A group of five of us made it. It's a memory quilt."

The man and the woman leaned closer to look at the details.

"In memory of a particular person?" the man asked.

"Yes." Blanche's throat narrowed. To gain a moment she pointed at the buttons. "We used buttons from her favourite outfits to add texture."

The man looked at her in a way that made her heart speed up. "Can you explain a few of your ideas?"

Was he really interested or merely being polite?

"My daughter died recently." Blanche swallowed. *Don't cry now. Keep going.* "When I was sorting her things, I wondered what could be done with them. Something to remember her by, something significant. I could have made the quilt myself, but there were others mourning Esther's death too." She lowered her head to catch her breath. "I thought making the quilt together would help all of us."

She'd have to get used to talking about Esther if she was going to teach a class on memory quilts. It was easier each time. The more she talked, the more she remembered Esther wasn't dead. She was more than alive—just in another place.

"Bible verses," said the man. "'I am convinced that neither death nor life …'" His finger traced the words and he quoted the bits they hadn't embroidered. "'Neither angels nor demons, neither the present nor the future, nor any powers, neither height nor depth, nor anything else in all creation, will be able to separate us from the love of God.' That's one of my favourites too." His eyes moved over the surface of the quilt. "The more you look the more you see."

"And the wildflowers," the woman said. "She must have loved them? I do. Where can I buy the embroidery patterns?"

Blanche blushed. "I made the patterns."

The woman's eyes widened. "You've got a great gift. Those are complex." She peered closer at the waratah. "Do you teach stitches?"

"I only started working here last week, and I'm only part-time. I'll have to check with my boss. She's having lunch at the moment."

As if on cue, Naida came in waving a sheaf of brochures.

"Perfect timing," Blanche said. "We've been discussing the memory quilt." She indicated the brochures. "I'll start teaching two classes on it in a fortnight. Would you be interested?"

"I'll have to think about it." The woman chuckled. "My skills are nothing like yours."

"Can you sew?"

The blue-eyed man answered for her. "She's more than competent. She's made children's clothes and done that, you know—" He swished his hand across his chest, his wedding ring glinting in the light. "—that coloured thread embroidery on babies' dresses—"

"Smocking?" Blanche asked.

"Yes, that's it," he said.

"Stop being a distraction, Anton," the woman said playfully, and came forward to the counter. "I don't know about a memory quilt, but I'd love to make something similar, perhaps with wildflowers and verses?"

Blanche looked across at Naida and raised her eyebrows. "The process would be the same. I don't see why not."

Naida nodded in agreement and spoke to the woman. "Leave your details, and we'll contact you if we get the numbers for the class to go ahead." She held out a sign-up sheet and a pen, and the woman took them.

While she wrote her name, the man stuck out his hand to Blanche. "Anton Turek. Delighted to meet you."

Those steady blue eyes were hard to ignore. She smiled and shook his hand. "Blanche Macdonald."

He held her hand fractionally longer than was necessary.

"Turek. What's the origin of your surname?"

"Czech," he said. "The family moved to Australia in the 1950s."

That explained the ghost of an accent. What did he do in life, or was he already retired? She wasn't going to ask the questions queuing up in her mind.

Naida took the completed sheet from the woman and read the name. "Helena." She smiled at her. "Here's the brochure. We look forward to being in contact soon."

As the door closed behind Helena and Anton, Blanche breathed a sigh of relief.

"What do you reckon?" Naida grinned. "I'd guess married for twenty-three years, four children, recently retired, lots of time on his hands to accompany his wife shopping."

Blanche's heart was still racing. She nodded, not daring to speak. Naida was probably right. It was a good thing he was married. Safely married to a beautiful and charming woman.

"Oh, and before you get back to your buttons ..." Naida said.

Blanche stopped in her tracks.

"Did I hear correctly that those patterns are your own design? Could you draft them all out? We could easily sell them."

"I'm not sure they're good enough for selling."

"You've got to be joking," Naida said. "They're terrific. I'd be delighted to be your exclusive agent."

Blanche flushed again. Since when had she blushed so often in one day? Had receiving praise been so small a part of her life? She'd always fitted her life around William's. Being a separate entity seemed odd.

Odd but good.

CHAPTER 21

*R*eg held up a pair of faded overalls. "Before you cover yourself in sawdust, we'd better get you properly attired. I went digging into my son's things and found his overalls. I think they'll be big enough." He handed them to William. "I also found a couple of his old T-shirts."

They were clothes William wouldn't normally be caught dead in, but he didn't want to ruin anything expensive. It had been obvious from his first weekend on the island that his clothes were unsuitable. He'd abandon the tie this Sunday, but he was stuck with his Italian leather shoes. He couldn't wear joggers with suit trousers.

"Won't your son mind?"

Reg paled beneath his tan. He took a shaky breath. "My son was killed in a plane crash two years ago."

"Davy's father?" William blurted into the silence.

The muscles in Reg's weathered cheeks tightened, and he brushed away a tear. "Yes. And his mother."

William's mouth opened but nothing came out. His blood

pulsed in his ears. What could he say? What could anyone say? He'd always avoided dealing with other people's grief.

"Davy should have been with them, but he had chicken pox. We assured my son and daughter-in-law they must go on their long planned-for trip. We'd look after Davy." He smiled grimly. "Davy was mad about it at the time, but I've always been grateful for his chicken pox."

Reg leaned down to pick up a screw from the floor, took a deep breath, then turned and walked out the door. "The other church on the island got rid of its pews, and I bought nearly the whole lot," he said over his shoulder. "They were silky oak, and the wood is not only beautiful but already planed."

The second shed was crammed to the top with carefully stacked planks. Reg pulled out a selection of planks. The grain was beautiful, a browny-orange with lines and marks like the watermarks William had seen on the tideline at the beach. He stroked his hand over the smooth surface of the pew. Reg must have used these to make the dining room table and chairs he'd seen last night, meticulously crafted and built to last for generations.

Reg pulled out several more long pieces that had once been the back or seats of pews. "We can cut these up for the top, bottom, and sides."

"Don't you have other work to do?" William still wasn't sure he wanted to try something he'd certainly be ham-fisted at.

"I'll get back to it in a moment, once I've given you the plans. You can measure it up and cut it."

Thirty minutes later, Reg was working in his corner and William was nervously measuring boards, using a pencil and ruler to mark them. It wasn't too dissimilar to how he'd seen Blanche make a dress pattern. He'd heard her mutter something to Esther one day about cutting the fabric in the correct direction. Perhaps fabric was like wood grain.

Once he'd finished, he called Reg over to inspect his work.

"Terrific." Reg said. "And very little wastage. Nice."

Once again Reg's praise oozed warmth into his heart. Not that any success had much to do with him. Reg had made the measurements clear on the drawings, and following instructions and diagrams was something he could manage. The table saw looked much more frightening. Those shiny teeth could cut through an unwary finger in a millisecond.

"I'll show you how to do the first cut while you support the end. The sawing will get easier as the planks get shorter."

Reg showed him how to stand and demonstrated how to keep his hands safe.

After three hours, with lots of supervision, William had all the pieces cut.

Reg dusted his hands on his overalls. "Time for lunch. I'm sure Ivy has something ready."

Reg and Ivy were simple sandwich people. Nothing like the food Blanche always had ready for him. "You don't have to feed me. I've got plenty at my place."

"It's no trouble at all. Ivy loves nothing better than showing hospitality."

He didn't see how he could avoid the sandwiches without being rude, and Reg was obviously the linchpin in the church. He needed to keep in with him. Otherwise, this whole experience would be a disaster.

They washed up at an outside sink and trooped onto the verandah.

"Sawdust spreads everywhere, so we'll stay out here." Reg pulled out a comfy chair and offered it to William. "I normally shower and change in the back of the shed before I go into the house. I don't want to give Ivy unnecessary work."

William avoided looking at Reg. He'd never considered Blanche's workload. When he was busy, he left things all over the house for Blanche to tidy up after him. He lowered himself into a chair that sagged comfortably.

Ivy pushed a tea trolley out the door. "I've already had mine, as I'm off to visit Mrs Payne." There were piles of homemade sandwiches on chunky farm-style bread, fruit, and cake, all covered by a lace cloth.

"Just put the things back on the tray afterwards and push it into the hallway. I'll deal with it when I get home." She left them to it.

Reg folded up the cloth and sniffed appreciatively. "Fresh bread with egg salad or ham."

He bowed his head and thanked God as though he was eating at Sydney's best hotel. William couldn't understand it. They were sandwiches, for goodness' sake. The most ordinary of food. Something he hadn't eaten in years.

William took a bite. His eyes widened in surprise as his teeth bit into the crusty goodness. Ivy certainly knew how to cook, like his grandmother used to. He finished the first sandwich and reached for another.

"I appreciate the time you're taking with Davy." A smile crinkled up the skin around Reg's eyes.

William swallowed his mouthful. "He's easy to have around." He chuckled. "He intends to drag me on one of the hikes on Saturday."

"Hope you brought your camera. The seabirds are spectacular." Reg offered William another sandwich. "Do you have children?"

William stopped mid-chew. "Two adult daughters." The words were spoken before he thought about them. It had been years since he'd admitted he had more than one daughter. He took a slice of cake his waistline didn't need and stared towards the back shed. *No more questions, please.* There were deep, dark places he didn't want to go.

"The other leaders asked me to speak to you about the sermons for the next seven weeks."

His stomach throbbed. Another topic he'd prefer to avoid. Sunday's sermon had gone badly, but he'd improve.

"Because we are a church that survives on interim ministers, we could easily have too many random sermons." Reg scratched the side of his nose. "That's okay occasionally, but we really need a series. Meat-and-potatoes kind of sermons. We've recently finished Genesis, and we're keen to do a series in Acts. One of the leaders did Acts 1 to 3. Would it be too much to ask you to do sermons from Acts 4 to 10?"

William's heart dropped to his knees. A series? He didn't preach series on whole sections of the Bible. It didn't suit his style.

Reg kept talking. "You might have noticed I read the whole chapter on Sunday even though it was rather long."

William nodded. He certainly hadn't missed that. It had annoyed him at first that Reg was taking up valuable time to read the whole chapter.

"We read whole chapters because then we get through signifi-cant chunks of scripture over the course of the year. Some church members can no longer read—"

William turned a laugh into a cough. It would have been hard to miss how many were geriatric.

Reg shrugged. "It's hard to keep doctors out here, and it's expen-sive to go and see a specialist on the mainland. People shouldn't go blind, but they do. Once that happens, the Bible reading becomes hugely important. Ivy's gone to read the Bible to one of the ladies who lost her sight two years ago."

William munched on fruitcake as delicious as the sandwiches.

"I remind myself," Reg said, "the Bible reading is the one time during the service God can speak his words, without any explana-tion, into our lives."

William leaned back in his chair. He'd never thought about it, but if the Bible was God's word, then what Reg said was logically true. If so, what was the point of the preacher? He didn't know if he could bring off the kind of sermon Reg was expecting.

"It probably wouldn't surprise you to hear we've had quite a few preachers who struggle to connect with our folk."

William laughed nervously. "Most of us are city blokes."

"Mmm," Reg said. "Some of our folk have never left the island."

William coughed as a crumb went down the wrong way. It was mind-boggling. This wasn't the nineteenth century and the days of sail.

"Of course, we're not completely cut off, what with TV and the newspapers." Reg gestured towards the beach. "And you've seen the tourists."

A group of people walked past the front gate, talking loudly.

"I guess young people either work in the tourist trade or leave the island," William said.

Reg grunted assent, stretched out his legs, and put his hands behind his head. "Before we knew you were coming, I prepared all the Bible studies on Acts. Would you like to look at my material so you can see what I've already covered?"

Sunday had shaken him. It wouldn't hurt him to look at what Reg had prepared—he could always ignore it.

"I used to read a lot of commentaries and use a lot of what they said, but it bored the congregation," Reg said. "I've learned sermons based on narrative passages work best. I made a lot of mistakes, but the locals were patient."

"So you didn't grow up here?"

"No. I was raised in Port Macquarie and answered an ad for a carpenter. Once I saw the place and met Ivy, I never wanted to leave." He sighed with what sounded like contentment. "It's a paradise for children."

William raised his eyebrows. Yes, if you had the sort of children who loved the great outdoors and had no real ambitions or desire to learn any of the myriad of things the island couldn't offer. "My daughter, Esther, would have loved it."

"Why doesn't she come out and visit?"

William swallowed past the tennis ball-sized lump in his throat. "Too late for that." His chest tightened. "She died a few months back." He gripped the arms of his chair and stared at the big tree across the lawn.

Reg leaned forward and laid a hand on his shoulder. "I'm so sorry. I thought it was your mother who died."

"No." William's voice came out rougher than the rasp on Reg's tool bench. "Mum's alive and well. Esther died. Cancer."

Don't ask how old she was. Please don't.

"How old was she?"

"Not yet thirty." There was a ringing in his ears.

"That must have been hard."

"I'm trying not to think about it." William's voice came out in a tight whisper.

Out the corner of his eye, William saw Reg wipe his face.

"William ..." Reg recovered himself and sat up straight. "I'm so, so sorry. After my son died, I cried so often I thought I was cracking up. If I wasn't crying, all I wanted to do was talk about him for hours." Reg glanced over at him. "I expect you've been through all that. But if you need someone to listen, well—"

William clenched his fists. He had things under control. If he started talking about Esther, the drawers in his mind would open and who knew what mess would spill out? Ian and his father. Rachel and his mother. Esther and Blanche. It was like a dune of shifting sand threatening to cascade over him. Suffocate him.

William cleared his throat. "I'd appreciate looking at the Bible study material."

Reg got to his feet, slipped off his boots and opened the front door. He put a finger to his lips. "Don't tell Ivy."

William got up and gripped the verandah railing. He had about two minutes to pull himself together. His eyes stung, and he bit his lip. He was not going to cry, and certainly not in front of someone he'd only known less than a week.

He could hear Reg opening and closing a wooden door in the house, then his steps coming back down the hall. The front screen door squeaked as Reg stepped outside.

"Here they are. They should all be clearly labelled."

William squared his shoulders, turned around, and reached for the manila folder in Reg's hand. The folder shook as he took it, eyes averted.

"And William," Reg said gently, "if you need someone to listen, you know where to find me." He placed a hand once again on William's shoulder. "I know it's often hard to find someone to talk to when you're in ministry."

William looked at his feet. Part of him wanted to sit down and talk. Reg would be safe, and who else in his life could he say that about? But it could ricochet badly if Reg talked to the wrong people. No, he'd leave it. He nodded wordlessly and turned away.

CHAPTER 22

It was only nine on Wednesday morning, but William had already had breakfast, written to Blanche, and been snorkelling with Davy. Today the dawn sky had been awash with a delicate pink, like the inside of a seashell. He never grew tired of snorkelling the same patch of coral. The variety of life and the way the water caressed his skin was always changing.

He was due to meet Reg at the front gate in a few minutes to walk to the midweek Bible study. Everything was walking distance in this place. Reg had said he was happy to take the first study, and William hadn't objected. He had no plan to make a mess of things again.

Reg had asked him to remind the attendees of the previous story from Acts 3:1–10 so they could better discuss chapter four. Normally he would have laboured over jazzing up the story, but he suspected Reg wouldn't be impressed. He was a 'just the Bible' kind of man. He'd spot any additions or deletions, like Esther had when she was in preschool and William read her Bible stories before bed. If he changed even one word, she'd scrunch up her face and tell him to read it again.

Reg's screen door shut with its distinctive thud. William picked up his Bible, notebook, and pen, walked out his front door, and locked it. Locking up now felt odd. Maybe he'd stop bothering soon.

As he walked over to Reg's, William muttered the story he'd prepared. He'd always preferred retelling to reading, and he wasn't going to attempt to read after hearing Reg on Sunday.

The house where the Bible study was to be held was built out of fibrolite and corrugated iron. At the gate, they met three old people struggling out of a single car. Reg offered his arm to support the most doddery. William hung back, awkward as a teenager on a first date. Victory had almost no retired people. They'd either died or gone elsewhere. Old people were too attached to hymns. Victory attracted musicians and singers who liked modern songs.

Inside, the living room needed a facelift as badly as its owners. An elderly couple were already seated. The vacant seats were a saggy sofa or vinyl-covered chairs. If he'd had a spray bottle of anti-septic, he'd have used it. Most people chose the harder chairs. Smart. It would take a forklift to get some of them off the sofa.

Getting everyone a cup of tea took an age. When the tea came, it looked strong enough to dye socks and tasted like it too. William placed the cup under his seat. He should have brought his own thermos, preferably with a shot of something to get him through the next hour.

Reg started the meeting by asking someone called Bob to pray. He droned on for a century or two, and William's mind wandered. His mother was over eighty now. She must be like these people. Why did the rest of his family like her so much?

"William—"

He opened his eyes. The prayer had ended, and everyone was looking at him. He'd nearly missed his cue.

"—has come to help us out, as we know," Reg said. There was a smattering of applause, the kind suggesting they were merely being polite. "Let's all introduce ourselves. Bob, why don't you start."

The names were easy enough, as William had always had a good memory for such things. The women had mainly been housewives, nurses, or teachers. Two of the men had been fishermen, one had worked in the post office-cum-shop, and another had been a chef. Nothing unexpected there, but the way they used their time now raised his eyebrows. One woman was translating a theological book from German, another was a ham radio enthusiast, and three more wrote letters to prisoners in Long Bay prison.

"As William has just arrived and I'd already prepared the Bible study on this section, I'll still lead this morning," Reg said. "William will take over next week."

It had been years since he'd merely been the participant of a Bible study. If he treated it as a lesson in cross-cultural communication, he'd get through it.

"William, if you'd remind us of the story prior to chapter four, that would be great," Reg said.

This time the group were wide awake, as though Sunday had never happened. They were a totally different group.

He didn't understand. He'd been so dramatic on Sunday, even using actions to show the stone slinging and sawing off Goliath's head. He'd improved the story, so why were they so riveted by the dull version?

Improved?

The word gave him a jab like a tiny electric shock. Would he appreciate it if someone improved on what he had written?

He brought his mind back to concentrate on Reg, who was asking Betty to read the first half of the new passage. She read with reverence, like she was sampling a rare cheese. A task she would not hurry for anyone.

William shivered and goosebumps rose along his arms.

Reg continued the passage. "'When they saw the courage of

Peter and John and realised that they were unschooled, ordinary men, they were astonished, and they took note that these men had been with Jesus.'"

William's face heated. The words seemed to echo in his head. Would anyone say that about him?

Where were these questions coming from? He shifted in his seat. It creaked. It was likely as ancient as its owners.

He squinted in concentration.

"'Then the Sanhedrin called them in again and commanded them not to speak or teach at all in the name of Jesus,'" Reg continued. "'But Peter and John replied, "Which is right in God's eyes: to listen to you, or to him? You be the judges! As for us, we cannot help speaking about what we have seen and heard."'"

There was a reverent silence before Reg handed around a question sheet. Eight handwritten questions. *Handwritten.* William winced. This really was in the sticks. Surely the library and bigger hotels must have a photocopier. Victory had two, always in constant use.

"Who opposes Peter and John and why?" Reg asked and then waited.

William had led Bible studies with discussion questions before, a long time ago. There'd been too many silences and it was hard to control what answers were given or asked. This group didn't hesitate to answer.

"The religious leaders—" the man next to him said, wheezing.

"Not the ordinary people," his wife said, almost inaudibly.

Jock, the ham radio enthusiast, slapped his knee. "They're jealous of all the attention the disciples are getting."

Reg looked around the group, and Nell, one of the women who'd been fairly silent up to this point, spoke.

"They don't want anyone talking about Jesus, because they crucified him." She hung her head and then raised it again. "If he really rose from the dead, then they're in trouble—"

"—because they've opposed God," Jock said.

A few more people added answers before Reg asked the next question. "How does Peter answer the men opposing and threatening them?"

Everyone searched their Bibles and called out answers. William sat and listened. Questions of his own were mounting, but he wasn't sure he was willing to ask them out loud. He was supposed to be the one with all the answers.

The Peter in Acts 4 was radically different to Peter who denied Jesus three times. What had changed him?

The group members were gazing so intently at their large-print Bibles they wouldn't have noticed an earthquake. William flicked back to the end of John and skimmed the story of Peter's restoration. Jesus dealt with him so gently, never once mentioning his failure or saying, "I told you so". It wasn't the way he'd have dealt with things, but maybe Jesus' way was part of the reason Peter became so courageous. Peter remembered the pain of his failure and was now thankful and determined never to fail Jesus again.

The group moved on to a third question, or was it the fourth? They were discussing the pressure tactics the religious leaders employed to keep Peter and John from preaching.

What puzzled him was why Peter and John provoked their accusers, as if they welcomed persecution or had a death wish. Yet they'd backed down only a few chapters earlier. If there was any situation where he'd choose to become vague and placatory, then this was it. William certainly made vague responses when challenged on live radio.

As if Reg had read his mind, he asked, "The opposition used threats to silence the disciples, but how did they respond? Start from verse twenty-three."

Jock was always quick to jump in as though he'd prepared the study beforehand. "The first thing they did was pray."

"Yes, but what did they pray?" Reg looked at them over his

glasses. "Did they pray for the pressure to ease off or for the religious leaders to drop dead?"

That is what William would have asked for, but he didn't remember exactly what they'd prayed. He looked down, finger tracing from verse twenty-four.

SOVEREIGN LORD, YOU MADE THE HEAVENS AND THE EARTH AND THE SEA, AND EVERYTHING IN THEM. YOU SPOKE BY THE HOLY SPIRIT THROUGH THE MOUTH OF YOUR SERVANT, OUR FATHER DAVID: "WHY DO THE NATIONS RAGE, AND THE PEOPLES PLOT IN VAIN?"

"They praised God for who he was and reminded themselves God had warned them tough times were ahead and were perfectly normal for believers," Betty of the blue-rinsed hair said.

These folk looked old, but they were quick to answer, and he hadn't been struggling to stay awake as he'd anticipated.

"They didn't pray for God to take their suffering away," one of the men said. "Instead, they asked for boldness to share in the midst of the pressure."

Crazy. William choked and covered his reaction with a quick cough.

It stirred a memory for him, though. Hadn't Nick come to him with a garbled story about Esther saying something similar? Something about Peter and John—or was it James? He surreptitiously turned the pages until he found chapter twelve. Keeping one ear open to the discussion, William scanned the chapter. Ah, now he remembered. Esther had apparently made a big deal about the fact that it wasn't only a story about Peter's rescue. She was right. Verse two said James had died. William frowned. Nick had mentioned Esther often talked about how sometimes God didn't rescue, about how he sometimes allowed someone to die.

A jagged knife-thrust of pain speared him and he struggled to breathe.

James had died. He took a big breath. And so had Esther—despite everything they'd done.

He'd told Esther it must be her fault, but what if it wasn't? What if she'd been faithful, like James? Faithful, yet she still died.

What kind of God did that? And more importantly, why?

CHAPTER 23

*B*lanche's first class had gone well yesterday, with ten happy older women who'd chatted easily and worked for two hours. Today Naida had gone to an early lunch, and this class would be a single hour over lunchtime.

Helena was the first to arrive, and Blanche nearly dropped the scissors she was holding when Anton came in with her.

He kissed Helena briefly on the cheek. "I'll be back in an hour."

The easy affection between them was like needles in the pincushion of her heart. William had never shown affection to her in front of others. In fact, a bystander wouldn't have known she was his wife in public except on the rare occasions when he'd stand next to her as they greeted guests.

Blanche turned her back and put the scissors down before anyone could notice her flushed cheeks.

"I came early to help." Helena placed her supplies on the table. "If you needed any, that is."

"Oh, thanks. That's kind of you," Blanche said. "Would it be too much to ask if you could wipe down the table and dry it while I put out the chairs?"

Blanche found her a clean cloth and a towel.

"I'm really excited about the class," Helena said. "The article you sent to us gave me heaps of ideas and got me thinking about colour schemes." She wiped the far corner of the table. "I've decided to do a quilt in memory of my parents, and I'm considering a mix of flowers and places from Czechoslovakia and Australia. Some Bible verses, too, and places that were special to them from their honeymoon in Paris. The Eiffel Tower should be easy enough to stitch."

So Helena's family were from the same place as Anton's. Perhaps their families had known each other before they migrated.

"You could add a café table and striped awning somewhere," Blanche said.

"I knew you'd have more good ideas." Helena grinned and looked at the clock on the wall. "There's a little bit of time. Do you think I could lay out what I've got and start to choose the fabrics? Have you got time to advise me?"

Blanche glanced around the room. Everything was ready for the six participants. "Of course."

They moved towards the rolls of cloth.

"Mum loved lace handkerchiefs, and I've brought several to use as panels," Helena said.

"The other women might like your idea as well."

Helena dropped her voice. "I hope the verses and the song I want to include might lead to discussion."

Blanche's heart sped up. It was still new for her to talk about Jesus with anyone, let alone someone she barely knew. She looked towards the door to check they were still alone and said in an undertone. "You sound like a Christian. How did you get to know Jesus?"

"Our family had been Roman Catholic for generations. At fourteen, my greatest ambition was to be a nun." Helena laughed. "Anton became a Christian first and, before long, influenced me.

145

Mum and Dad were horrified. They thought leaving the Catholic Church would condemn us both to hell."

Blanche leaned in, eyes wide. "And did they change their minds?"

"It took a few years, but they watched us." Helena laughed self-consciously. "They couldn't fail to notice how we changed. Especially the fact we had even more time for them than before. They agreed to come with us to the Billy Graham Crusade in 1979." She smiled. "They went four nights in a row, and on the final night they both went forward."

"Oh," Blanche said, hand to her mouth. "You must have been thrilled."

Helena's eyes shone. "We were. It brought us all so much closer."

The bell above the shop door gave a jangle, and then another. Blanche looked up and smiled at the women coming through the door, laden with sewing bags. "Welcome," she said. "Come in and have a seat."

There was soon fabric all over the table.

Helena helped Blanche hand out the equipment they'd need and the linen squares for their memory patches.

"Have you had a chance to read the information I sent?" Blanche asked, and they nodded. Teaching such a motivated group would be a breeze. When it came time to share about their projects, Blanche discovered two were making quilts to remember their husbands, two were remembering parents, and the final two were remembering a child. No one was recently bereaved, which should be easier—more good memories than emotional outbursts.

The ladies had brought clothing, military patches, and photos to generate embroidery ideas. One lady was going to print photos on fabric for half her panels. Another had a collection of her father's ties to incorporate into her design.

They were soon working on their easiest panels and swapping ideas.

Helena was seated to Blanche's right.

"Why don't you do the verse panels first?" Blanche said. "That might be the easiest way to get started."

"I would, but my writing is horrible," Helena said. "Would you have time to write them for me?"

Blanche managed to get six verses written in between helping and advising the others. "Helena, if you leave the others with me, I'll do them at home," Blanche said.

"I don't want you to go to too much trouble." Helena looked mildly embarrassed but also pleased.

"Believe me, I need projects to keep me occupied at the moment."

And it felt good to be needed. Blanche had minimal housework to do, and writing to William every few days didn't take much time. Christmas presents this year would be easy because being around this shop every day gave her so many ideas for quilts. Naomi needed one—her bedspread was looking tatty, and a quilt was something personal she could give to Rachel. She'd make a queen size. Who knew when it might be needed.

The hour was soon over. Anton arrived moments after the other women left. "Did you have fun?"

"It was super," Helena said with a grin.

"What about you, Blanche? Did Helena and the others behave?" Anton asked in a teasing voice, a twinkle in his eye.

Blanche suppressed a giggle and said in her best school teacher's voice, "They behaved impeccably. They're ready for afternoon tea at Buckingham Palace."

The banter continued, bouncing back and forth like a lively tennis match with the score about even. In no time at all, the three of them were laughing like old friends.

On the way home that night, Blanche walked with a lighter step and a warm feeling in her chest. It had been a long time—too long a time—since she'd had friends who didn't know she was a pastor's wife. Friends to laugh, cry, and banter with. Friends who seemed to like her for her personality rather than the fact she was married to Victory's senior pastor.

CHAPTER 24

illiam detested pastoral visits, but pastoral visits were part of the job he'd agreed to, so there was no escape. After his first year at Victory, he'd assigned pastoral care to the elders. What was the point of enduring endless cups of tea and rambling stories about a person's latest surgery?

Reg had handed him the list of all the people he prayed for and told him they'd all appreciate one visit while he was here. William had selected Jock, the ham radio enthusiast, and Betty and Stan as the least likely to put him to sleep.

Betty and Stan lived in a bungalow surrounded by flowers and neat lawns.

"Come in, come in." Stan looked as pleased as if he were welcoming a king.

At their age, visitors were probably the highlight of their day. William shuddered. He didn't want a retirement like this. He'd prefer to work until he dropped. No long lingering twilight.

"Betty has the kettle on, and she baked a cake."

William wasn't much of a cake eater. Not with the number of business lunches he had to attend.

The sunroom was a little too warm and lined with photos of grandchildren. Something else he'd have to pretend enthusiasm for.

A memory of Esther as a baby cooing in his arms lanced him between the ribs. He bit the inside of his cheek. He was not going to think about Esther now.

Betty passed him the tea in a delicate china cup and saucer. He sipped. Too strong for his taste. He chose the smallest piece of cake.

"The pastor normally asks us a couple of questions." Stan's false teeth clacked.

William stared at Stan over his glasses.

"About our spiritual health and such like." Stan returned to munching his cake.

What kind of questions did one ask about spiritual health? How much they prayed or how many chapters of the Bible they read? Or something else entirely?

"We've had some answers to prayer recently, haven't we, Betty?" Stan said.

Betty nodded. "One of our grandchildren has terrible asthma, but last month she didn't have a single hour away from school."

William smiled, more because he thought it was required than for any real enthusiasm. Every mention of grandchildren was sand-paper across his heart.

"Even better, the eldest one recently became a Christian."

William's shoulders relaxed. They'd given him a lead-in. "How did that happen?"

Stan put down his plate. "He's been skipping school and staying out late at night. Our son and daughter-in-law were pulling their hair out, and we're too far away to do anything."

"So we've been praying hard," Betty said.

Stan smiled gently at his wife. "The best thing we could have done."

William's chest tightened. "And how did God answer?"

"One of his friends got drunk and smashed himself up in a car accident. The boy survived, but he'll always walk with a limp. The whole situation gave our grandson the wake-up call he needed. A few weeks later, he came to his Dad to talk things through—"

"—and his Dad pointed him to his need for Jesus," Betty said.

Need for Jesus. Interesting phrase. William had always thought in terms of need for peace, or forgiveness, or healing.

"Do you want to hear how we came to know Jesus?" Stan asked.

William nodded. That should use up plenty of time. He'd forgotten to ask Reg how long island pastoral visits were supposed to last.

Betty pointed her chin at Stan, and he cleared his throat. "My family attended church because that's what people who considered themselves good did. Church was their equivalent of a social club."

William's father had always treated church in the same way. A place to nurture his networks.

"We considered ourselves Christians and therefore good people. At least better than average." He winked at Betty. "But boarding with Betty's family while I did my training for the post office challenged all my assumptions."

"Another cup?" Betty asked, raising the pot.

"No, thanks," William said. He still had another visit and probably more tea. Hopefully weaker than this brew.

"Betty's family read the Bible every night at the dinner table," Stan continued. "I listened in for a few months before I dared to ask questions."

"But it didn't take you long once you started questioning," Betty said.

"Because there was a match between the words I was hearing and the way your family lived." Stan turned to William. "Their family actually followed Ephesians 4 and didn't let the sun go down on their anger. Every day truly was a new start." He patted Betty's hand. "A principle we've followed."

Their simple affection made a lump in William's throat. How

many times in his marriage had he gone to bed angry? They'd said harsh words. No, that wasn't strictly true. Blanche hadn't said anything harsh. She'd expressed her opinion, and he hadn't appreciated it.

William leaned forward. "What do you do when you disagree about something?"

Stan chuckled. "In the early years of our marriage, I thought too much of my opinion and too little of Betty's. I had to learn the hard way that Betty was God's gift to me."

"But how often do you disagree?"

"Not often now, but we had grand clashes at the beginning." He winked at Betty again and she blushed.

"Betty came from a family of debaters, and her father treated the girls as equals. Which they are, of course, but it was a radical idea in our generation." Stan chuckled. "Early in our marriage, I tried to make Betty submit to my decisions and opinions." He shook his head. "That was a disaster. It only destroyed the trust and love between us and made me feel wretched."

"Five years into our marriage we were making a mess of it," Betty said. "We had to seek counselling with an older couple in the church."

William raised an eyebrow.

"They taught us how to pray through decisions and to ask ourselves if there were any biblical guidelines on the issue."

"I learned how to listen to Betty and not to manipulate her to do what I wanted." Stan laughed. "Betty is a treasure of godly wisdom."

A treasure? He'd never considered Blanche a treasure or even a true partner.

"Now, hadn't we better pray together so you can go and do your other visit?" Stan said.

To his surprise, William found himself praying sincerely for this couple and being prayed for in turn. He blinked away a tear. The visit he'd dreaded had turned out to be both short and interesting.

Even worthwhile. This couple weren't gritting their teeth and enduring each other. Rather, they still wanted to be together even after fifty-plus years.

*J*ock's house was festooned with radio antennae. Starting a conversation here should be as easy as pressing play, although pressing stop might be harder.

Jock led William out to the wide verandah at the back of the house and offered more cake and too-strong tea.

"This house feels old. How long have you been here?" William asked.

"It was my parents' house and my grandparents' before them." Jock's voice had a slow pride-of-place burr. "We raised our family here. The children scattered to the mainland, and Jean went home to Jesus two years ago." His voice quavered.

William glanced out the window. Was Jock going to cry? And if he did, what was he supposed to do about it? This was one of the main reasons he avoided pastoral visits.

"It hasn't been easy, but I've come to appreciate my church family even more. My daughter wants me to come and live with her, but I can't do it." Jock's eyes swam with tears. "Too many memories here. Good memories." He indicated the roof. "And there wouldn't be room for all my equipment."

William's first boss had always urged them to ask a person about their passions. "How did you get into ham radio?"

"I wasn't always a homebody." The corner of Jock's mouth lifted. "I had no intention of burying myself on an island with three hundred old fogies. It was the big city for me." He put his feet up on the coffee table. "I made all the mistakes a country bumpkin can make and ended up wasting too much time and money on things that aren't worth anything."

William would never have guessed Jock had been a rebel.

"One night I was driving when I shouldn't have been behind the wheel." Jock whistled between his teeth. "At the time I would have called myself lucky, as I only ran into the curb. I was so out of it, I fell asleep right there. Sometime during the night, I woke thinking someone was speaking to me." He grimaced. "I must have bumped the radio control, because it was one of those middle-of-the-night radio shows and someone was sharing their story. It could have been mine."

William watched Jock's expressive face intently.

"He used a phrase that caught me like a possum in the head-lights. The man said, 'I was wasting my life on alcohol and fast women. Investing in tinsel instead of gold.'"

"'Investing in tinsel instead of gold.'" William rolled the phrase around his mouth. "That would be a good line to use in a sermon."

"I've used it with a couple of my friends over the years." Jock held his hands together in front of him. "God had me on the hook and reeled me in." He acted every phrase. "Despite my befuddled state, by the end of the man's explanation, many things I'd heard as a child clicked into place. I parked the car in a better spot, slept until morning, and set about making wise decisions. For me, that meant leaving the unhealthy relationships I'd made and eventually coming home."

William loosened his collar. He was tempted to put his feet up as Jock did, but that went against years of rigid discipline in appropriate ministerial behaviour. "And how did radio fit in?"

"There now, I went and forgot to answer the original question. Used to get in trouble at school for the same thing." Jock scratched his arm. "Since I became a Christian through radio, I wanted to support radio ministry. It wasn't long until I became interested in the engineering side."

Jock gestured towards the hall. "You might have noticed the map covered with coloured pins."

William nodded.

"I talk with people in the Philippines, India, Hawaii, and the Pacific," Jock said. "They start as strangers, but they soon become friends. Several have come to visit."

It seemed a weird way to make friends.

"I have lots of opportunities to talk about Jesus," Jock said. "Two or three have eventually become Christians. It's one of the ways I can be involved in something beyond island life."

"The church also supports two missionaries." Jock reached for another piece of cake and laughed. "One of them presented us a gold award for being the best letter writers. There's also ten of us who write letters to prisoners."

"Oh?" William said, eyebrows raised.

"Lots of people in prison either don't have family or don't receive letters. We get together once a month and pray for each of the people we're writing to. One of my guys became a Christian this year. Then we have the fun of coaching them in the basics of following Jesus." Jock rubbed his nose. "How to read their Bible and pray and such things. They're sometimes reluctant to contact the chaplain."

William could understand that. One of his radio guests had been an ex-con.

"Many have a real sense of inferiority. They struggle with how God can accept someone who has done what they've done."

A clock inside struck the hour and William jumped. He'd never have believed the time could pass so quickly.

---

*R*eg was applying a coat of varnish to his latest project. "Just about finished," he said, with long, smooth strokes of his brush.

William pulled out a stool and sat down. There was something soothing about watching such a high standard of craftsmanship. Reg didn't hurry himself for anyone. He knew what needed to be done and he did it.

"Are you going to continue working on your dovetails, William?"

A week ago, William hadn't even known what dovetails were. Reg had given him a short lesson, and they'd made the first few together. Such a clever way to connect pieces of wood without using nails. He'd loved puzzles as a boy, and this was similar.

"Would you check them all before I cut them?"

"Happy to."

And he would be too. Reg was infinitely patient. He'd be Mr Popular at the local school where the older primary-school children were given a few basic woodworking classes.

William got to work. The only sounds were the scratch of his pencil on the wood and Reg's tuneful whistling.

With Reg's guidance, his project was looking good. He'd only give it to Blanche if it reached a decent standard. Otherwise he'd abandon it in some dark corner.

He wasn't sure how he felt about Blanche working. What if she became so independent she no longer needed him and left their marriage forever? How would he explain her leaving to his elders? He was too old to start another job. His pencil dug in too deep, and he leaned forward on the counter. She had to come back to him. She had to. He'd write tonight and tell her about Stan and Betty and Jock. That would show her he could still connect with people who were no use in furthering his career.

"How are you going?"

He jumped. Reg had crossed the workshop on silent feet.

"Nearly finished, I think." He held his breath while Reg checked his work.

"Looking good," Reg said.

GRACE IN DEEP WATERS

Two small words. It again shocked William how much he valued something so ordinary.

"How did your visits go?"

"I quite enjoyed them."

Reg looked over his spectacles at William. "Thought you might. Those ordinary folk are solid gold."

William nodded. He'd never considered people as treasures. He certainly hadn't considered Blanche as a treasure until she'd left him.

Or perhaps he'd simply never taken the time to dig.

CHAPTER 25

DEAR WILLIAM,

*W*riting to her husband still felt stilted. They'd been around each other constantly from the time they'd met, so letter writing hadn't been a major feature of their relationship.

William's first letter had arrived at midday, full of flowery descriptions of the island, amusing notes on the accommodation and congregation, and humorous accounts of his jaunts. It was a letter worthy of publication, but all froth and bubble. Nothing beneath the sunny surface.

Disappointment settled in her gut. Would William ever grieve as she'd been grieving, with tears and moans and never-ending heartache?

Sorting boxes and sewing the memory quilt had helped, but didn't stop her almost calling out to dark-haired strangers who walked as Esther had, or storing up amusing incidents at work to share with her. Esther had insisted laughing beat crying, and they'd shared a wheelbarrow-load of giggles and laughs in Esther's last months. Sometimes she wished she'd kept Esther at a distance, so the pain would be less now.

She bit her lip. No. At least this way she had an abundance of good memories to treasure in her mind.

Repressed grief must be eating into William's insides. Blanche sat up straight. She'd write about how she was feeling. William might not appreciate her words, but writing them would at least benefit herself.

I WONDER, HOW ARE YOU REALLY GOING? I HAVE TO PUT ON A CHEERFUL EXTERIOR AT WORK. I BEGIN TO UNDERSTAND WHY YOU AND NICK WORKED SO HARD LAST YEAR. HARD WORK KEEPS THOUGHTS AT BAY.

BUT LIFE IS NOT ONLY WORK, NO MATTER HOW MUCH TIME IT TAKES. EVEN WHEN I'M NOT A WEEPING MESS, MY HEART IS FRAGILE.

Blanche tapped her nails on the table.

I'M REMINDED CONSTANTLY OF ESTHER, AND EACH REMINDER IS A NEEDLE IN MY HEART. YOUR MOTHER IS A ROCK OF UNDERSTANDING. SHE NEVER TELLS ME I'VE TALKED TOO OFTEN ABOUT MY MEMORIES.

Blanche's recollections of Esther were a series of small things. Private moments of no significance to others. Small things mattered so much in the bonding between parent and child.

Cuddles that had left her breathless with wonder. The feel of a tiny hand in hers as they'd crossed the street. Esther's first tooth. Her first day at school, with Esther holding herself stiff in her new uniform, determined not to crinkle it. Recollections William didn't share because he'd seldom been there.

What memories salted her husband's wounds? William remained a closed box—polished on the outside but possibly empty inside.

She tapped on the table again. Her task reminded her of the worst kind of English homework. The essays she'd had to grind out one painful paragraph at a time.

I'M THOROUGHLY ENJOYING WORK, BUT THE BEST PART OF MY WEEK IS SATURDAY AFTERNOON. MUM, RACHEL, AND I MEET WITH TWO OF ESTHER'S FRIENDS, AND WE READ THE BIBLE AND PRAY TOGETHER. I DON'T KNOW WHY I HAVE NEVER DONE THIS BEFORE, BUT I HUNGER FOR IT. IT MINISTERS TO A PART OF MY HEART THAT I NEVER KNEW NEEDED IT. THERE IS SOMETHING ABOUT COMING TO GOD'S WORD AND LOOKING AT IT IN THE ORDER IT WAS WRITTEN, EVERY VERSE INSTEAD OF BITS AND PIECES.

She gnawed her lip. If she said anything more, William's hackles would rise. She scribbled off a final line and signed her name before addressing the envelope.

Rachel was there as Blanche put the envelope on the hall sideboard ready to take to the post box.

"Mum, I don't know why you bother. Dad will never change."

Blanche looked Rachel in the eye. "You changed. I have to believe God can change anyone."

*B*lanche walked up Anton and Helena's stone path. Was it a mistake to visit? There might be a rule about fraternising with customers, but she wasn't going to ask. Not when she had so few friends and liked Anton and Helena so much.

The house with its blue-and-white themed garden somehow managed to avoid fussy formal and to achieve elusive elegant instead.

Helena had suggested Blanche bring her sewing. She clutched the bag in her hand. Having something in her hands had soothed her since she was a little child. Even if her father had thrown plates on Saturday, she could sit and sew by Monday.

The door opened before she reached the front verandah. "We're so glad you've come," Helena said. Anton's face beamed from behind Helena's shoulder.

It hurt to see his smile. Why couldn't William welcome her like that? Instead, she always felt she was a sort of trophy. Never an equal. Her thoughts left a nasty aftertaste as though she was being disloyal. Anton was a married man. She shouldn't be thinking about him at all.

The living room was covered with photos. She didn't want to appear overly curious, but one looked like a photo of Helena and Anton in their mid-teens. They must have been childhood sweethearts. If so, they had broken the 'too early married always ends badly' cliché. Their relationship was strong.

"I'm nearly finished making dinner," Helena said.

"Do you want any help?" Blanche asked.

"No, thanks. Everything's under control. Why don't you and Anton go and choose the music for the evening?" She handed Anton a plate of olives, cheese, and crackers.

"This way." Anton led her towards a room at the back of the house.

Blanche's eyes widened as she entered. A cello sat on a stand. There were several instrument cases on a shelf to the right. The stereo and speaker system were William's preferred brand.

"Who plays all the instruments?"

"The violin and clarinet are mine, and the cello and French horn are Helena's."

"I'm impressed."

Anton gave a tiny smile. "European families often created their own mini orchestras."

"Like Bach's family."

He nodded. "Those long winters meant you had to entertain yourselves." He walked over to a series of shelves. Groups of records were separated by alphabetical dividers.

"That's one big record collection."

His laugh reminded her of long summer evenings. "It could have been much bigger, but Dad always said, 'Don't just buy any record of a piece. Only buy the best, or you'll have to buy another later.'"

"Makes sense."

He turned towards her. "What would you like to listen to?"

She flushed. "I like music, but I'm not very educated about it. Why don't you choose a favourite?"

"You mentioned Bach. We can't go wrong with that." His long fingers moved along the "B" shelf. "Dinner's not ready yet. There's enough time for the Toccata and Fugue in D Minor."

Blanche laughed nervously. It sounded like some sort of elaborate dessert.

"You'll probably have heard this somewhere. So, if you sit here and we place the crackers and cheese here, you'll be set up for the best experience." He guided her to the best chair, treating her like some priceless musical instrument, making sure she was settled comfortably.

He dusted the already pristine record and took his time placing it on the turntable. "Ready?"

She nodded.

He settled himself in a chair. "Don't be embarrassed to shut your eyes. I usually do."

The opening three notes, played on a pipe organ, were immediately recognisable. William had never been an organ fan. Said it was an instrument for old fuddy-duddies. He'd obviously never heard a master like this. As the torrent of sound poured over her, she risked a glance at Anton. His eyes were closed and he swayed, as though caught up in a trance. Such a handsome, aristocratic face. What was his story?

She closed her eyes and let the music take her along like a leaf carried on a surge of water. Agony and ecstasy, joy and sorrow, pain and beauty. The music unlocked a part of her tightly curled for too long.

After the record ended, there was a long silence.

"Dinner is ready," Helena said.

Blanche jerked herself out of the fantasy world in which she'd been immersed. She opened her eyes to see Anton offering her his hand. Her face heated. She covered her confusion by fussing with the wrinkles in her skirt.

In the dining room, crystal glasses and silver cutlery gleamed in the candlelight. Elegant and understated, like Anton and Helena. They weren't at all lovey-dovey but obviously cared for each other. A violin concerto on another record player accompanied the main course, and they had dessert listening to a canon, whatever that was. Anton quietly announced each piece before it started with details of composer and dates. He must have a prodigious memory.

They chatted about music without Blanche being made to feel ignorant. The food was delicious, and they were soon laughing like they'd known each other all their lives. She even related witty stories about Rachel and Esther. The sting that once had her gasping with the pain of loss was diminishing, and she didn't break down once.

The only family member she didn't mention was William. There was nothing she could say that wouldn't put a dampener on the whole evening.

After the meal, Anton shooed them back to the music room to chat while he cleared the table and stacked the dishwasher. Helena predicted he'd soon bring them a pot of tea. What a man. Blanche couldn't remember a time when she could simply sit back and relax.

Some time later, Anton came back into the music room carrying a tray with tea things and after dinner mints. "Helena and I often play music in the evenings. Would you like that?"

Blanche sat up straight. "You mean my own private concert?"

He chuckled. "Something like that."

"I'd love it. Would it offend you if I sewed?"

"Not at all. You go right ahead." They all had a cup of tea before he reached for his violin and tucked it under his chin. Helena moved to her cello stool.

After a short time of tuning, they launched into a piece of music Blanche didn't recognise. Whatever it was, it was a perfect accompaniment for the panel she was sewing—more wildflowers for a quilt for Naomi. This one would be all wildflower panels, twelve of them. Naida was turning her first three designs into packs that included pattern, instructions, fabric and thread. She was predicting good sales.

Blanche stitched and sneaked occasional glances at the musicians. They played as one being, communicating with raised eyebrows, nods, and tiny gestures. Why had she and William never been like this? One flesh, but never really one.

Had she and William reached a point of no return? The first time she'd had this thought she'd gasped with the pain, but now it seemed the only sensible way to go. At what point did someone decide to give up and admit some marriages can't be saved or aren't worth saving? Was theirs such a marriage?

CHAPTER 26

$\mathcal{T}$he knock came at half past six in the morning. William yawned. Goodness, the kid was keen. He was up as early as the sun. After several weeks of being nagged, William had promised Davy they'd go hiking this morning. Proper hiking, Davy called it, out to the cliffs to see the seabirds.

Davy was hopping up and down on the doormat. "Are you ready? Are you ready?"

Watching Davy exhausted William. The days when he was young and full of energy were long past. Some mornings it took iron discipline to get out of bed. "Let me grab my pack first."

"Grams gave me enough snacks for both of us."

No surprise there. Ivy and Reg had been looking after William like he was family. Close family.

William laced the boots Reg had loaned him, stood up, and pulled the door closed behind him, not bothering to lock it.

Davy was already pushing his bike through the gate. William quick-marched over to the shed, grabbed his bike, and set off in pursuit. He still needed a light jacket, but the cloudless morning promised another stunning day.

They rode north towards the start of the walk, parking their bikes under a bush before setting off through the low-lying scrub. Davy skipped ahead and around a corner, and William couldn't see him. Maybe he should have loaded a few rocks in Davy's pack.

"Hey, Davy. Slow down a bit."

No sound. William's heart rate sped up. Davy was his responsibility, and he mustn't lose him. He ran forward, tripping over roots, his backpack thumping against his back.

"Boo!" Davy leaped out from behind a rock, laughing.

William ground to a halt, his mouth dry and his breath coming in ragged gasps.

"Scared you, scared you," Davy chanted.

"Whad'ya do that for?" William shouted.

Davy went pale and took a step back.

The look of fear seared William's gut. He wheezed out a shaky laugh. After a moment, Davy joined in.

William had leapt out at his father once, many years ago. He'd never made that mistake again.

Davy spoke over his shoulder as they set off again. "Did you have a little boy like me once?"

There was a sudden lump in William's throat. "Just a daughter." His voice came out a croak. He still found it so hard to admit he had two daughters. What was it about Rachel that he preferred her dead to alive? His parents had lost one child and ignored the second. Now he was doing the same.

He shook his head. If only he could clear his thoughts so easily. Blanche's letters always included titbits of news about Rachel. Like she was determined to force him to remember. Maybe the adult version of Rachel was different, but they used to fight every time they laid eyes on each other. Her leaving had been a relief.

But what kind of father leaves a fifteen-year-old on the streets?

Ever since he'd arrived here, such unwelcome questions had intruded more and more frequently. In Sydney he'd succeeded in locking his thoughts away, out of sight and out of mind. Here, he had so much free time that thoughts kept surfacing. Thoughts were dangerous. Thoughts led to questions he couldn't answer. He'd never liked unanswered questions. He shivered. Unanswerable questions.

"Only one child in the family, like mine." Davy said.

It was tempting to let Davy live with his assumption but, somehow, he couldn't lie. He was out of practice talking about Rachel.

Hadn't dared to mention her?

Blast. There was another of those errant thoughts. Why were they coming to the surface now? He'd always been a good husband to Blanche. He'd never questioned her spending or criticised her housekeeping. He'd given her everything she needed.

Everything?

Had he made Blanche as happy as Reg made Ivy, or Stan made Betty? Silly question. He and Blanche were different. Their marriage didn't have to be like anyone else's.

"I had two daughters," William said.

"What do you mean 'had'?" Davy persisted.

"It's a bit hard to talk about." He swallowed loudly enough to hear himself gulp. "One of my daughters left." He couldn't say her name out loud. "I haven't seen her for many years."

"Why did she leave?"

His hands were sweating. "We didn't get along very well, and she was angry."

Davy stopped so abruptly, William nearly crashed into him. The kid turned around and gazed at him with a piercing eye a high school principal would die for.

"Why didn't you forgive her?"

"Sometimes it's not that easy."

Davy frowned. "Gramps says it's never easy, but we have to do it anyway. I didn't find it easy to forgive Ben when he lied and got me in trouble. Or Nate and Julie when they bullied me."

Davy turned and walked forward again. William followed. Did Davy inherit his maturity, or had losing his parents forced him to grow up in a spurt-like jump?

The examples Davy mentioned were trivial, but he had a point. Perhaps Davy practiced forgiveness on smaller cases, so he hadn't been angry at God when his parents died. He'd assumed Davy was too young to be angry at God, but Reg had shot the idea out of the water. Said all of them had struggled through the normal whys. Why had God allowed Davy's parents to die? Why had God allowed Davy to be too ill to join them on the plane? Or was that only coincidence?

William had no answers to these questions. He stamped his boot on the dead leaves in front of him. No answers. He'd always had answers. At least, he'd had plenty of answers until Esther's surgery. He'd been struggling since.

Esther had asked him why God wasn't healing her, and he hadn't had any answers. Not that he'd told her. He grimaced. He'd spouted all sorts of possibilities.

Spouted. He snorted. That's what he'd done. Spouted, when his answer box was empty. Esther's questions and doubts had left him floundering. That was unfamiliar. He was Mr In-Control-At-All-Times. Cancer had taken control away, so he'd ignored it. Not that ignoring the cancer had made any difference. Esther had still died.

He crushed the thoughts underfoot like the discarded palm fronds strewn over the ground, dry and long dead.

Death. One more thing he didn't want to think about. William skirted a puddle left over from last night's rain and hurried to catch up with Davy.

"This is one of the best spots on the island for growing these palms. Gramps says they get exported all over the world." Davy's voice thrilled with pride. "Gramps loves to come hiking, but he said I should take you today. He says it's good for you to see God's creation."

What else did Reg say to Davy? Probably not much, but the man definitely had an agenda. In anyone else, William would have labelled it meddling, but he'd been drawn to Reg and Ivy from the first time they offered him a meal. Their warmth, their simple trust, their goodness. No pretension, no harsh judgement, no impatience. Rare in his experience.

"Every time Gramps comes with me, he tells me, 'Learn from the trees, Davy, learn from the trees.'"

"What does he want you to learn from the trees?"

Davy put his head to one side. "Lots of things." He reached out and let the fronds of a young palm run through his stumpy fingers. "You know. Things like growing tall and straight, pruning ... things like that."

Davy pointed at the dead fronds. "Last time, he talked about how things had to die for there to be life." He kicked a stone. "I don't understand that yet."

They walked on.

"Gramps knows I learn best from stories. I don't always like being told what to do." He hung his head. "Maybe that's why I sometimes get in trouble at school."

Was there anyone who appreciated criticism? Certainly not William or anyone else he knew. Being told what to do always felt like a criticism or an attack and made him push back against the command. Maybe he hadn't opened his mother's letter because he dreaded another telling off like the ones she'd given him in the past.

Even Esther had thrown around criticism, which was why he'd overreacted and given her an ultimatum that led to her moving out. If he'd known she'd end up at his mother's house, he'd have curbed his tongue.

The light was strengthening as they came out of the shade of the palms. Cliffs plunged into the sea and rose far above them. Birds wheeled across his vision, rising on the thermals.

"Red-tailed tropicbirds," Davy yelled above the clamouring bird calls.

Their tails were unlike any William had seen on a bird before—more like a stick or a rudder than a tail.

Davy pointed behind him. "Did you see all those burrows?"

"Looks like you've got a rabbit problem," William yelled.

Davy giggled. "They're not rabbits. They're muttonbirds. They come in at night."

Davy insisted they get their binoculars out and look at the different birds. They shuffled like geriatrics in ill-fitting boots on land, but were all aerobatic grace when flying.

Davy spread his arms apart like wings. "Don't you wish we could fly?"

William reached down and smoothed Davy's recalcitrant cowlick. "It would certainly be a good view."

Davy knelt down and crawled towards the edge.

"Are you sure going right to the edge is a good idea?" William called.

"It's how Gramps taught me. Come on. It's safe." Davy lay down and peered over the edge.

William had never been afraid of heights, but crawling seemed like a good idea, even if it muddied the knees of his trousers. Below them, the blue-green water sparkled in the sun. Bird after bird dive-bombed, seldom missing a catch.

This cliff would be high enough to be the local suicide spot. Bile rose in his throat. Not a question he'd ask Davy, and not something he'd do. Knowing his recent luck in life, he'd only cripple himself and be far worse off.

Davy wriggled back from the edge. "We'd better get going."

They toiled on. At least, William toiled. Davy bounced and skipped like he was strolling on a city footpath. William pulled a handkerchief out of his pocket and wiped his forehead. The higher they climbed, the better the view, but he refused to stop and look now. He had the beginnings of a blister on his heel. That's what came of wearing someone else's boots, but he didn't have any of his own. He'd never needed them.

"Yahoo," Davy called.

William looked up. Davy had taken off his pack and was leaping around like a mountain goat. Did the boy never stop?

William put his head down and pushed on. His leg muscles objected every step of the way. With a last surge, he made it to the crest and gasped at the 360-degree view.

"Those are the Admiralty Islands," Davy said, pointing.

Volcanic pinnacles of rock rose out of their pale blue setting with sparse vegetation clinging to their crown.

"Gramps says that's some of the best diving in Australia, but—" Davy frowned "—I have to wait 'til I'm bigger."

William, too, had spent all his high school years wanting to be bigger and smarter and faster, although his motive was different to Davy's.

"Now turn around. Slowly," Davy said.

Sea and more sea. Aquamarine near the shore, and darkening the further out William looked. The beauty of it caught in his throat. Not a single cloud interrupted the view, all the way across the waist of the island where they all lived. More islands set in opalescent sea.

Davy was pointing again. "There's Mount Lidgbird and Mount Gower."

"What kind of bird is a Lidgbird?"

Davy choked on the mouthful he was swilling. "It's not a bird—it's a name. One of the early explorer guys."

William laughed, more relaxed than he'd been in years. Davy was as refreshing as the water in their bottles. They sat down on the top of the hill and munched on fruit cake and apples.

After half an hour soaking in the view, they headed back. William still had to go over his sermon for tomorrow. Reg seemed to think the last two weeks had been a big improvement on the first week's disaster. If he didn't meet the church members' expectations they weren't afraid to say so. The biggest crime in their eyes was to wander from the passage, and he hadn't dared after the second week. The passage for this week was a long one, all of Stephen's story. He didn't know what to make of it. Why did God allow such a man to be killed? Surely the God who created the universe and raised the dead could have saved Stephen.

William stumbled as he avoided a muttonbird burrow.

Where were all these questions coming from? The image of his mother's letter still hidden in the pocket of his suitcase flashed into his mind. Could that be it? Would the questions end if he read it, or would his disquiet only increase?

CHAPTER 27

"Follow my lead. I'll talk you through it," Anton said to Blanche.

She took a deep breath. Her dancing experience was limited to two balls, decades ago. She could manage a waltz and a polka, but the thought of a tango or rhumba tied her insides in knots.

The music started, and Anton counted her in. "Three-two-one, here we go."

She faltered and then his calming voice was in her ear, "One, two, three, one, two, three, very good, well done, Blanche ..."

She relaxed into his arms. All her fear of making a fool of herself ebbed away. Helena was Anton's usual dancing partner. What did she think about Blanche being here tonight?

Helena whirled by in the arms of another man. She fluttered her fingers towards Blanche and gave a broad smile. Maybe Helena wasn't the jealous type. Not that there was anything for Helena to be jealous about.

Anyway, Anton and Helena were showing her what marriage should be like. Companionship with mutual respect, mutual trust, and loads of laughter. If her marriage was like theirs, she wouldn't still be living at Naomi's.

Blanche hummed to the familiar music. Anton had played her Strauss the week before. She smiled to herself. In the past few weeks she'd been to a concert, another dinner, and an art gallery. She'd had more fun in the last month than she'd had in years. These invitations were not because of who her husband was or because she was the head of a church committee, but simply because Anton and Helena liked being with her. And she liked being with them. A lot.

Sometimes she came home with her ribs aching from laughter. Naomi and Rachel had both noticed she was glowing. She was having fun, and why shouldn't she? It wasn't as if William cared. He'd always indulged his own interests and never bothered to find out they didn't interest her.

He was writing regularly and sounded like he was developing new hobbies. Snorkelling and hiking, and he even mentioned getting around on two wheels. It would be amusing to see him on a bicycle.

The music drew to a close. Anton bowed to her, and it seemed appropriate to curtsey back. He smiled, and a tingle of electricity zipped up her arm. She quickly turned and headed back to where she'd placed her water bottle. Anton followed.

"How was that?"

"Great, great thank you," she said too heartily, keeping her back to him. "I didn't think my feet would remember how to dance."

"Do you want to dance the next one or sit it out?"

"What about Helena?"

He grinned. "Don't worry about her. She has people queuing up."

They danced three more in a row before she danced with one of the other men—because it was more than time to dance with someone else. Her stomach heaved and she shivered. Coming dancing had been a mistake. This was too intimate. She was responding like a teenager, craving Anton's touch but terrified at the same time. There'd been a mutual connection with him from the first day. She should have seen trouble coming. No wonder Naomi had looked concerned the other night when she'd arrived home. She'd recognised the glow on Blanche's face and knew it had nothing to do with William.

Blanche stumbled and trod on her new partner's foot. "Sorry."

"You're doing well for a first timer."

How had things come to this? She'd never have let this friendship flourish if Helena hadn't been around. She flushed. Had Helena seen what she hadn't? Surely not. She'd never given any indication of being the kind of woman who would encourage her husband to romance someone else. And it had been a romancing, though up to now Blanche had been too blind to see it.

Her neck prickled. What was going on? Neither Anton or Helena had given the slightest inkling something wasn't right between them, and Anton must know she was married.

The dance finished, and Blanche retired to the seats around the wall. Anton was by her side before she'd swallowed her second mouthful of water.

"One more dance before the one I'll do with Helena?"

If only she could refuse, but she couldn't do it now without unpleasantness. She'd have to talk to them, or to Helena. If she'd misread the whole situation she'd not only look a fool but might lose a valued friendship.

She allowed herself to be led to the dance floor as the music started again. Another waltz. Good. She wasn't going to be much use with anything more complicated.

"Just relax, Blanche."

If only she could. He looked into her eyes. Why did he have to have such marvellous dark-blue eyes with flecks of grey? She looked down.

"Is anything the matter? You seem tense."

"I'm okay," she said as brightly as she could. "Getting rather tired."

She hated herself for the lie, but this wasn't the place to sort things out. She forced herself to follow him.

He leaned in, much closer than a mere friend would lean. How could she ease away from him without causing a scene? Oh, if only she didn't have to. He was all she wished William would be. She tightened her grip on Anton's hand. If William hadn't treated her as he did, she wouldn't be in this fix.

Helena and her partner passed by. Helena turned her head and grinned at them. Something was off, really off. What kind of woman seemed happy her husband was cuddling up with someone else?

Blanche lurched back, stepped on Anton's foot, and gasped in pain.

Anton stopped. "Are you okay?"

"I've twisted my ankle," she blushed. "Right when I crushed your foot."

"My foot is fine, but how bad is your ankle? Can you put it on the floor?"

She put her foot down and took a tentative step. Pain stabbed her outer ankle. "Ouch."

The other dancers still twirled around them. Anton was watching the couples pass by. He beckoned one of them. "Matt, can you check Blanche's ankle?" He took her arm. "Matt's a paramedic. Let me take your shoes off."

He crouched down and eased off her shoes, and the two men helped her hobble to the side. It turned out to be only a minor sprain.

Anton sat down next to her. "I'll let Helena know what's happening, buy an ice pack, and then drive you and your car home."

Her eyes welled with tears at the warmth in his voice. "I can take a taxi." She didn't trust herself to be alone in a car with him.

"I wouldn't think of it. Helena can drive our car. I want to make sure you get home safely." He smiled in a way that melted her to her toes. "After all, it was my foot that caused the damage."

CHAPTER 28

*B*lanche was placed in the front seat of her car like Anton considered her a priceless Ming vase. Fifteen minutes of smooth efficiency from the moment she'd done the damage. Now to endure the twenty-minute drive home. Saying nothing wasn't going to be an option. Twenty minutes seemed a long time for awkward silences, but was it long enough to sort out the mess she'd inadvertently placed herself in? How could she raise the topic when she suspected Anton was making a pass at her—or worse? Perhaps she wasn't even safe in the car with him.

Lord, give me courage. I need help to get out of the mess I'm in.

Courage was something she'd been requesting since Esther had first been diagnosed with cancer. Courage to face Esther's illness, courage to face her past, courage to confront William. She'd asked for the courage of Shadrach, Meshach, and Abednego, and her prayers had been answered every time.

Her sprained ankle might give her the perfect excuse to clear things up.

"Thank you so much for all your care," Blanche said. "I'm sorry I've ruined your evening."

Anton glanced across at her. "You have in no way ruined my evening." He paused. "I hope I am going to have the pleasure of caring a lot more for you."

Help. It didn't sound like she'd been mistaken.

"What will Helena think?"

"I'm not sure I get your meaning." His accent was more noticeable than usual. "She'll be delighted. She's been encouraging me since we met."

Blanche swallowed. This was awful. Worse than her one disastrous date as a sixteen-year-old, long before being swept off her feet by William's determined pursuit. At sixteen, she'd eaten too much ice-cream and followed it with a rollercoaster ride. A very messy disaster indeed. Bile rose in her throat.

"Are you and Helena divorced?"

She heard his gasp in the semi-darkness, then he started to laugh. And laugh. "Oh, my goodness."

This was one joke she was missing the punchline. Her jaw ached with tension.

There was a gasping snort and more laughter. "Have you thought Helena and I were married all this time?"

He pulled the car over and parked it on the side of the road under a streetlight. Then he turned to look at her. "I am so sorry. I shouldn't laugh." He took her hand.

Blanche gently withdrew it.

"I assumed you knew," Anton said. "Helena is my sister."

Blanche let out her breath in a long whoosh. Her legs trembled. How could she have been so very wrong about their relationship?

"I told Helena several times sharing a house would cause confusion." Anton shook his head. "Perhaps this isn't the best place to talk. I don't want your ankle to blow up like a balloon."

"It's barely hurting now, and the ice pack you bought is working wonders."

"What if you put your seat back and I find something to put under your ankle?"

He undid his seatbelt and leaned across to find her seat lever. She held her breath at his closeness.

He sat up. Even in the darkness, she could feel the intensity of his gaze burning into her soul. She needed to avoid looking at him if she was going to get through this with any dignity. "But you talked about your children."

"My children, Helena's nieces and nephews. I was married for thirty years. Six years ago, Enid ..." He paused. "Enid was my wife. She died of melanoma."

A tear glistened on his cheek, and she had to sit on her hand to stop herself brushing it away.

"I thought I'd never recover." He sat for a few moments. "I endured two years on my own, but I was so lonely. Eventually Helena suggested we share her place. She'd never married, and we'd always been close."

He tapped the steering wheel. "Actually, it's been a great arrangement." He chuckled. "Except for the confusion it's caused you. I assumed Helena had told you."

Nausea surged in Blanche's stomach. "And she probably assumed you'd told me."

"Didn't you look at the photos in the house? I always look at people's photos."

"I didn't want to pry."

"If only you'd been less polite then we wouldn't find ourselves in this situation with me having to convince you it's okay for me to love you." He reached over and brushed her cheek.

Tears welled in her eyes and her stomach heaved.

"That's just it. It isn't okay."

He withdrew his hand as though she'd slapped him. "What do you mean?"

"I believed you were married, and you aren't—" A horrible

strangled sound erupted from her throat. "And you believed I wasn't, but I am."

His eyes opened wide in pools of hurt and confusion. Oh, this was worse than she'd imagined. She'd assumed she had talked about William at least once, but perhaps she hadn't. She'd been in so much pain herself and hadn't wanted to dump her troubles on new friends. Friends that seemed happily married. She'd talked often about Esther and Rachel and Naomi, but she must not have mentioned William. It had been stupid, but she had not meant it to lead to this desolation. This desert.

She touched her ring finger.

"Yes," he said looking at her hands. "That's what convinced me you were a widow. No rings."

She clasped her trembling hands together. "The diamond was loose and the jeweller got extra busy, so I told him he could put them on the back burner."

He stared out the windscreen. "You'd better tell me about your husband." His voice was a mere whisper.

She put her hand to her chest. It was tight, and she ached all over. What a mess. Now they had a mountain of pain to deal with.

She pushed the small of her back against the seat.

"You know Esther died earlier this year."

He nodded.

"William didn't handle the situation well. In fact, he barely had anything to do with her once the cancer recurred."

"I don't understand at all. What man doesn't drop everything to spend time with his daughter when she needs him?"

Tears pooled in Blanche's eyes and overflowed. Anton had put his finger on the issue that had given her the most pain. She opened the glovebox and rummaged around for the small packet of tissues she kept there for emergencies.

"I haven't really understood either." Her stomach ached, and she wrapped her arms around herself. "I think the reasons are more complex than they appear on the surface."

"What was the surface?"

She sighed. "William is the senior pastor at Victory Church—"

"Oh," Anton said. "He's made his reputation claiming God heals, and God didn't heal his daughter."

Bless Anton for understanding.

She hiccupped. "He didn't even come to Esther's funeral."

"And how did that make you feel?" His voice was tight.

"Angry. Angry enough to remain at my mother-in-law's."

"Why were you there in the first place?"

She didn't want to go into the details, to be disloyal or say things that made the situation between her and William any worse.

"You don't have to tell me."

He must have sensed her reluctance to talk. She squeezed her stomach harder. "It's been horribly complicated. William expected me to go home and behave as if nothing had happened."

Did Anton whisper "dolt" under his breath? She covered her mouth with her hand. The corner of her mouth twisted upwards with the glimmer of a smile. The man was sensitive to her every mood, but she mustn't let Anton get any closer. He was close enough already. Dangerously close.

"I told him I couldn't go home until he dealt with the issues, and I've been stuck in limbo ever since." She blew her nose. "The time away has been good for me in dealing with the grief of Esther's death, but I'm not sure whether William has made any progress."

"I have a friend who attends Victory, and he mentioned the senior pastor was away."

"Yes, he's doing an interim ministry on Lord Howe Island."

"Is that what he calls a break?"

She nodded. "Breaks aren't really his thing."

"What's next?"

Was he asking because he wanted to know for her sake? Or was he hoping against hope he had a chance? Was he the kind of man who would marry a divorcee? Was she the kind of woman who would get divorced? She didn't know the answer to that question herself. It wasn't a question she'd thought about before.

"Well, my mother-in-law and a few other women are praying for William." Looking back, Blanche's prayers had been more perfunctory since she'd met Anton. "I guess we haven't got a Plan B. We've been praying and trusting God to meet with William." It sounded lame. God could change people and circumstances, but what if they didn't cooperate? If William never changed, would she remain separated from him or would it be better to formalise the split? *Quit the euphemisms, Blanche.* Would they get a divorce so both of them could move on?

A warmth spread up her neck. Was Anton a man who would wait?

CHAPTER 29

*T*he letter from his mother had been on William's mind the entire weekend. No matter whether he hiked with Davy or preached this morning's sermon, he couldn't forget it. For whatever reason, he was afraid of his mother's censure. Odd for someone his age. Blanche had nothing but respect for her. Perhaps his mother had changed. Blanche certainly had.

William sighed. He still had a month on the island. If the letter angered him, he'd have plenty of time to simmer down. Once back in Sydney, he'd be running from one appointment to the next with no time to think. No time for anything but preparation and presentation. This was the best time to deal with it.

He went into the spare bedroom, squatted, and hauled the suitcase out from under the bed. The suitcase stuck midway, as though it was as reluctant to come out as he was to open it.

Once clear of the bed, it only took seconds to unzip. William sat on the floor, head in hands. Did he really want to do this? Only he and his mother knew about it. If he threw the letter away or burned it, he could pretend he'd never received it.

But you won't stop wondering about it.

Right. He couldn't fool himself. There was one main reason he couldn't burn it—what if the letter contained a last message from Esther?

All through Esther's memorial service, he'd sat in his car parked in a back street. He hadn't had the guts to let anyone at the church know he hadn't gone to the funeral, and he hadn't corrected anyone who'd assumed he'd gone. It was unforgivable not to have farewelled Esther, but he hadn't been able to summon the courage to go. Instead, he had stared at a random clump of trees, totally numb.

Two hours after the service should have ended, he'd roused himself and driven home on automatic pilot. He didn't notice other cars. He didn't notice any traffic lights. He drove as though there had been an apocalypse and he was the only person in an empty city.

Disconnected scraps of memories from that first night still appeared in his nightmares. The hum of the garage door. The semi-darkness as he sat, mouth slightly open, fixated on the tools he could vaguely see in front of him. All angles and steel in systematised rows. Each in the precise spot where he'd placed them. A total contrast to his life.

He had no notion how long he'd sat there. Eventually he had gotten out of the car and gone to the kitchen. He remembered the ping of the microwave as he robotically prepared a meal. It had tasted like cardboard. He had been home, but it was no longer a place of welcome. It had been a sleepless night.

Then Kylie had put the letter marked 'Strictly Personal' on his desk at the church.

There was no escape now. He had to read it. William fished in the suitcase and grasped the letter. His hand shook. No, he'd read it later. Tomorrow. He nodded twice. Yes, that would be better. He'd be much fresher in the morning. More able to cope with emotional things.

He tossed the letter onto his dressing table and went into the lounge where he surfed through the television channels. Nothing made any impression. Flashes of light and confused sound bouncing off the bowling ball of his skull. Totally unintelligible. Nothing penetrated. Nothing caught his attention.

It was no use. He turned off the TV and walked stiffly to his room. He was a robot. Preprogrammed to shower, do his teeth, and fold back the covers. He shivered as he lay in the darkness staring towards the ceiling. He missed Blanche.

He squirmed, trying to find a comfortable spot.

The letter.

It burned in his mind as though it glowed in the dark. Why couldn't he fall into the oblivion of sleep? Random pictures dropped into his mind like a slideshow of memory—Esther, laughing in happiness after her engagement announcement. Esther, sitting in the living room with bowed head as the elders prayed around her. Esther, her face full of hurt and sadness the day he'd kicked her out of home. That was his last vivid memory—one of pulsing pain and shame. Would he ever be able to forget the look on her face? The look he'd caused because he'd insisted on being in control.

Why?

Whys were the questions that terrified him. Asking why was dangerous. Like poking a stick into a hornet's nest and exposing himself to a swarm of stinging fury.

Half an hour passed. Then another. He fought the urge to look at his digital clock but still found himself looking at it every hour on the hour. His sheets became a tangled cord, winding around him, tying him down.

The letter.

Still sitting on the dressing table. He'd hoped a little distance would make him forget. Impossible. Invisible cords of curiosity bound him to its smooth surface.

At two o'clock, he abandoned all attempts at sleep, switched on the bedside lamp, leaned across the bed, and snatched up the letter. He tore open the envelope and smoothed out the pages.

DEAR DAD,

He gasped and scanned to the back page. Yes, the writing might be his mother's but the letter itself was from Esther. His heart thumped in his chest. What if he had a heart attack right here with no one around to help him? His fingers were slick and stuck to the pages. There was now no question of not reading the letter. For in it, his daughter reached out from beyond the grave. He'd failed her in life. He wasn't going to fail her again in death.

THIS LETTER MIGHT BE A SHOCK. LET ME SAY FIRST, IT COMES WITH ALL MY LOVE. NO MATTER WHAT WE SAID TO EACH OTHER, I'VE NEVER STOPPED LOVING YOU AND HAVE PRAYED FOR YOU CONSTANTLY.

Tears leaked out of ducts long dry. No man was less deserving of his daughter's love.

AS A CHILD, I ONLY WANTED TO PLEASE YOU. I WHOLEHEARTEDLY ENDORSED EVERYTHING YOU SAID. AFTER ALL, THERE WAS NO REASON TO QUESTION IT FROM MY COMFORTABLE COCOON. MY ENGAGEMENT TO NICK SEEMED THE CROWNING EVIDENCE OF BLESSING. I SELECTIVELY READ MY BIBLE AND FOUND PLENTY OF

CHRISTINE DILLON

EVIDENCE TO SUPPORT MY VIEWS. I WAS SWEPT UP IN THE SUCCESS OF VICTORY CHURCH.

William knew where Esther was headed. She'd said it all before, but he'd ignored her.

Steamrolled her?

Where had that thought come from? He pushed it away.

He'd been wrong not to go to the memorial, no matter how awkward it might have been. The family could have pretended everything was normal. After all, they'd had plenty of practice.

MY DIAGNOSIS WAS A RUDE SHOCK, BUT I REASSURED MYSELF IT WOULD BE A TEMPORARY BLIP. SURELY GOD WOULD BRING GLORY TO HIMSELF BY HEALING ME. WHEN I WASN'T HEALED, IT CONFUSED ME. WEREN'T WE FAITHFUL ENOUGH?

YOU MADE ME ANGRY BY SAYING THE PROBLEM WAS MY LACK OF FAITH. I KNEW I'D DONE MY BEST, SO WHY WASN'T GOD COMING THROUGH FOR ME?

Esther hadn't been the only one who was confused. He'd had the same questions, but his whole life and ministry was built on the assertion that God blessed the faithful. Any problems had to be due to sin or lack of faith. After all, how could the problem rest with God?

He kept reading.

JOY WONG WAS GOD'S GRACIOUS GIFT. I DIDN'T SEE IT IMMEDIATELY. AT THE TIME, I THOUGHT SHE WAS THE LAST STRAW. HER QUESTION, "WHY DO YOU THINK GOD MUST HEAL?"

WOULDN'T LEAVE ME ALONE. BY THE THIRD SLEEPLESS NIGHT, I
KNEW THE ONLY WAY TO DEAL WITH MY DISQUIET WAS TO PROVE
HER WRONG, SO I WENT BACK TO THE GOSPELS AND READ ALL OF
THEM AS FAST AS I COULD. I NOTICED THINGS I'D NEVER PAID
ATTENTION TO BEFORE. IN PARTICULAR, THE REPEATED THEME—
THE WAY TO LIFE IS NARROW AND STEEP. WE MUST PICK UP OUR
CROSS AND FOLLOW JESUS.

Those words of Jesus had always bothered him too, but he'd
glossed over them. Pushed past them onto more comfortable teach-
ings. He stuck with topics relevant to his congregation.
Relevant?
"Shut up," he muttered.

SURELY PICKING UP A CROSS COULD BE NOTHING BUT PAINFUL,
DIFFICULT, AND HUMILIATING. AS I READ, I WAS CONFRONTED BY
THE UNPALATABLE TRUTH. I HAD BELIEVED A LIE. JESUS WAS
CRUCIFIED, SO WHY SHOULD WE EXPECT ANYTHING LESS?

Esther's question leapt off the page. It pierced William's soul,
stabbing through layers of self-protection. All he wanted to do was
rip the pages into shreds and fling the scraps into a fire. His own
questions, the ones he had tried to shut away, were written on the
pages before him in stark black on white. Had he deceived himself?
Worse, had he deceived others?
He didn't want to see himself under this harsh light.
Didn't want to, or didn't dare?
Again troublesome thoughts poured out of him, like bats from a
dark cave, flitting through the cracks of his mind. He'd stamp on

them. He'd capture them somehow. He must, he must, he must! If he didn't, what would he have left?

Desperate for distraction, he kept reading.

MY PRIVILEGED LIFE IN AUSTRALIA HAD BLINDED ME TO WHAT LIFE IS LIKE FOR BELIEVERS THROUGHOUT THE WORLD. JOY TOLD ME ABOUT CHINA. LIFE IS TERRIBLY UNFAIR FOR FAITHFUL CHILDREN OF GOD, YET THEY REMAIN JOYFUL, FOR THEIR EYES ARE FOCUSED ON JESUS.

DEAREST DAD, BY THE TIME YOU READ THIS, I WILL BE WITH JESUS. HE HAS BECOME DEARER TO ME THAN LIFE ITSELF. I WILL NO LONGER BE SUFFERING, AND MY HEAVENLY FATHER WILL WIPE AWAY MY TEARS. MANY OF THOSE TEARS WILL HAVE BEEN FOR YOU.

His daughter had cried for him. Why? The question echoed in his darkness. He bent double, gripping under his knees. He dug his fingernails into his skin. Outer pain felt much better than inner pain. His heart pounded uncomfortably, and he shut his eyes. He couldn't open the hidden drawers of his mind. It would destroy him. He'd finish the letter and never look at it again. Ever.

But it was too late. The words were already seared in his memory. Flaming letters a hundred metres high. The bitter taste of failure was on his tongue. He'd failed his daughter because he hadn't dared to face himself. Or was it, he hadn't dared to face God?

William gnawed his lip and kept reading.

DAD, SUFFERING ISN'T TO BE AVOIDED OR DENIED. IT'S TO BE EMBRACED. PART OF LIVING IN THIS SIN-SOAKED WORLD.

Dearest Dad, I fear for you. Though it hurts me to do so, I must warn you. You claim to be God's spokesman, but your words are out of step with his. Please don't miss out on one day sharing my joy. God accepts the meek and humble who cry to him for mercy. Have you done so? I close with all my love and forgiveness.

Your daughter, Esther

William's breath came in tight, shallow gasps. Esther's questions pinned him in a blazing spotlight. No matter how he squirmed and wriggled, he couldn't escape. He stood naked in the light before a mirror, all his imperfections glaringly visible. No, not imperfections. It was more than time for correct labels. They were not merely imperfections. It was sin.

Sin.

A simple, stark word. A stark word for an ugly truth. Bile rose in his throat, and he feared he'd vomit all over the carpet.

Sin.

His life was consumed with chasing glory. Building himself up so he'd feel worthy of his father's attention. It had never been about Jesus, not really. Everything was for William B Macdonald in his run-over-everyone-else-trample-their-faces-into-the-mud pursuit of glory. He'd cut off anyone who'd dared to warn him so they could never criticise him again. His mother. His daughters. In the end, even Blanche. All those people who had only been guilty of loving him.

His whole jaw ached with tension. He hadn't wanted love. He'd wanted control. Control of their thoughts. Control of their tongues. Control of their hearts. He'd wanted robots. Robots who bowed to the golden image of himself that he'd created.

Hot tears poured down his cheeks. Tears of grief and shame. The innermost corners of his heart were dark ugliness, full of deep-rooted pride. Like Adam and Eve in the garden, he'd tried to cover his inadequacies with fig leaves. He'd gone about in tailor-made suits and kept his body trim, but he'd neglected to make his heart fit for service. Along the way, he'd destroyed good people and led too many astray. His life was one huge failure.

Paroxysms of grief shook him. His muscles ached. His bones ached. His very soul ached. Could someone die from this kind of pain? He moaned. If only God would strike him down. It would be a mercy.

A wave of darkness and despair broke over him, threatening to smother him.

He fell to the floor and lay there, plunging into a mist of pain and shame. Time passed but he didn't know how long. Finally he came back to confused consciousness.

He disgusted himself. No wonder Blanche didn't want to come home. No wonder Rachel had run away. They'd be better off without him. Blanche was beautiful both inside and outside. He didn't deserve her. She needed someone who would better appreciate her qualities.

He stumbled to his feet and headed for the door.

CHAPTER 30

*B*lanche was woken by the sound of the toilet flushing. Her ankle throbbed. She'd cried herself to sleep last night after her talk with Anton. Now she'd woken far too early. She squinted towards the darkened window. It wasn't even dawn. Why couldn't Naomi have left the toilet unflushed?

She was being unfair. Naomi was more than considerate. She was cranky because she hadn't had enough sleep and her emotions were in turmoil. She turned over. Could she get back to sleep?

The kettle clicked off. How was it such tiny sounds could pull her out of the doze she'd drifted into? She may as well get up. Maybe a cup of tea would make her feel better.

It was cold. Winter was coming, so she took her dressing gown off the hook at the back of the door. She'd snuck home a few weeks ago and collected it, staying as short a time as possible. The place was musty and echoed with loneliness. She'd been glad to escape.

Naomi was in the back room with a throw rug over her knees. She didn't seem surprised to see Blanche. Why was that? It wasn't as if Blanche made a habit of wandering around at unearthly hours of the morning.

"Grab an extra cup, dearie. I've made a pot and there's plenty for both of us."

Tea wasn't the only thing there was plenty of. A pile of buttered wheatmeal biscuits were on a plate.

"Are you okay, Mum?" Blanche sat down.

"I'm not sure. I was woken up an hour ago with an urgent feeling we must pray for William."

Blanche peered at the clock on the wall. "At four o'clock in the morning?"

"The hour wasn't my choice, but I never ignore these calls to urgent prayer. I had one when Melissa at church nearly died in labour and another when four of the young people were involved in a head-on crash."

Naomi hadn't mentioned these experiences before. "And you feel we should pray urgently for William. What danger would threaten him at this hour?"

Naomi poured her a cup of tea and added milk. "I've no idea. I've never been told why to pray, just who to pray for."

"But do you always get it right?"

"I don't remember. But it won't hurt to pray, even if William is in no danger whatsoever. Will you join me?" She handed Blanche a buttered biscuit.

"Did you make these for me?"

"I figured if God woke me up to pray for William, he'd probably get you up too."

Blanche shook her head. It was too early in the morning for all this, but who was she to question her mother-in-law? If they believed in the God of the Bible, they had to believe in a God who could summon people to prayer.

"What have you been praying?"

"I started by praying for William's protection, but I've switched to praying for his salvation."

Blanche's arm jerked and her tea sloshed into the saucer. "You think he isn't saved?"

"I've been thinking a lot about Jesus' illustration of the tree and its fruit."

Blanche took a sip of tea.

"Jesus said a person is recognised by their fruit. A good tree can only produce good fruit and a bad tree, bad fruit."

"And William's behaviour suggests he doesn't know Jesus." It made sense. More sense than any other explanation.

"It's easy to substitute churchgoing and serving others for truly knowing Jesus."

Blanche nodded. "Esther said that was what she did for far too long."

Naomi put down her tea cup. "Let's get to it, shall we?"

Blanche pulled her chair closer to Naomi's and they clasped hands. If Naomi thought they should pray, then pray she would.

"Dearest Jesus," Naomi said. "We don't know why you got us out of bed, but we trust you. We don't even know what's happening at the moment. William might be tucked up safely in bed and I got this call to prayer wrong, but we pray anyway. Lord, you know everything about him. We know so little about what is really in his heart. Lord, have mercy. Bring him to yourself in repentance and submission."

Naomi squeezed Blanche's hand and continued. "Everyone needs to submit to you and accept your death in our place. All of us need to repent so we turn away from our stubbornness and turn 180 degrees towards you. Have mercy ..."

Naomi prayed for a while and Blanche followed. The tiredness had left her. Now urgency gripped her. Without Jesus no one, not even William, had any hope of real change. "Remind William of your words of truth. Help him to call out to you. Replace his passion for his own reputation with a passion for your reputation."

They prayed on while the light grew in strength. Every so often, they fortified themselves with more tea or biscuits.

Naomi prayed again, pleading that Jesus' power save William and bring him to repentance. "He's my son and he's precious to me, but he's much more precious to you."

How had Naomi persevered all these years? It had been four decades since she'd last seen her son, and yet here she was, praying as fervently as if they'd had dinner yesterday. Never giving up, never losing hope. How was it possible?

"We pray all these things in the name of your son, Jesus. Amen."

Naomi let go of Blanche's hands and they smiled at each other.

"I think we can stop now," Naomi said.

Blanche rubbed her eyes. "Why now?"

"The urgency is gone. Don't ask me to explain—I can't. It's a mystery, and it's one many people I know have experienced."

Blanche had to go to work. She'd be a total zombie from lack of sleep, but this had been the right thing to do. She reached across and put her arms around Naomi. "I am so glad I found you. I wouldn't have coped with the last months if it wasn't for you."

Naomi patted her shoulder. "Don't give me too much credit, dear. If I hadn't been around, your loving heavenly Father would have provided someone else."

Blanche sat up straight again and stretched. "I know that's true, but I'm so grateful for everything you've done." The clock struck seven. "Mum, are you ready for breakfast?"

---

*B*lanche sliced a banana over the top of the cereal, poured milk on it, found a spoon, and handed the bowl to her mother-in-law. "Please eat," she said. "And tell me how you've persevered in prayer for forty years."

"It's simple really," Naomi said. "I remind myself constantly of the words the angel spoke to Mary when she'd asked, 'How can this be since I'm a virgin?' The angel told her, 'Nothing is impossible with God.'"

Blanche looked out towards the garden flushing with the colour of the new day.

"If God could give a virgin a baby then nothing is impossible— even William changing." Naomi took a mouthful of cereal and chewed.

"But forty years is a long time."

"Yes, but not as long as Abraham and Sarah waited for their miracle. When God announced they would have Isaac, he also told them nothing is too difficult for God."

Blanche put her head to one side. "They'd only waited twenty-five years."

"Yes and no. It was only twenty-five years since God promised they'd be the ancestors of a great nation, but they'd been waiting for a son since they were married. It was closer to seventy-five years." She looked across at Blanche. "Imagine what it must have been like. Seventy-five years of pitying looks. Seventy-five years of gossip and unwanted advice."

Seventy-five years was a lifetime. Blanche had only been waiting a few months, and already she'd drifted away from William and towards another man. Sweat prickled her hairline.

"Can you think who else in the Bible had to wait but discovered God was faithful?" Naomi asked.

Blanche scrolled through her Bible starting from Genesis. "Rebekah and Isaac ... Hannah ..." She paused. "Oh! And what about Daniel waiting in Babylon and wondering why God had allowed him to be taken into captivity?" Daniel had become one of her favourite stories. One she'd read over and over.

"And what about the people in Jesus' time?" Naomi said. "Barti-maeus begging by the road, the woman bleeding twelve years."

The bleeding woman had been one of William's most used

197

stories, but he'd always preached on the miracle rather than the twelve-year wait in silence and shame. The woman hadn't known she'd eventually be healed. She'd expected to be ostracised for life.

"I'd better stop chattering on and let you get ready for work," Naomi said.

Blanche stood up, leaned over, and kissed her forehead. "I love your chatter. You've given me lots to think about."

As Blanche cleared the breakfast things away, she came up with more examples, not least the stories of her own daughters. Esther's wait hadn't ended the way they'd hoped, but Esther herself came to accept her cancer as a gift, not a curse. A gift because it had opened Esther's eyes to what was most important and drew her closer to Jesus.

The question was not whether God was the God of the impossible, Blanche knew he was. The question was whether she wanted to persevere in believing it. What if God asked her to persevere in prayer for William for ten years? Or twenty? What if he wanted her to be like the people of faith listed in Hebrews 11, who never saw what they'd been promised while they remained on earth? God might be asking her to give up having a husband at all. To remain single until she died. Was she willing to trust him, trust he'd provide her with everything she needed?

Was it so wrong to long for an Anton? Someone who loved her for herself, not what she could do for them. Someone who'd adore her. What could be wrong with that?

illiam shivered. Sand crunched underfoot, cool and
clammy. Silver moonlight shone on the edges of the
waves frothing on the beach. The waves murmured, calling his
name.

He stepped into the water and drew in a hissing breath. A
breeze wafted the scent of flowers across his skin. It was a stunning
night. Cold and serene and beautiful.

He walked in up to his knees, then his thighs, and hesitated
before he took a deep breath and dove forward with flailing arms.
The cold squeezed his chest and his breaths came in short gasps. He
swam ten rapid strokes and ten more, then settled into a steady
rhythm, heading straight out from the beach.

He'd always been good at swimming. Now he would prove it.
He angled towards the island, hidden somewhere in the darkness.
Even when he was swimming he needed a goal.

His arms cut through the water.

He'd been a driven person from his earliest memories. For him
there'd only ever been one competition. The competition for the

approval of a man whose life philosophy was that no one remembers who came second.

William was no longer cold. There was something satisfying about his rhythmic strokes and the slide of the water over arms honed by years of swimming laps.

Left stroke, right stroke, breathe with the next stroke. Right stroke, left stroke, breathe.

He'd been smart, he'd been sporty, but he'd always been second. All through high school, he'd believed Ian's death had given him a chance. He'd fooled himself. His father had awarded Ian the gold trophy years before.

Left stroke, right stroke, breathe.

How far had he swum? Time flowed past with the water. He could have been an ant swimming in a bathtub. It was quieter than he'd expected. He turned on his back. Far off to either side, the shadowed bulk of the headlands was vaguely visible under the silvery moonlight. The dark water around him sparkled.

It was a suitable metaphor. To outsiders, his life sparkled, but it was the sparkle of cheap Christmas tinsel. His heart was as dark as the sea around him. The only sparkle he remembered was when his horse had won the Melbourne Cup. For a few glorious days, he'd hugged the win to his heart and wouldn't have dreamt of spending his silver shilling.

Success was a drug and he'd hungered for more. He could never get enough of it. He'd competed in every area he'd had a chance to shine, clawing his way to the top of the pile.

In marketing, aiming for success had been acceptable. In the church, he had to change the language to disguise his addiction. Everything became 'for God's glory'. He rolled over and continued swimming.

He snorted, bubbles fizzing out of his nose. Success. What rubbish. He was a failure by any measure that mattered. A failure as a husband, a failure as a father, and a failure as a pastor. He'd certainly failed to understand Blanche. Failed to encourage her to be the woman she was created to be. He'd bullied, manipulated, and browbeaten her. All so he could feel good about himself. Prove he was in the right and she was in the wrong. How could he have made it such a childish battle that demanded she choose between Esther and himself? He deserved the scorn Blanche poured on him.

Left stroke, right stroke, breathe.

When Esther had needed him, he'd abandoned her. Abandoned his own flesh and blood because he was unwilling to lose his reputation as someone to whom God listened.

He huffed an angry breath into the water. Why had he thought such a thing was important? How could reputation be more important than a daughter? And not just one daughter, but two. He'd failed Rachel just as badly—worse even, because she'd been much younger.

He hadn't even bothered to search for her. What kind of father would do such a thing? If she had died, as happened to many teenagers on the streets, he'd have been a murderer. In one sense, he had murdered her. He'd denied her existence and buried her as deep as if he held the shovel. All to protect his reputation.

William raised his head, trod water, and strained his ears. He was approaching the island. Last chance to stop. He shivered. Attempting to land on a strange beach in the semi-darkness filled him with dread. What rocks waited below the surface to shred his skin like grated cheese?

He laughed grimly. What did it matter? Being ripped to pieces or attacked by sharks or swimming until cold, cramps, and sheer exhaustion took him. The end would be the same. How did someone end a life on an island where there were no fast roads and no gas ovens? Where even the knives in the kitchen were blunt and the cliffs weren't quite high enough to guarantee anything more than a severe injury. Carbon monoxide was out. Even if he'd had a car, Davy would have been the most likely one to find him. Davy had enough death in his life already.

Swimming made the most sense and would leave enough doubt about his purpose. Blanche didn't need any more grief. She'd be better off without him. And Rachel? She would probably dance a jig on his coffin.

He kept swimming.

It wouldn't take Blanche long to find a new man, one who'd treat her the way she deserved.

Swimming was harder now. Was he tired or was he caught in a current? How long could someone of his fitness swim? Swimming until he dropped had sounded romantic, but the reality would likely be different. He shut his mind and ploughed on, one stroke after another, in a mind-numbing rhythm.

His upper back and arms began to ache. The water tugged at him. He dug deeper. He'd once swum three kilometres, nearly thirty years ago. One kilometre was his usual distance, and he must be long past that now. The light was strengthening. Dawn was coming.

The saltiness on his lips and tongue made him long for a drink of fresh water. He began to count, switching to breathe every second stroke. Sometime after 400, he lost count.

The strokes became a mindless drumbeat in his head. *Failure, failure, failure.*

He switched back to breathe every third stroke, but it wasn't any better. *Set them free, set them free, set them free.*

The current pushed against him, and he struggled to make any leeway. He angled away from his line of movement, but after five minutes he gave up. The current was too strong and broad to escape. He dug his hand into the water again.

The light continued to strengthen. Did he imagine a welcome warmth playing across his skin? How far had he swum now? Two kilometres? Three?

A hot stabbing pain gripped his left calf. Argh. He rolled onto his back and grabbed for his toes, splashing as he struggled to bring the cramp under control. He eased it out and turned to continue on his way. Three more strokes and his right leg cramped.

It took two minutes to sort this one out. He rolled back to start swimming, but the current was strong enough now to require all his energy. Anything less would mean he'd be pushed back towards land, towards the island he'd passed an hour ago. Maybe two. He didn't remember when.

Another cramp hit his right calf. By the time it eased, his legs were aching along their entire length. He didn't trust himself to use them. He'd rest on his back a moment.

The sun was rising over Lord Howe Island, a sunrise of golden glory, bathing him in molten gold. A gold more real than any he'd chased. A gold available to anyone with eyes to see. Tears welled in his eyes.

God, do you see me out here?

He'd never bothered to memorise scripture, but now verses from somewhere dropped into his mind.

Where can I hide from your Spirit? Where can I flee from your presence? If I go up to the heavens, you are there; if I make my bed in the depths, you are there.

An anguished howl spewed from him and was swallowed up in the immensity of the ocean. A bed in the depths was exactly what he'd intended. Yet, God would be there before him. No matter where he went or what he attempted, he couldn't escape. He'd have to face the Judge of the universe and he wasn't prepared.

Jonah had failed when he had attempted to flee from God. Why had William thought he'd have better success?

He checked over his shoulder. He should be thankful he'd been spared the giant fish.

Okay God, you've got my attention. Now you'll have to complete the job.

If he could turn himself onto his front and make himself as streamlined as possible, the current might carry him to the island— or, at least, close enough to swim in. There should be a tour group arriving before midday.

He experimented with extending his arms in front of him. They ached, but he still had the energy to roll and breathe when he needed. The current pushed him closer. He yawned. Now was not the time to sleep. He needed his wits about him.

One hundred metres from the tip of the island, he rolled into an upright position, treading water. *God, which side—seaward or land-ward? Help me make the right choice.*

Landward might take more energy, but he'd be more protected. He angled towards the landward side. The current weakened but still assisted him enough to keep him moving. He doggy paddled, scooping with his hands. It wasn't pretty, but it worked.

He inched forward, down the length of the island, changing from doggy-paddling to a new stroke and back again as each one exhausted him. *God, help.*

There it was, a flash of golden sand. His mouth twisted. One sort of gold worth striving for.

He managed the last hundred metres on prayer alone. The waves were minimal, so he only scraped himself a few times as he headed for shore. The last few strokes seemed to take an eternity. Finally, he lay exhausted, half in the water and half out. He gathered his strength and, putting his arms beneath his body, used the waves to lever himself higher up the sand. Blessed warmth. He'd have a killer sunburn tomorrow, but the pain was a price he'd gladly pay. In the dark hours of this morning, he hadn't intended there would be any more tomorrows.

CHAPTER 32

*B*lanche jumped every time she heard a firm footstep outside the shop. Could it be Anton? Their customers were predominantly female, but it seemed every male in the area had decided to buy Blanche's cross-stitch designs in the last few days. Naida was crowing in delight because they were selling like ice cream on a blazing summer's day, but every male voice sent Blanche's heart rate up and made her blush.

"Blanche, is something bothering you?" Naida asked in a quiet moment.

"Just a few things I'm dealing with," Blanche said as she folded up the piece of fabric in her hand.

"Well, I've been praying for you, and I'm here if you want to talk."

"Thanks," Blanche said with a tight smile.

Every time she looked up and saw a man passing, Blanche experienced jabs of pain like she was sitting on a red-ant nest. Thousands of little stings, but no killing blow. Would Helena turn up to the class tomorrow? Would Anton pick her up?

CHRISTINE DILLON

When Blanche had assumed Anton was married, she'd concluded he was either a super attentive husband or Helena couldn't drive. Now both of those assumptions had proven to be incorrect, so he must have been coming to see her.

One part of her was thankful he'd be unlikely to come anymore, and another part grieved. Again. Why was grief the backdrop of her current existence? A gnawing, relentless ache that ebbed and flowed when she least expected it. Maybe her attraction to Anton was the result of the tiredness, loneliness, and grief leaving her open to temptation. Or was it something deeper? Would she have always been susceptible to a man like Anton? A man who cared.

That was what hurt. A man like Anton didn't deserve the pain her words had given him. If she'd had the faintest inkling of his feelings, she'd have quashed them early. She certainly wouldn't have spent so much time building a friendship. Helena was loyal to her brother. Would Blanche lose her friendship too?

She'd had a couple of crushes in high school, but a boyfriend would definitely have put her head above the parapet. Boyfriends might ask questions and want to visit her family. Boyfriends might see what she'd kept hidden. Blanche hadn't known the word domestic violence back then, but she'd known the shame and fear. She'd isolated herself behind a frozen smile.

Blanche moved over to tidy the rolls of fabric.

She'd been in early primary school when she'd first swallowed the lie that conflict should be avoided at all costs. It was linked to all the Saturdays she'd hated as a child. Saturday nights turned her father into a stranger.

It had always started with being woken late at night by the squeak of the gate. Slow, stumbling steps would come along the footpath, and then there'd be a thump on the front door. She'd draw her blankets over her head and curl up in a tight ball, knees hugged to her chest, as if by being as small as possible, she could somehow disappear. It never worked.

Minute by slow minute would drag by when nothing happened. She'd be hopeful. Maybe not this week. Then there would be a crash. Tomorrow there'd be more plates missing from the cupboards.

She always stuck her fingers in her ears and squeezed her eyes shut as though this might somehow prevent any more bad things happening. Would he stick with just smashing plates?

Thud.

Was the night going to be a one-hit night or would there be two or more?

Slap. Thud. Why did her mother wait up for him? Why did her father hit her? He always said he loved her mother, yet the next day Mama would have new bruises. New reasons to stay inside.

Blanche had never known what Mama had done to displease him. Probably nothing. Nowadays much research had been done into these things, but she always avoided thinking about her past. It hurt too much.

When her father was sober, he always hugged Blanche and called her his little princess. She'd believed she was safe, and so one night, she'd reasoned maybe if she went out there, he'd stop. Maybe she could be the one to save Mama. To save them all.

A surge of courage propelled her out of bed. She grabbed her dressing gown and tiptoed out into the hallway and down towards the kitchen. Dad had his back to her and a plate in his hand. He shifted to the left and her mother saw her. Her eyes widened full of frantic fear. "Get out," she mouthed.

Dad spun around and threw the plate. Blanche ducked. It hit the cabinet behind her and spattered her with slivers of china.

"Heads that poke above the parapet get shot," he yelled.

She didn't understand what her father meant, but she still dropped to her knees and scuttled backwards. The plate slivers crunched beneath her and cut her palms and knees, but even the fear, pain, and blood didn't slow down her movement.

Her father whimpered, scaring her far more than the plate throwing.

"Baby, I didn't mean to hurt you."

He staggered forward and grabbed her. She tried to push him away, heart pounding, as her hands left smears of blood on his shirt. She turned her face away to avoid his foul breath.

"Princess," he blubbered as he patted her knee, "I would never hurt you."

She hadn't believed him. Not then and not ever again. She'd learned to be quiet and submissive like her mother had urged and to keep her head down. Her father's lesson had been successful. Much too successful. She'd paid the price for decades after.

William had never asked anything much about her. She hadn't thought it odd—she was relieved. His lack of interest in her background gave her permission to block it out and pretend it had never happened. She'd known exactly where she was with William. No alcohol. No hiding inside. No money worries. Instead, she was the wife of a respected man with a good reputation.

She desired to serve Jesus, but oh, she empathised with the woman who had wanted to have her cake and eat it too. If this was a novel, she'd type William out of the story. In a suitably heroic way, of course. Then, after an acceptable period of mourning, she could eat her cake. A wedding cake.

Why did real life have to be so difficult? Reading about the way of the cross being narrow and steep was poetic. But the reality was anything but.

What if she phoned Helena? It wouldn't be her fault if Anton answered, and she could close her eyes and imagine his arms around her and his cheek close to hers.

She shivered. No, that wasn't a good idea. But she would like to talk to Helena. Perhaps they could go out to lunch. Lunch sounded nice and safe. Then she could allow Helena to talk about her brother. There wasn't anything wrong with that, was there?

It wasn't like she would follow through with any of her imaginings.

CHAPTER 33

*W*illiam woke in his own bed. The tour guide had wanted to take him to the clinic, but he'd insisted he was fine.

Someone was moving around in the kitchen. His skin burned and throbbed. A damp sheet covered him.

He turned his head and spotted the bell on his bedside table. Did he have the energy to reach over and ring it? He fumbled and knocked it on the floor. Footsteps creaked across the wooden floors, and Ivy popped her head around the corner.

"Good. You're awake." Her smile was like a lighthouse. "I've got a cup of water for you." She was back in moments with a tall cup. "Try and finish all of it."

If he did, he was going to have another problem, and he wasn't sure if he could get out of bed.

"I'll go and call Reg to help you get up. You'll be stiff and sore." She grinned. "But you're obviously tough."

He didn't feel tough. His arms shook when he held them up. He let them flop back onto the bed. He flexed one knee experimentally. Everything hurt, but he'd live. He gave a crooked grin. Now he'd decided to live, even pain felt good. It reminded him he was alive.

William slept most of the day, waking now and then, aware of Ivy and Reg taking turns to watch him. After a dinner of soup and custard, Reg pulled up a chair at right angles to his bed and put the things he was holding on the floor. "Want to talk?"

William glanced away from Reg's direct look. He did and he didn't. Who wanted to stand out in the open with all their faults on display? There he went again, calling sin faults, as though his failures were minor mistakes. Excusable things of no importance.

"You weren't going for an overly ambitious swim, were you?" Reg asked gently.

William shook his head. He was afraid he'd bawl like a baby if he talked. He'd never bawled in his life.

"I'm sorry I wasn't more sensitive," Reg said. "I knew you had things on your mind, but I didn't want to push."

"I wasn't ready to say anything." His whole life, William had denied his emotions and kept things stuffed in the drawers of his mind. Drawers full of memories. Drawers full of unresolved conflict. Drawers full of denied pain. He'd feared opening the drawers, even a crack, in case he released something scary. Something even he couldn't control.

Reg stretched out his legs, settling himself in the chair. "But something pushed you over the edge." He paused. "Do you think you can talk about it?"

William blinked back tears. If only he'd met Reg years ago—not that he'd have been smart enough to value him. What a fool he'd been. Judging books by their cover and never opening the prizewinning stories inside. Reg helped him sit up and attempt to get comfortable.

"I'll have to start right back in my childhood."

"Can I whittle while you talk?" Reg sat down and picked up a piece of wood and knife from the floor. "It helps me listen."

William nodded as he cleared his throat. "I was the second son."

He closed his eyes while he shared things he'd never told another person, about his father and his brother and how Ian had drowned. He talked about all the complicated relationships in their family and how his parents had fallen apart after Ian died. The only sounds were the knife on wood and Reg murmuring in all the right places.

He related the story of his marriage and Esther's cancer and how he'd treated Blanche.

Reg let him talk and talk. Somehow, opening up drawers which had always been locked no longer seemed impossible. Something had changed, but he wasn't yet sure what.

"Why don't you tell me why you swam out to sea? More importantly, tell me what changed your mind."

William sighed and told him about the letter. "After wrestling all night, my only thought was my life wasn't worth living. The best thing I could do was to free both my family and the church."

Reg looked up from his carving. "And where do you think those thoughts came from?"

William rubbed his nose. "I guess my desire for my father's approval."

"I dare say that was part of it, but I was thinking beyond you, right back to the enemy of our souls."

It was an old-fashioned word, but William knew who Reg meant. Satan. William had never thought much about him. Maybe never even believed in him except as a way to threaten those who looked likely to stray outside the boundaries William himself set.

Reg dug his knife into the wood and scraped out a hole. "Satan always opposes God's purposes. He started with Adam and Eve when he convinced them God couldn't be trusted, that God was withholding things from them."

William wasn't sure what Reg was getting at.

"Satan loves to confuse us. To make us think lies are truth and truth are lies."

The silence stretched out as William reviewed his life. What lies had he believed? Probably too many to count, but he was sure Reg considered some more foundational than others. The gears in his mind were stiff today.

Reg scraped the wood in his hand. "Why don't we talk about your relationship with your father."

William's shoulders tensed. He couldn't recall a single time his father had cared for him or seen him for who he was. "I thought a lot about my father out there." He gestured towards the ocean. "I wasted too many years trying to gain his approval."

Reg stopped whittling. "It's normal for sons to want their father's approval, but many fathers can't give it. Your mother might know more about why."

William had already put his mother on the to-be-dealt-with-later shelf. Blanche was his first priority.

Reg turned the piece of wood in his hands. A shape was gradually emerging from the formless lump. "Human fathers are never going to give us what we seek. You fell for one of Satan's lies. You were seeking the approval of the wrong father."

William bent his knees up to ease his back. "I presume you mean God's approval?"

"Mmm," Reg said, nodding. "Although what he approves isn't always what we expect."

William frowned. His mind was too sluggish this evening for all these riddles.

"What changed your mind about ending your life?" Reg's questions probed like William was the block of wood in Reg's work-worn hands.

"A combination of things. A current pushing me back towards shore. Cramps." William crossed his arms across his chest. "But really it was the words dropping into my mind after I'd cried out to God."

Reg's hands stilled, and he looked directly at William. "What words?"

"'Where can I hide from your Spirit? Where can I flee from your presence? If I go up to the heavens, you are there; if I make my bed in the depths, you are there.'" William gave a nervous laugh. "I couldn't remember the exact Psalm, but I saw I wasn't only trying to escape the consequences of my choices. I was trying to escape God, and it wouldn't work. Even at the bottom of the sea, I'd have to meet him." A tightness, like a belt, encircled his stomach. He groaned. "I don't think I'm ready to face God."

"And what makes you think you're not ready?"

William hesitated. If only the fog in his brain would lift. If only he could be sure.

Reg leaned forward. "Before we talk any more, I'd like to pray."

A lump blocked William's throat. Could Reg sense his desperation? A darkness pressed him down, smothering light, crushing hope.

"Dearest heavenly Father, King and Saviour. You are light and in you there is no darkness. Shine on us today. Give us wisdom to see the real issues here. Help William see you …"

Reg prayed on and William echoed. *Give us light, give me light. Help me see clearly.*

Reg said "Amen" and leaned down to pull his Bible out of the plastic bag on the floor. "Why don't we start at the passage God placed in your mind?" He riffled through the pages. "Here it is. Psalm 139." He ran his finger down the page and then slid it back to the top. "Let's start at the beginning."

Reg sat up straight and read, "'O Lord, you have searched me and you know me. You know when I sit and when I rise.'" He paused. "'You perceive my thoughts from afar. You discern my going out and my lying down, you are familiar with all my ways.'"

The skin on William's arms rose in goosebumps. God hadn't been fooled by his designer clothes, his flashy smile, or his confident assertions. God saw the real William.

"'If I rise on the wings of the dawn, if I settle on the far side of the sea, even there your hand will guide me, your right hand will hold me fast. If I say, "Surely the darkness will hide me and the light become night around me," even the darkness will not be dark to you; the night will shine like the day, for darkness is as light to you.'"

William had aimed for the far side of the sea and for its dark waters to hide him. He remembered the moon and the glorious golden sunrise. God had seen him. The God who sees every sparrow fall had seen a tiny speck in the vast ocean and rescued him. Why? Why waste his time with a man such as him? A fraud and failure.

"'For you created my inmost being; you knit me together in my mother's womb.'"

William's grandmother had been a champion knitter. One careful stitch at a time, working to a pattern, a pattern he could never work out until she finished. Did God still have plans for him?

"'Your eyes saw my unformed body; all the days ordained for me were written in your book before one of them came to be.'"

All his days? Even all his failures? He hadn't earned even a silver medal or a bronze. He grimaced. He hadn't been running in the right race. Instead he'd been a confidence trickster who had led people away from the light into his own darkness.

William reached over for a drink of water. He needed Jesus like he needed the water, but how could he ask? He had a PhD, sure it was in church growth and organisation, not theology as he'd let people assume, but he'd always been proud of his achievements. How did he admit he was still wandering, lost in the dark? Why was pride the hardest thing to kill? Like attempting to squash a leech but having it ooze back every time.

"I wonder ..." Reg said.

Reg was a man who measured his words. Was his hesitation because he was praying? Probably. Prayer was his life blood.

"Did you head out to sea because you only travelled halfway?"

More riddles. William raised an eyebrow.

"Did you only see your failures and your sin? Is that why you wanted to end it?"

His failures were like an oily sludge coating the feathers of a bird trapped in an oil spill. The sludge suffocated him. "I couldn't see any hope at all." His words were little more than a croak.

"Like Judas. He couldn't imagine his betrayal could be forgiven, so he ended it." A tiny smile crinkled the corners of Reg's mouth. "But Peter clung to hope."

"How did Peter hang on?"

"I don't know." Reg looked up from his whittling. "Maybe God protected him from being overwhelmed by his betrayal."

Peter's betrayal somehow seemed worse than Judas'. Judas had been disappointed in Jesus and had betrayed for gain, but Peter had been Jesus' close friend and betrayed Jesus out of fear. Not once, but three times.

"I love the way Paul expresses things," Reg said. "'While we were dead in our sin, while we were God's enemies, he died for us.'"

William had always treated God as if they were best buddies. He'd never considered himself an enemy of God, let alone dead in sin.

Reg laid down his carving. "My family attended church every week, and yet not one of us understood these great truths. We thought of others as blind and ourselves as seeing clearly." He laughed ruefully. "So many people think the same. They think of people as having a sickness, then Jesus comes along and heals it."

"And doesn't he?"

"Yes and no."

Jesus used to avoid directly answering questions too.

"Of course Jesus heals, but our spiritual condition is more serious than a mere sickness. If we were simply sick, there might be things we could do to get well. The reason why so many people work to improve themselves is because they think sin isn't nearly as serious as it is."

William swallowed. He'd been like that.

"But what if we can't? What if we keep doing what we don't want to do, or not doing what we ought to do? If we work hard at improving ourselves, we're assuming we can save ourselves by our own efforts." Reg paused for a long drawn-out moment. "If we can save ourselves, why did Jesus have to die?"

The question echoed in William's heart and pounded in his head. Why did Jesus have to die? Why?

"It doesn't make sense, does it?" William whispered.

He no longer cared what Reg thought about him. He wanted to know the answer more than he cared about anything else—his work, his pride, even his reputation.

"One of Satan's major lies is that we can save ourselves by our own efforts," Reg said, picking up his wood again. "In order for us to believe this, we have to be blinded to the seriousness of our situation."

William had been blinded. He'd been the blind leading the blind.

"Paul's description of our being 'dead in our sins' helped me. If we only use the blindness imagery, we can fool ourselves into believing there is some contribution we can make."

William flushed. He'd believed his contribution was the most important part. After all, he'd worked hard to attain his high status.

"No one can raise the dead. No doctor, no king, no miracle worker. Jesus came because only his death in our place results in spiritual resurrection."

William leaned forward and groaned as the skin on his back stretched.

"Would you be better sitting in a chair?"

"Probably." Did he dare to admit his utter ignorance? He'd mostly preached on Jesus' miracles or a few other favourite passages. He'd seldom talked about Jesus' death and resurrection.

But what did it matter if Reg thought of him as an ignorant fool? William took a deep breath. "I've never fully understood how Jesus' death saves us."

Reg chuckled. "Does anyone? When God created the universe, he set it up so if we chose to reject him and go our own way, the penalty was death."

"Why?" The question burst out of him.

"Perhaps because God is the only source of life. If we sever contact with God, we are no longer connected to life."

Oh. He'd always been puzzled why Adam and Eve hadn't dropped dead when they ate the fruit. God had said they'd die, and so they had. First spiritually, then physically.

"The Old Testament gives us lots of clues as to what Jesus' death would mean."

William had rarely bothered with the Old Testament except as a series on ancient heroes. No one he knew read it much.

"What do you remember about the Day of Atonement?"

"Not much," William muttered. It was getting easier to admit his ignorance on things he should have known. He'd tried to read Leviticus once and given up, as he couldn't see what all those laws had to do with the modern world.

"Have you got a piece of paper and a pen?" Reg laid down his carving.

William dug one out of the bedside table drawer, wincing as he twisted.

Reg sketched a simple rectangle. "The Tabernacle had two main rooms. The smaller one at the back was especially important."

William might have ignored parts of the Bible, but he did know something about the Holy of Holies.

Reg drew a wriggly line across the rectangle. "The line represents the curtain separating the Holy of Holies from the rest of the temple. Can you remember what that was meant to teach the Israelites?"

William was on more stable ground here. "The separation between God and people, because God was perfect and people aren't."

Reg nodded. "The Day of Atonement is all about how God solved the problem."

There was something about priests and lambs but the details escaped him.

"I'm sure you know all this."

Reg was too kind.

"The high priest only went behind the curtain once a year. First, he had to make special preparations, including bathing and spotless clothes."

The meaning of those regulations was clear enough.

"The most important thing was two perfect lambs. One as the scapegoat, to symbolically carry their sins far away, and the other to be killed and its blood taken into the Holy of Holies." Reg paused. "The Bible later asks whether the blood of a lamb can truly forgive sin."

William shook his head.

"So what was the point?" Reg asked.

William was finally joining the dots. "Jesus was the real lamb. The one who was much greater than a mere animal, and so he could truly bring forgiveness. One death for all time."

Reg leaned back in his chair and put his hands behind his head. "Isn't that something to celebrate?" He unclasped his hands. "So the most important question is, are you ready to respond?"

And all at once, William was. A tremulous joy fluttered in his heart. Like he was dancing on the edge of the most important moment in his life. Now was the time to dive off the edge into a new future. William had always loved pomp and show. Yet now he simply bowed his head.

"God, I have never really understood your salvation. I've picked and chosen the parts of your word I wanted for my own ends. I've hurt others, including my own family." It was hard to mention his sin out loud, but he persisted. "Thank you for Reg, who dared to speak the truth to me. Thank you for dying for me and helping me see I have no good deeds I can contribute. The gift is one hundred per cent your work for me."

William finished his prayer and breathed out a gusty breath before he looked up at Reg. He'd never prayed such a humble prayer, but it was right and proper that it should be in this way and with such a man.

CHAPTER 34

$\mathcal{T}$he typed envelope gave no clue as to the sender. William turned it over. The address on the back was Victory's. His chest tightened. Could they possibly have heard about his suicide attempt?

He counted back on his fingers. No, not possible. Even if Reg had rung the church, a letter couldn't have made it here this quickly. Phew.

He reached past the breakfast marmalade and picked up a clean knife to use as a letter opener. The letter inside was a crisp sheet of double-spaced typing. He scanned to the bottom. It was from the board of elders. His heart-rate sped up.

Dear Reverend Macdonald,

Was their formality a good or a bad thing? He had major decisions to make, but he didn't want to be fired.

WHEN ARE YOU COMING BACK? NUMBERS ARE DOWN WEEK BY
WEEK, AND NOTHING WE'VE DONE HAS REVERSED THE TREND.
PEOPLE NEED YOU HERE.

Once he would have been excited by such a letter, but now it concerned him. If the church had been built upon the foundation of Christ, it shouldn't matter who preached. Yet if the church had been built on his gifts—not to mention his ego—it was no surprise it was crumbling.

JIM AND ERIC HAVE SOLDIERED ON, BUT NICK HASN'T BEEN THE
SAME SINCE YOU LEFT. THIS MORNING WE RECEIVED HIS
RESIGNATION LETTER.

Resignation! William inhaled a toast crumb and coughed violently. Of course, he'd known Esther's death had stirred up Nick's doubts and emotions, but he'd assumed things were heading in the right direction.

HE SAYS HE'S RESIGNED BECAUSE HE'S NOT IN THE PLACE
EMOTIONALLY TO KEEP SERVING IN THIS CAPACITY.
    DO YOU KNOW ANYTHING ABOUT THIS? HE PLANS TO TAKE A
BREAK THEN FIND ANOTHER JOB. THERE ARE NO INDICATIONS OF
WHETHER HE MEANS A CHURCH-RELATED JOB OR ANOTHER KIND
OF EMPLOYMENT. THE YOUTH ARE DEVASTATED. CAN YOU
CONVINCE HIM TO STAY? WE FEAR IF HE GOES ELSEWHERE, THE
YOUTH WILL FOLLOW HIM.

Did it really matter where the youth went as long as they went somewhere? He could hardly blame the elders for their concerns. He'd chosen leaders like himself, and now they were thinking like he did. Like he used to. It had only been a few days since he'd submitted his life to Jesus. It wasn't only asking Jesus to save him. It was more a final bowing of the knee to someone he had claimed to submit to for most of his life. How easy it had been to fool others. Confidence and smooth talking went a long way. Too far. It was even easier to deceive oneself. All those years he'd sat firmly on Jesus' throne and demanded others serve him.

He read the last few lines.

WE KNOW YOU STILL HAVE THREE WEEKS THERE, BUT CAN YOU RETURN SOONER? THE SOONER YOU'RE BACK, THE SOONER THE HOLE IN THE DIKE CAN BE PLUGGED.

YOUR TEAM AT VICTORY,

All the elders had signed their names. He counted. Yes, every single one. They were serious.

William bowed his head and closed his eyes. *Lord, I wanted time to realign myself with your word and will.* Paul had taken three years, but it looked like he wouldn't even get three weeks. *Lord, give me wisdom. I'd prefer to stay here, as there's still so much I could learn from Reg and the others.* Even young Davy had a way of making him think.

---

*R*eg wasn't in his workshop. William closed the door and wandered towards the house. A snipping noise came from around the corner of the verandah, and a voice called out.

"We're round here, having our hair cut."

William poked his head around the building to see Davy rubbing the back of his neck. "Hi, Mr Macdonald."

"If you wait, young man," Ivy said, "I'll brush the hair off the back of your neck."

"Ben's waiting for me. We're going to build a fort in his back garden."

Ivy dusted his neck with the corner of the sheet she'd tied around him and rubbed his head. "Get on with you then."

Davy jumped up, clattered down the stairs, and scampered across the garden towards the gate.

Ivy laughed. "It takes all our energy keeping up with him."

"Well, you've done a wonderful job. He's a great kid."

"We've done a lot of praying," Reg said as the sheet was draped over him. "Were you looking for me?"

"I was, but I'm happy to talk to both of you."

"Can I cut at the same time?" Ivy asked.

William settled himself in the chair Reg had vacated. "Don't let me stop you."

Ivy got to work. It was obvious she'd done this before. A smooth rhythm of comb, trim the hair, and move on to the next section.

"Something on your mind?" Reg asked.

William held up the letter. "The elders want me to return as soon as possible."

"What's the problem?"

"The youth leader has resigned, and more people are leaving every week." He shook his head. "They're nervous I've been away too long."

"And what are you thinking?"

"I had hoped to have a few more weeks to pray and discuss things with you. I have major decisions to make."

Decisions he was terrified to make. Decisions which would most likely affect his marriage. His ministry. His entire life.

"Don't rush into anything."

William didn't intend to. He'd write to Nick and let him know what had happened to him. The whole story, not an edited version.

"Is it a problem if people are leaving?" Ivy asked, getting out a shaver.

William shook his head. "Not really. Not to me, although it would have bothered me last week." He grinned. Even his grins were different. They were genuine responses of simple friendship or joy, not used to express an appreciative opinion or gain favour.

Ivy brushed the back of Reg's neck and whipped off the sheet.

"Now my hair is cut, why don't we go to the shed, finish putting your box together, and spend time praying?"

"That would be good."

Praying was something William had always managed to promote without actually doing much of it himself. Everything in his life needed to be rethought and recalibrated.

Would Blanche rejoice in what had happened to him, or was it too late for them? His stomach ached. He'd have no one else to blame if Blanche had run out of patience. Sometimes it can be too late for forgiveness and new starts.

CHAPTER 35

"Good morning, Blanche," a male voice said. The voice she'd been longing to hear. The voice she'd been dreading to hear.

Blanche looked up into Anton's deep blue eyes. Her stomach fluttered, and her heart started doing cartwheels.

"I'm dropping off Helena and bringing these for the shop." He held out a bunch of yellow roses. "Helena mentioned it was the tenth anniversary of the opening."

A tentative smile tugged at the corners of his mouth. She didn't trust herself to smile back but reached out and took the roses.

"Thank you, so thoughtful. Naida ..." She kept her eyes down. "Naida will love them. Everyone will."

Oh, the stiffness between them was horrible. They'd been so comfortable before, and now she didn't want to meet his eye. Didn't want to see love or hope. She mustn't give him hope. She bit the inside of her cheek. It was so unfair that their friendship was threatened. Why was it men and women could seldom be good friends without anything more? If it wasn't one of them falling for the other, it was other people gossiping and wrecking a good thing.

And it had been a good thing. A friendship of music and laughter, encouragement and respect. A friendship like she'd never had with a man and hadn't known she was missing. Now a new hunger gnawed at her.

Anton lowered his voice to talk to Helena. "See you after class."

So Blanche would have to see him again. It all felt too hard. Perhaps she could duck out to the bathroom and avoid him. Or was she behaving like a teenager? Probably. She hadn't had enough experience to know.

Helena touched Blanche's elbow briefly and gave her a friendly smile as the last of the class members entered the shop chattering like a parliament of lorikeets. Blanche squared her shoulders and clapped for attention. "Take a seat, ladies, and let's share your progress."

The class had been a resounding success since the first week, and Naida was already scheduling the next one. All the women had been highly motivated and did most of their projects at home. There'd been much laughter and not a few tears. Naida now kept boxes of tissues in the storeroom, something she said she'd never expected to be part of a quilting store's supplies.

Each woman held up the square they were working on and explained how it fit into the whole. Two ladies had already started putting their quilts together. They only had two more weeks of class scheduled, and they still needed to do the borders, backing, and finishing touches.

"If we can clear the table, I'll lay out a quilt and demonstrate the next steps," Blanche said.

She took a steadying breath. She should be able to hold herself together if she stuck to business and didn't look towards Helena. Her friend also avoided looking back. Blanche was confident it wasn't personal, but rather practical, so that both of them could function. *Lord, get me through this.*

he same evening, Blanche asked Naomi if they could talk. Rachel was out for dinner, so they had privacy.

"I've sensed you had something on your heart," Naomi said. "If you'll light the fire and bring my slippers, I'm all yours."

Sydney was never really cold, but this evening a cold change had blown through. This sort of cold usually meant the mountains to the south had received a significant fall of snow. Blanche fetched her own and Naomi's slippers and set a match to the kindling. The flame danced across the paper and caught the wood shavings. Blanche blew a series of gentle puffs with the bellows and the flame spread, eating into the paper and twigs and licking at the bigger sticks. She breathed in the invigorating smell of eucalyptus, cut from a tree toppled during the summer storms. It was dead but still gave out fragrance and warmth. Like Esther. Only this week, Gina had shared how much Esther's life was still impacting hers.

Blanche got up off her knees and manoeuvred her chair around to face the fire. Perhaps a mother-in-law wasn't the best person to discuss her problem with, but who else did she know so well? Naomi could be counted on to offer biblical advice.

The fire was burning strongly now. Tongues of red, orange, and yellow intertwined amidst a constant barrage of pops and crackles.

"It's always hard to start, isn't it?" Naomi said. "What's bothering you?"

Blanche had considered sharing her situation with a "what if" hypothetical, but Naomi would see through it straight away. What she ought to do was clear, but it was how to do it that caused the struggle.

"I've been writing to William twice a week as you suggested, and as you know, he's been writing back."

Naomi nodded. Collecting the mail was one of Naomi's household tasks.

"I don't sense any changes in him apart from him being more relaxed and gaining new hobbies. He hasn't responded to any of my sharing. We're stuck on the superficial."

"We've always known he needs a miracle," Naomi said. "Which is why we've majored on prayer. The letters were a way of keeping the channels open so there were possibilities for the future."

Lead settled in Blanche's limbs. That was just it. Was there any future? Rachel didn't think so.

"Do you think there is any way forward?"

Naomi moved the cushion behind her back. "Probably not from a human point of view, but Jesus always brings hope to any situation. Remember Sarah and Hannah and Elizabeth."

"They were all waiting for children." Blanche shrugged her shoulders. "Is there any biblical story of hope for a marriage like ours?"

"Do you think those marriages were all rosy? Just because the details aren't there, do you imagine the strains weren't?" Naomi stretched out her hands towards the fire. "Hannah's story certainly gives us clues about the strain on her marriage."

"You mean the second wife?" Blanche asked. Yes, it wouldn't have been much fun to have a rival who constantly mocked.

"You can be certain Peninnah paraded her pregnancies and children in front of Hannah at every opportunity." Naomi turned her hands over to warm the back of them. "And what about Hannah's husband, Elkanah?'

Blanche had forgotten the names of the minor characters, but wasn't Elkanah like Anton? "Wasn't he a treasure?"

"In most ways, but he didn't understand why Hannah's barrenness was such a big deal. Remember? He asked her, 'Don't I mean more to you than ten sons?'"

"The problem with all these stories is that we know what happened." A heavy lethargy filled Blanche's heart. "Knowing the ending makes us forget the pain of waiting."

"Is that what it feels like?" Naomi asked.

Blanche nodded. "And there is no guarantee we'll resolve our situation. I don't believe in divorce, but I can't go home with things as they stand between us." Her stomach soured. If only God would get a move on instead of leaving her in limbo. "If I go home, I feel like I'm endorsing William's behaviour."

"I do agree going home now would allow William to ignore his need to change." Naomi reached forward and placed her now toasty warm hand on Blanche's arm. "Waiting for God to work is hard, but he does promise he'll provide the courage and contentment you need, whatever happens."

A tear trickled down Blanche's cheek and she swiped it away. "I'm having a hard time being content at the moment."

Naomi looked at her for a long moment. "What's happened?"

"You know my friends, Helena and Anton?" Even saying his name gave Blanche a pain in her stomach. It was so not fair.

"Oh, yes." Naomi smiled. "You must invite them over sometime."

Blanche's mouth twisted to the side. "That's just it. They're not married. Helena is his sister."

"Oh." The word dropped between them. Like a stone dropping into a deep pond and causing ripples.

"And Anton didn't know I was married." Blanche raised her ringless hands. It was her own fault. She hadn't noticed Helena's ring finger was as bare as her own.

"Didn't you tell him about William?"

"I thought I had, but obviously not. I talked often about Rachel and Esther, but talking about William was too painful." A throbbing pain crept up the back of her neck. "Anton has been gently wooing me, and I didn't even know until it became crystal clear the night I went to the dance with them." A tear trickled down her cheek. "I hurt him badly."

Naomi stroked the arm of her chair. "But you sorted it out?"

"Well, we sorted out he wasn't married and I was, but it isn't that easy."

Naomi sat motionless. She'd always been a good listener.

"Oh, Mum. I like him. Far more than I ought to." Her heart pounded as the words poured out of her. "When I thought he was married I indulged in a little 'what if' fantasy. I knew it was wrong but deceived myself that his being married made me safe."

Naomi said gently, "It never is right, is it?"

Another tear slid down Blanche's cheek. "I know. I knew it then too, but I was tired and lonely. It made me feel better for a short while, although I always felt wretched afterwards." And ashamed. She'd only wished William were different and wondered what it would be like to be married to someone like Anton, but it still had been a step too far. It could so easily have led further. Further than she'd thought she could go.

She'd always looked down on people who had affairs. Now she knew how they happened. It wasn't one huge jump but a series of tiptoed steps and experimental slides.

"Thank you for trusting me with this," Naomi said. "I know it wouldn't have been easy to share it with anyone, least of all me."

A log shifted in the fire, and a flurry of sparks flew upwards. King Solomon had known what he was talking about when he likened lust to a fire. It started with a spark, but spread until it became a mighty conflagration that burned both parties and everyone near enough to its heat.

Blanche covered her face with her hands and wept. Oh, why did it have to hurt so much? The loss of friendship, the pain she'd inadvertently caused, and now the extra pain accompanying her choice to remain faithful to promises she'd made as a young woman. There were no guarantees William would change. No guarantees her future held anything more than long years committed to an unhappy, unfulfilling marriage. Long years stuck in the awkward state of separation where she would be considered neither married nor single.

Naomi's knees creaked as she got up. She shuffled across to Blanche and drew Blanche's head towards her. Naomi's stomach gurgled, a reminder of life. Blanche would live through this, but how long would the pain last? What if God asked her to hold on until death did them part?

She clasped Naomi around the waist. "Thanks for being here."

"Is everything sorted out with Anton?"

Blanche lifted her head. "I'll have to talk to him this week."

"Not on your own, I hope."

"No, I'll ask Helena to be in the room."

Blanche didn't trust herself to be alone with him. Anton was an honourable, godly man, but the two of them were only human.

CHAPTER 36

*T*he paintbrush glided over the surface as William added the final coat of varnish to the chest he'd made Blanche. He'd written his usual letter to Blanche this morning. She'd be disappointed, once again, by the lack of depth in his sharing, but he wasn't ready to tell her what was happening. First he needed a few more days to realign his life with much prayer, much Bible reading, and long talks with Reg. *Reg.* He got a lump in his throat thinking about the man.

William brushed one final fluid stroke, a relaxed movement from one side to the other. There. Who would have thought he could make something with his own hands?

He capped the tin and laid the brush in the turps. Then he washed his hands and whistled a tune he'd heard on the radio.

"You're sounding jaunty," Reg said as he crossed the workshop.

"Jaunty." William tried the word out on his tongue. "Not a word that's described me since I was five."

Reg peered at the surface of the wooden chest. "Your third layer looks great. All the hard work of sanding prepared the way."

"I find sanding relaxing."

Reg's eyes twinkled. "I wonder if God finds it so?"

William chuckled. "I doubt it. We wriggle and squirm and complain."

Reg had used many woodwork analogies in the last week. God had needed more than sandpaper to cut William down. He'd needed an axe. Hopefully sandpaper would be the only thing God would find necessary in the future.

"Ready for lunch?" Reg handed him a towel to dry his hands.

They crossed the lawn and settled on the verandah with their roast beef and salad rolls.

After they'd both eaten a few mouthfuls, Reg said, "Talk me through your choices."

A flicker of fear danced down William's spine. "Whatever I decide, there are major implications. I don't want to be pushed into too much public ministry too soon." Not before he'd read through the entire Bible and reconsidered what he believed. There were hundreds of lies he'd accepted, which must be recognised and dealt with.

"I'll need to resign from the radio programme. My absence should have already prepared the way. I don't see how it can continue with its current format and content. I no longer want to promote what I've been promoting."

"Could it be changed?"

"Probably. It could become more of an interview and testimony programme, but the station would have to rebrand and retitle the whole thing. They might not be willing to gamble on me again." William sighed. "Something new might be a total flop."

"Does failure still worry you?"

"Not like it once did." Would this sense of peace remain once he returned to the Sydney rat race?

"What about church?"

Church was what made it hard to get to sleep. It was hard to think straight when his whole lifestyle and reputation was bound up in the job.

"Reg, I need every prayer you can pray. Victory is a manifestation of what the old me was like. It's a corporation based on slick marketing, self-promotion, and sophisticated programming." Nausea slow-boiled in his stomach. "There isn't anything worth keeping."

William took another bite of his roll and chewed slowly. Reg followed his lead. One of the things he appreciated about Reg was his ability to be silent.

"The question is whether I'm the man to bring about the changes or if I should get out of the way."

"Are you thinking of resigning?"

William blew out a gusty breath. "It's a terrifying thought. I'm almost at retirement age. If I leave, I won't get another job. My name will be mud. No other church would touch me, and what else am I still qualified to do? No one hires people in their sixties."

"You mentioned many of your mistakes were because you cared more about your reputation than God's. Did I remember correctly?"

William nodded.

"We had a preacher here, years ago. I've forgotten his name, but I remember him saying we must only do things for the audience of one."

Audience of one. William was worried about the thousands of church members and listeners to his radio programme.

"Most of us worry about what others think, and it cripples us," Reg said.

Yes, crippled was an appropriate term. Crippled by an addiction to the approval of others. His father, his colleagues, his congregation. Crippled by his views of himself. The old him had been a hollow sham of a man. How might life be different if he lived for the only audience who mattered? If he lived for God's approval alone?

Reg offered him the fruit bowl, and William chose a Golden Delicious and cut a slice. If he lost his job, he'd have little to offer Blanche. They'd almost certainly have to sell their home, get a second-hand car, and simplify their lives. He wouldn't blame Blanche if she opted out.

"Do you think God might have a plan in this situation?"

William saluted Reg. "You always bring me back to the correct focus." He nodded emphatically. "I do trust he has a plan, but I'm not sure what I'm supposed to do."

"I always find it best to keep praying until I'm crystal clear what the next step is."

"I'm already praying hard." William said. "Perhaps the next step is for me to write to Blanche and tell her what's been happening." He stared at the ants working together to shift one of the crumbs from his lunch. Today his problems seemed as huge as the crumb was to the ants. Yet they were moving it, as they worked together. If only Blanche would be willing to stand beside him. Probably a vain hope, but he could ask, couldn't he?

"You know, your coming to Lord Howe was a miracle," Reg said.

William looked sideways at Reg and raised an eyebrow.

"Our denomination is strict about who we can ask to fill in. I never thought they'd allow you to come."

"How did that come about?"

"Well, you know we hadn't had anyone for over a year. That was one factor. The more I prayed, the more I became convinced we needed to wait. My burden to pray lifted on the morning your letter arrived, as if my prayers had already been answered."

"I know I used to think I was the answer to everyone's prayer." William chuckled. "But I don't see how I could have been thought to be the answer to yours." William ticked off on his fingers. "Firstly, I was the wrong denomination. Then, I'm a total city boy.

Thirdly—and the major reason—I didn't truly know the One I was supposed to teach about." That one reason alone should have slammed the door in his face.

"Well," Reg said. "I didn't know about the third reason, but the others were obvious from your letter and …"

Reg was astute. He'd probably read between all sorts of lines in the application. William hadn't been in a good place. Who knew what he'd written.

"And?"

"Well, it was obvious you were running from something."

"You haven't mentioned the fact I was arrogant and thought I was better than everyone on the island. I was hardly a sensible choice by anyone's standards." William stretched out his legs and put his hands behind his head. "So why did you accept me?"

"When I read your application I was convinced God wanted you to come. That you needed us, even if we didn't need you."

William laughed. The sound still amazed him with its lightness and joy. "It's like Psalm 139. God knows his plans for us before one of them comes to pass."

He sat up straight. "Let's talk about tomorrow's hike up Mount Gower with Davy and then about Sunday."

Reg laughed. "Prayer first, William. Prayer first."

How long was it going to take him to learn not to jump into action without prioritising prayer? He had too many bad habits to count, and they all needed rewiring. Prayer must be first. His first response to trouble, his first response to joy, His first response to any and every happening in his life. Prayer had to become as natural as breathing.

CHAPTER 37

*L*ast time Blanche had knocked on this door her stomach had skipped in excitement. This evening it fermented with fear. *Lord, help me to be kind, clear, and faithful. Remind me I'm your daughter and you're right here with me. Every minute, every breath, every step.*

The door opened, and Helena pecked her on the cheek. "I'll be praying the whole time you're talking. Remember we're your friends."

Helena led her into the living room where Anton was standing at the window. He turned when they entered, gave her a tight smile, and crossed the room towards her. Her heart squeezed. He'd never been anything other than a total gentleman.

"Helena is bringing tea." His voice cracked.

How Blanche hated this. She longed to put her arms around him and comfort him. *Help me, Lord.*

The chairs were arranged differently than last time, into a private nook but with a small table between them. Wise man.

Helena came back with tea and a homemade lemon slice. She poured them each a cup and withdrew to the bay window, where she sat down at her sewing machine with her back to them. She'd thought of everything. They had all the privacy they'd need, and the hum of the sewing machine would prevent Helena overhearing their conversation. What a friend.

Anton cleared his throat. "Are you okay?"

She clasped her hands and nodded. It wasn't true yet, but it would be. It had to be. God had promised to give her the strength and wisdom she needed, and Helena and Naomi were praying for her.

"I'm sorry I came to the shop the other day," Anton said. "I wanted to check you were okay." He rubbed his eyebrow. "It was selfish of me. I saw that the minute you looked at me."

Had he seen what she wanted to hide? That she cared—too much. She twirled the shiny rings on her finger. She had picked them up this morning.

Anton glanced down at her hands and winced. He knew what they meant as well as she did—just as his now-empty ring finger signalled he was ready for a new start.

"It's not going to be possible is it?" Anton said. "For us to remain friends?"

She shook her head, not trusting herself to speak. Hot, unshed tears pooled in her eyes, ready to betray her at any moment.

"I—we'll miss your friendship more than anything."

"Me too." Her voice wobbled. She reached for her neglected tea and took a long sip, and then another.

"I'm sorry for all the mix-ups. I would never have willingly hurt you." He brushed a finger over the corner of his eye.

She nodded again still unable to speak.

"This is the tough bit of following Jesus. Doing the right thing when we don't want to." He squared his shoulders. "Jesus knew what would happen when we met, yet somehow he's allowed it."

He looked across at her. "Even though we're hurting now, I want to say it has been my privilege to know you. You're a special person, a light that burns brightly. Don't let anyone tell you differently."

She swallowed the golf ball-sized lump in her throat. She wasn't going to say anything about him. It would cross a line, and there was no way she could do it without a deluge of tears.

"I admire you even more because of the choice you've made," he said.

Blanche covered her eyes with her hand and bit her lip.

"I asked Helena if she'd be willing to pray for you and William," Anton said. "Would that be okay?"

She couldn't have borne it if he'd prayed for her. It would have been as intimate as a kiss, but Helena was a good choice. Praying put Jesus where he should be, right in the middle of this whole mess.

"Helena," he called.

Helena jumped to her feet, came across and squeezed Blanche's hand quickly. Empathy shone in her eyes.

"This will be short, because it's all I can manage."

They stood equidistant from each other, heads bowed.

"Heavenly Father, thank you for loving and saving each of us. Thank you that when you ask us to do hard things you promise to give us the strength we need."

Oh, how she needed God's promised strength. Blanche wrapped her arms around her waist.

"You know Blanche desires to be reconciled to William. Please do a miracle and bring about the transformation needed." Helena's voice caught and then softened to a whisper. "In your name, Amen."

Anton put his arm around Helena. "Thank you," he whispered.

Then he turned towards Blanche. "Will you be okay driving home? Helena can take you and your car home if you need it."

That was Anton, consideration to the very end. She gave a crooked smile. "I'll probably have a good cry first, but I'll be fine."

He stooped to pick up the teapot. "Blessings on you, Blanche." He spun on his heel and walked out of the room.

It was done. Hard, so, so hard, but also surprisingly heart-warming. These two had been real friends. Friends who desired to honour Jesus more than follow their hearts' desires. Friends in a million.

Helena walked her to the door and hugged her. "If things change, call me. I'll miss you. Remember, I'm your friend even if we have to be apart."

Blanche squeezed her back. "I know, and I'm sorry we can't stay in touch. You know I'd love to remain your friend." The first of the tears she'd been holding back ran down her cheek. "Thanks for everything."

"You know we'll be praying often for you and William."

Blanche bit her lip. Anton and Helena had grit. Praying for God's will to be done and praying for William when both Helena and Anton had dreamed of another outcome. Blanche had known from the day they'd met that these two were special. That was one thing she'd got right. If only she hadn't got everything else in a tangled mess.

CHAPTER 38

*W*illiam ambled across his garden, through the gate, and towards his final lunch with Reg, Ivy, and Davy. It was a few days earlier than planned, but not as early as Victory's elders had wanted. This morning he'd preached his final sermon on the island.

His first Sunday, he'd despised the congregation. Looked down on their substandard singing and their lack of sophistication. Today he'd only seen friends—family, really.

He'd once thought he'd die of boredom here, but he was beginning to understand how they could love this speck on the map. The beauty, the birds, the people. This place would always be special to him.

He clattered up the stairs, whistling. He hoped he'd caught Reg's good habits, like how much he loved and studied the Bible and the way he prayed over everything. Every little thing. Things William had once thought too trivial to bring to God's attention.

The door was open, and he walked in.

To a crowd, clapping.

It was a flea to an elephant comparison with the thunder of

applause he'd often heard at Victory, but the warmth on everyone's faces made the difference.

"Don't think you're the only one we do this for." Jock winked. "We always have a potluck when interim pastors leave."

Trust Jock to bring him back to earth. Jock and various others had been his teachers when he'd had no clue what to do. Pastoral visits might be his new favourite activity, especially hearing how people came to know Jesus. It didn't make any difference whether they were dramatic stories like his own, or more mundane stories of becoming Christians at the knees of their mother or father.

"Let's pray," Reg shouted over the hubbub. "Then we can eat."

William would miss this simplicity back at Victory. Church dinners had become impossible once they'd passed three hundred members. Even before three hundred members, their dinners had to be formal affairs, yet another occasion to show off their 'success'. Victory had never had a simple potluck meal.

The oldest church members sat at the dining table, and he, Reg, and Ivy served them. Then they went with the rest to the serving table and lined up.

"Make sure you get a scoop of this creamy scalloped potato. My Betty makes it, and it's the best on the island," Stan said. William helped himself and had to sample everyone else's specialities too. Soon he was stuffed tighter than the local butcher's sausages.

Once the dishes were cleared from the tables and stacked in the kitchen, Reg clapped his hands. "If everyone would take a seat, we're going to let William say a few words. Then we've got a gift for him and I'll close in prayer."

"No more sermons, young William," Jock called.

William laughed. "I'll do my best not to put you to sleep."

"You had us awake this morning. Your sermons have improved every week."

"Hear, hear," Stan said with the loudness of someone hard of hearing.

The new sermon style Reg had taught him fed his soul so much more than his previous way of preaching. Being forced to preach on every passage in a book meant he had to wrestle through it, whether he wanted to or not. When he'd only preached his favourite passages he could cruise on autopilot. Reg's way was a discipline where he had to dredge the ocean floor instead of skimming the surface like a catamaran.

Someone coughed and William's face warmed. "Missed my cue. I was so busy thinking how much I'll miss all of you, I forgot you're waiting for me to speak."

A wave of friendly laughs rolled around the room.

"One of the things I'll miss most is hearing Reg read the Bible. If I can read it half as well as he does, I'll be content." William looked around at the individual faces. "I'll miss hearing all your stories and how God has answered your prayers. Thank you for teaching me how to do pastoral visits."

"Yes, you didn't seem too sure of yourself when you visited me," Jock said, ever irrepressible.

"My stomach will miss Ivy's cooking, and my heart will miss Davy's questions and all the snorkelling and hikes we did. Davy, thank you for showing me your magical kingdom."

Was he going to stick with politely saying thank you or should he say something more? Something more personal? *What do you want me to do, Lord?*

How would he have the courage to speak to the throngs at Victory if he didn't dare to speak to the few gathered here?

He took a deep breath and let his shoulders relax. "Most of you don't know how I ended up here. I was running away from my grief at the death of my daughter." Blanche had told him the more she talked about Esther the easier it became. He'd have to let her know she'd been right.

He looked up. Everyone was watching him, even Davy from his spot on the floor.

"My daughter loved Jesus, and her greatest fear was that I didn't. She'd tasted God's living water and could recognise someone who wasn't drinking it."

Reg's gaze was fixed on him. He gave a tiny nod as though to let William know he wasn't alone.

"Someone can sit all their lives in church and even be the pastor of a church and not know Jesus. For too many years, I was like Simon the sorcerer." He'd preached on the passage this morning. "I wanted the power and influence Jesus gave but didn't want Jesus himself. My own pride got in the way. I didn't want to stand in God's light because I was afraid of what I'd see."

He smiled towards Reg and Davy. "I'll be forever grateful to Davy and Reg. Davy asked questions and made me think." He crouched down to the boy's level. "Did you know someone your age could teach an adult?"

Davy shook his head.

"Well, you did." William ruffled Davy's hair. "Thank you." He stood up.

"And Reg introduced me to the Bible in a way I'd never experienced before. Next week, Reg will preach about a divine appointment between Philip and the treasurer of Ethiopia. Well, coming to Lord Howe was a series of divine appointments for me. I didn't see it at first." He hadn't seen anything at first. "But I can now." He looked around the room, meeting each person's eye. "Thank you for showing me that Jesus has his servants everywhere. If you're like me and have known about Jesus but never accepted him yourself, don't let it rest. Talk to someone." He smiled broadly. "God bless you all."

Thank you, Jesus, for giving me courage to speak your truth.

"Now we have a gift for you," Reg said. "It wasn't my idea at all." He put his hand on Davy's shoulder who was now standing beside him. "It was all Davy's idea. He wanted to make something for you."

Davy reached behind himself and picked up the box he'd been hiding.

"It's his first real woodworking project."

Davy flushed. "Gramps did the hardest part of it."

"But it was your idea and choice of design. Go on, Davy, hand it over."

Davy came towards him with the box, his chest puffed out.

William took the box and hefted its weight. "Can I open it now?"

"Davy might pop in frustration if you don't."

He opened the box, taking his time in case it was fragile. Two identical-sized objects were inside. He unwrapped the newspaper and gasped.

"It's a pair of bookends for all those books you read," Davy burst out, hopping in excitement.

It was a pair of bookends all right. Carved with an anchor on each—the anchor he'd seen Reg whittling the day after his rescue. William put the box on the floor and held up one of the bookends for everyone to see.

Everyone oohed and ahhed, and Davy went beet red.

"Come here, you," William said, his voice rough as he reached to hug him.

"You don't have to hug me you know." Davy smelled of the grass he'd been doing cartwheels in after church.

William grinned. "I know, but I want to."

Davy hugged him back so hard, everyone laughed. How he'd miss the boy. William broke off the hug and rubbed his eyes. He'd have to come back and visit Davy and the others soon. As soon as possible.

CHAPTER 39

$\mathcal{T}$he letter was for her, Blanche Macdonald, with the correct address, but other words were scrawled on the envelope.

Very important! DNTA.

Blanche raised an eyebrow. The letters were William's code for notes he'd left on the phone table. Do Not Throw Away. Had he suspected she might be tempted to treat his letters with disdain? Perhaps he was getting more sensitive to her feelings. She was tired of praying. If it had been up to her, she would have stopped ages ago, but she couldn't stop while Naomi pressed on. Blanche's heart was wrung out from crying at home and trying not to cry at work.

Helena hadn't come to the final class, but she'd sent a note.

My sister, keep trusting Jesus. We're doing the same.

There'd be no more communication. Helena and Anton were wise enough to know any contact hurt and made it harder for her to stick to her decision.

Blanche walked back into the house, holding William's letter. What was so important to William now? Was it another scheme, another plan? Maybe he'd written a book and wanted her to clap and cheer and tell him he was wonderful. Well, he'd be waiting a long time.

She'd been anticipating some new enthusiasm for a while. All that scenery and quietness could have driven him mad or led to all sorts of new projects. Her shoulders slumped. If wooing her back was on his to-do list, she'd shriek and refuse to participate.

She went into her bedroom, sat in the chair next to her bed, and opened the envelope with a sigh.

DEAREST BLANCHE,
ARE YOU SITTING DOWN? THIS WILL BE A LONG LETTER.

Up until now, William's letters had been a regulation two pages, as though he'd decided what was appropriate and wrote no more and no less. She moistened her thumb and counted the pages. Five. An essay. Probably full of enthusiasms that excluded her.

LET ME START WITH THE MOST IMPORTANT THING FIRST. I'M SORRY. SORRY FOR EVERYTHING.

Her mouth dropped open. She had never heard sorry cross his

lips. She'd doubted his mouth and tongue even knew how to form the word.

THIS LETTER IS NEVER GOING TO BE ABLE TO CONTAIN ALL THE THINGS I NEED TO SAY SORRY FOR. I HOPE TO DO THAT IN PERSON. LET ME WRITE THE BIG ONES. SORRY FOR TREATING YOU LIKE YOU HAD NO MIND OF YOUR OWN. SORRY FOR EXPECTING YOU TO SIMPLY BE MY CHEERLEADER AND BACK-UP. SORRY FOR NEVER ALLOWING YOU TO BE THE PERSON GOD CREATED YOU TO BE.

Blanche scratched her ear. Was this one more scheme to get his own way?

SORRY FOR HOW I TREATED ESTHER AND RACHEL AND FOR BLACKENING MY MOTHER'S NAME BECAUSE I DIDN'T WANT TO HEAR THE TRUTH. THERE HAS BEEN A TRUCKLOAD OF TRUTHS I HAVEN'T WANTED TO HEAR. SORRY IS VASTLY INADEQUATE.

Could he possibly be genuine? Naomi had been praying for these changes for forty years, but had Blanche actually expected the prayers to be answered? She laughed wryly. She was like Rhoda and the other believers in Acts, praying for Peter to be released from prison yet not trusting their own eyes when he turned up on the doorstep. What could possibly have happened to William to make him see his own sin and say sorry?

I'LL UNDERSTAND IF YOU'RE SCEPTICAL. I WOULD BE. I NEVER REALLY BELIEVED IN TRANSFORMED LIVES. I BELIEVED IN MIRACULOUS HEALINGS AND GOD CHANGING OTHERS, BUT NEVER SAW THAT I WAS THE ONE WHO MOST NEEDED TO CHANGE. I APOLOGISE FOR MY BLINDNESS. NO, I WASN'T MERELY BLIND. I WAS DEAD. DEAD TO ALL LIFE AND TRUTH.

She turned the page with trembling fingers. Could what they'd been praying for have happened? How? If the death of a daughter hadn't made him see himself clearly, what tsunami had God used?

BUT!!!

This was new. Despite William's marketing background, he despised those who wrote in capitals and exclamation marks.

BUT GOD. HE DIDN'T GIVE UP ON ME. EVEN THOUGH I HAD THE STUBBORNNESS OF PHARAOH, THE PRIDE OF NEBUCHADNEZZAR, AND THE RUNNING ABILITY OF JONAH, GOD REACHED DOWN AND SAVED ME. THREE TUESDAY EVENINGS AGO.

THAT MIGHT BE THE TIME OF MY SALVATION, BUT I NEARLY DIDN'T LIVE TO SEE IT. EARLY MONDAY MORNING, AFTER A SLEEPLESS NIGHT, I FINALLY READ THE LETTER ESTHER WROTE TO ME. DID YOU KNOW SHE'D WRITTEN?

She and Naomi had been puzzled about why William had never mentioned receiving or reading Esther's letter. They'd wondered if it had been lost, for how could someone read one of Esther's letters and not be moved?

I DIDN'T KNOW IT WAS FROM ESTHER BECAUSE THE WRITING WAS MUM'S. I DIDN'T WANT TO READ ANY LETTER FROM MUM, SO I'D BURIED IT IN MY SUITCASE.

GOD WOULDN'T LET ME FORGET IT, AND WHEN I FINALLY READ IT, IT WAS LIKE RECEIVING A MESSAGE FROM BEYOND THE GRAVE. LIKE A NUCLEAR BOMB HAD EXPLODED IN MY HEART. I SAW WHO I WAS, AND I HATED MYSELF. ALL I WANTED TO DO WAS END IT AND SET YOU FREE OF THE BURDEN OF BEING MY WIFE.

No, no, no. Bile surged in her throat. "Father, forgive me for wanting William to get out of my life," Blanche whispered. "For wanting my situation to work out like a happily-ever-after novel. All so that my life would be less painful and difficult." She turned over another page.

SO I WENT DOWN TO THE SHORE AND STARTED SWIMMING FOR THE HORIZON.

Blanche covered her mouth with her hand. *Oh, William.* How could her supremely confident husband have come to this? With a mix of horror and awe she read how God had stopped him and saved his life. By the time she read about how Reg had led him to Jesus' feet she was crying. She sobbed and held the letter away from her to avoid smearing it with her tears.

"Blanche, are you okay?" Naomi called from outside in the

corridor.

"I'm fine," Blanche said. "Come in."

The doorknob turned and Naomi entered.

"Come and sit on the chair." Blanche stood and moved across to the bed. "It's a letter from William. You're going to be crying soon."

"Good tears or bad?" Naomi said seating herself.

"The best." Blanche handed the pages over to Naomi. "It'll be easier if you read it yourself."

She sat and watched Naomi read. Expressions chased across her face like a videotape on fast-forward. Sadness to gladness to joy. Her tears started Blanche off again, and she reached for the tissue box.

Naomi looked up, her face damp but shining. "Do you remember which morning I woke up early?"

"No. Too much has happened since." Too many painful decisions resulting in tough days and even tougher nights.

"It was that Monday morning. The morning that William decided to end his life."

Blanche put her hand to her chest. What if Naomi hadn't woken, hadn't prayed? Might the outcome have been different?

Naomi tapped the pages in front of her. "Are you going to do what he asks in his postscript?"

Blanche peered at the postscript again. William was asking something which might be impossible. She shrugged. "I don't know if I have the courage."

"Would you be willing to tell the other ladies what's happening and get them to pray?"

"Of course. I'm going to need all of their prayers. Our get-together will be the day William returns. It gives me time to pray first."

"And you know I'll be praying."

Blanche laid a hand on Naomi's arm. "That's a given." Naomi had nearly worn her knees out over the years.

CHAPTER 40

*D*id the congregation notice something different about Victory Church that Sunday morning? Could they see William's fear, or was his lack of confidence hidden?

Gone were the usual musical flourishes designed to manipulate people's emotions. Gone was the proclamation of his full name and title. Earlier in the morning, William had searched through his extensive wardrobe. He'd found his first suit right at the back, forgotten. The suit he'd worn at his marriage and ordination. Wearing it seemed appropriate.

Now William stood in the pulpit, paused out of long habit, and bent his head. *Give me courage, Lord.*

He lifted his head and took a mouthful of water from the glass under the pulpit. "What do you see when I stand here, week after week? Do you see the successful image I've worked hard to portray, or are you more perceptive? Are you able to see as I could not? As I dared not? Do you see William Macdonald, suave and sophisticated, but with fathomless, subterranean caverns of fear and insecurity in my soul?"

Even from the stage, William heard gasps and stifled cries of "What?"

"My daughter wrote to me before she died of cancer. Due to a great deal of fear on my part, I didn't read her letter until a couple of weeks ago. Her letter was tender but hard-hitting. She was unwilling to go to be with Jesus without making sure I'd one day be with him too. God spoke to me through her, and I began to see into the depths of my caverns. It was not a pretty sight. Things I'd kept hidden, even from myself, spilled out. I've talked about honouring Jesus, but I have only honoured myself. Along the way, I've led others astray by being a pretentious preacher of pretty nothings."

There was frantic movement down the side aisles as several of the church elders headed for the front. William held up his hand. "Don't come and shut me up. I've not gone mad. For each of your own souls' sakes, you must listen." Several of the elders subsided into empty seats while others were pulled down by members of the congregation. William gripped the pulpit, knuckles white under the lights, praying for courage.

"Today, I stand before you a broken man. What would you think of a man who didn't attend his own daughter's funeral? Who left her to die without him? A man who yelled at his own wife for going where he should have been?"

Each phrase caught in his throat but once the words were out in the light, he felt freer.

"How could someone do such a thing, you might ask?" William stared right up to the top corner of the auditorium. "The roots of my failure stretch back many years. I started out eager to please God, but it all seemed too difficult. I allowed myself to be influenced by people who suggested shortcuts to success. Those men showed me ways to achieve my ambitions. Soon God's ways looked outdated."

If only he could cut bits out of his story, but if he did, past sin would keep him trapped. "My mother tried to warn me, so I cut her out of my life—for over thirty years. I blackened her name to keep my family away from her."

"I studied techniques to make me look and sound good. Sadly, people do listen more to someone who looks the part. And that's what I was playing—a part." He shook his head. "Even with my lovely wife. I didn't build her up and allow her to become the woman she was created to be."

William scrutinised the listeners. "I didn't want anything to mar my fantasy of the ideal family. After all, my message promised that God blesses his followers with visible gifts of health and wealth. I could not allow you to see me as less than what I preached."

Usually his pauses were for added effect. Today, they were to give him time for desperate prayers. "My fantasy of an ideal family was just that, a fantasy. For my pride had led me even further into error." His voice cracked. Could he keep going? His sin was not a single grain of sand but a vast desert.

"Do you remember I have an older daughter? Rachel couldn't stomach my Jesus, so she ran away."

William hung his head. "I pretended … no, I lied and said she'd gone to live and work overseas. Instead, she was lost to us for nearly twenty-five years. She rejected my Jesus but didn't know there was a real Jesus who loved her. She certainly never met Jesus in my house. I forbade Blanche from mentioning her name to anyone. After all, I had my image to protect." William mocked the words he'd once believed. "Then I lied to Esther, so she never knew she had a sister. I wish this was the end of the story, but it isn't."

William took another sip of water. "Pride and ambition are poor masters. By the time Esther discovered she had cancer, I'd already believed my own message. So I led you in prayers telling God what to do. How incredibly arrogant. When Esther wasn't healed, I didn't consider my thinking might be wrong. Rather, I castigated Esther for her lack of faith." He hung his head.

Was anyone listening out there, beyond the glare of the lights? It didn't matter. If the audience of one was pleased, he was more than enough. "But Jesus never abandoned my Esther. He sent a faithful witness called Joy Wong. Someone I would have looked down on— a hospital cleaner. Joy's words made Esther angry at first, but they forced her back to God's Word. She discovered Jesus promised a steep and narrow way, not a casual stroll along an easy path. He promised a cross and persecution to his followers, not a life of luxury and ease. Esther's life was transformed as she read the Bible properly."

William sighed. "To say I didn't appreciate her sharing what she was learning is an understatement. I rushed to raise walls of self-protection. Finally, the only way I could stop her talking was to give her an ultimatum—shut up or leave. Esther followed her conscience and left."

He paused. "I guess her growing joy and peace condemned me. Increasingly, I couldn't bear to be near her. I tried to force Blanche to cut herself off from Esther too. But thank the Lord, Blanche dared to follow her conscience and was there at Esther's side when she was needed."

His breath caught in his throat as tears streamed down his face. "I'm not worthy of Blanche. I may have lost her forever."

He choked and hung his head. As he struggled to gain control he heard a murmur in the crowd. The murmur grew in volume until he could no longer ignore it. He lifted his head. Someone was walking down the main aisle. Blanche. He swallowed and his vision blurred with tears. The last time he'd seen her walk down the centre aisle she was dressed in white. She was the most beautiful sight he'd seen in months. She walked up the stage steps and took his hand.

He'd asked her to come, but he'd never believed she would. Not after the way he'd treated her. Yet here she was, placing her hand in his. He squeezed her hand and held on, keeping his eyes staring at the floor. How could he look at her?

"William," she whispered.

He looked up at her. Blanche's eyes swam with tears. He swallowed again, and his stomach rolled. Precious, wonderful woman, standing here with him.

Blanche squeezed his hand and then leaned forward to adjust the microphone down to her height. She cleared her throat. "I've never been prouder of my husband than I am at this moment."

William gulped through his tears. What a woman he'd married. She mirrored Jesus in ways he didn't.

Still clutching Blanche's hand, he stepped towards the microphone again, tilting it up. "God's word says, 'Be sure your sin will find you out.' Well, mine has. It has shown me to be a sham. A tree without fruit. A cloud without rain. A spring without water. Offering nothing of any use to anyone."

A refreshing breeze seemed to blow through his heart. He was more alive than he'd been in years, like a hermit crab shedding its old, too-tight shell.

"I have seriously misled you all. A pastor should protect his sheep and be willing to die for them. Instead, I've been a false shepherd, exploiting you for my own ambition and pride."

His legs still trembled, but it no longer mattered what anyone else thought about him. Not the listeners today or those who would hear the gossip tomorrow. He had his inward eyes fixed on the one audience that mattered. At last.

"What I did to my family and you feels unforgivable, and for this I am truly sorry, but it is nothing compared to how I treated Jesus. I claimed to love him, but I only loved myself." His voice wobbled. He stopped and he took a deep breath. Blanche gently released his hand and stood back behind him. "I claimed to honour Jesus, but I dragged his name in the mud. I spat at him and crucified him every day with the things I said and did. I'm not even worthy to look at him."

He gripped the side of the pulpit, gathering his strength to finish what he needed to say. "Esther's letter spoke the truth in love, and it was a truth I almost couldn't bear to hear, but oh, how I needed to. Her precious heavenly Father has poured grace over our family, but for a long time it looked like I was going to miss out. What an appalling tragedy. It took the death of my daughter and coming face to face with my own failures to force me to wake up to my sin."

William raised his head and looked all around the auditorium. "No matter who we are, we are not worthy of anything but God's judgment. This is the message I should have been preaching all these years. 'There is no one righteous, not even one. There is no one who seeks God ... for all,' yes every one of us, 'have sinned and fallen short of God's glorious standards.'"

Reg would have said the words better, but he trusted God would enable his word to sink into their hearts. "Jesus died for us, his enemies. Unbelievable. The King of glory would die to save you and me. Such grace, such marvellous grace."

His voice began to crescendo. "There is no other name by which we can be saved. None, not one. A few weeks ago, Jesus saved me— William Macdonald—a sinner beyond measure. I intend to share one message for the rest of my life. Jesus is the only way. The only truth. The only life."

William gripped the pulpit and took a huge breath. "I will be resigning, effective immediately. Please choose a faithful pastor who will teach you the Lord's way. Perhaps one day, when I have learned what the Lord has to teach me, I'll serve here again."

He bowed his head for a long moment of silence, then turned towards Blanche and offered her his hand. And, oh joy, she took it. Hand in hand, they walked slowly up the main aisle.

Many of the congregation looked away. It hurt, but who could blame them? A few offered tentative smiles. Bless them. He clutched Blanche's hand. He was never going to let go of her again.

Jesus had brought him through deep waters. He wasn't drowning, but he was a long way from the shallows. There was more

work ahead of him—with Blanche, with his mother, with Rachel—
and no guarantees anyone would forgive him.

William raised Blanche's hand to his mouth and kissed it. Tears
spilled down her cheeks.

He'd relied on himself and behaved like he was the saviour of
the world for far too long. The scriptures were clear—there was
only one saviour. Only Jesus had the power to save. Only Jesus was
worthy of his praise and worship. Only Jesus could take him at his
lowest moment and raise him to life again.

His immediate future might be tough and certainly financially
less comfortable, but he'd place everything in Jesus' hands. His sin
and his failures, his past and his future.

He was going to trust Jesus. Following step by step wherever
Jesus led, right to the end of his earthly journey.

STORYTELLER FRIENDS

Becoming a **storyteller friend** will ensure you don't miss out on new books, deals and behind the scenes book news. Once you're signed up, check your junk mail or the 'promotions' folder (gmail addresses) for the confirmation email. This two-stage process ensures only true storyteller friends can join.

Facebook: As well as a public author page, I also have a VIP group which you need to ask permission to join.

www.storytellerchristine.com

Pinterest – many resources related to Bible storytelling and my books.

BookBub - allows you to see my top book recommendations and be alerted to any new releases and special deals. It is free to join.

ENJOYED GRACE IN DEEP WATERS?

Reviews sell books.

As this book is independently published, the only way it will be discovered by readers is if you get excited about it. Online reviews are one way to share your enthusiasm.

How to write a review – easy as 1-2-3

1. A few sentences about why you liked the book.
2. Perhaps one sentence about what kinds of people might like the book.
3. Upload a review - the same review can be used on each site. Possible places are Amazon, Goodreads, Bookbub, Kobo and Koorong (for Australians).
4. If you loved the book please also share your review on your personal social media, or feel free to tell others about it in any context.

NON-FICTION BY CHRISTINE DILLON

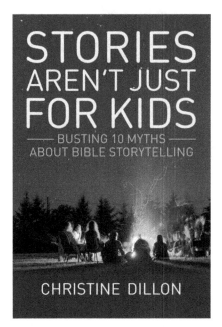

*Stories Aren't Just For Kids: Busting 10 Myths About Bible
Storytelling (2017). Free to subscribers and packed with testimonies
to get you excited about the potential of Bible storytelling.*

NON-FICTION BY CHRISTINE DILLON

1-2-1 Discipleship: Helping One Another Grow Spiritually
(Christian Focus, Ross-shire, Scotland, 2009).

Telling The Gospel Through Story: Evangelism That Keeps Hearers
Wanting More (IVP, Downer's Grove, Illinois, 2012).

All these books are available in Chinese too.

ACKNOWLEDGMENTS

People often ask me if writing gets easier. I'm not sure it does. Every book has its challenges. The idea for my first book (which became two books) was essentially given to me during a prayer day. This third book was a new story and it took a long time to come together. I struggled too to write such a difficult character as William. I am grateful that our God is a God of miracles. The God who could change a William ... or Jacob, or Peter or Paul ... can change us too.

One thing that gets easier is learning to work as a team. The first novel I stumbled through finding editors, cover designer, beta readers, proofreaders (those with 'eagle eyes' and a low tolerance for incorrect commas, spelling ...) and a launch team who did online reviews and raved about the book to their friends.

I am thankful that God led me to the right editors early on in this journey. Cecily Paterson is the character and dialogue queen. She keeps my stories real with her comments, "Nah, that doesn't work."

Iola Goulton is the queen of making sure that grammar, facts and many other things are correct. Both women are thoroughly professional but also people who care about the story. There is prayer and friendship in the mix too and they take the time to teach me. I keep hoping that the next book will require less editing but it seems that whenever I learn how to deal with one issue, another raises its head.

Joy Lankshear, thank you for another stunning book cover. I love looking at them as a set. Thank you for your friendship, generosity, and model of faithful service to our King.

The three people above don't see the book until a group of beta readers have read and made comments and suggestions. Thank you to Kate B, Debbie F, Sarah L, Jane P, Lizzie R, Claire U and Kristen Y. Thank you for being part of the team. We're learning how to do this. Having one google document allowed us to learn from each other.

The proofreaders have to work under a tighter time pressure. Thank you Kate B, Jane C, Katie D, Sarah L, Joy M, Suzanne R, Lizzie R, and Kim W. Each person has a different speciality and together it works.

Thank you too to the book boosters who write early reviews and tell their friends. I won't mention each of you but you know who you are.

Molly Whitelaw gave me a quiet place looking out on her garden to do the main editing and rewriting. Thank you for understanding how important that was and for being my greatest British fan. You single-handedly provide most of the UK sales. Let's pray that spreads.

As I commented last time, any miracles in these stories are based on real events. The prayer miracle in chapter 30 has happened numerous times within our family and among colleagues. The miracle in chapter 31 I've heard in various people's testimonies. Not exactly the same but close enough to for me to feel confident to use a similar story in this novel. I love the way that

God deals with each person differently and uses many people as 'links in the chain' of his purposes for our lives.

I am so grateful to be an author who is a Christian. I have a huge resource that non-Christian authors don't. Thank you to the people who pray for me as an author and for the books themselves. There are numerous times that I question why I'm putting myself through the stress and strain (I'm not one of those 'I've always wanted to write' people). Many times I've been unable to move forward. God has worked through your prayers to keep me going. So often you'll let me know you're praying, or send me a little encouragement, or tell me about someone who has been helped by one of my books. Thank you.

I am grateful too that my leaders have recognised that my writing is 'multiplying disciples one story at a time' and have now allowed writing to be part of my job description. This has been a tremendous encouragement and lessening of my load. Thank you.

Now on to the next. May each book bring Jesus the honour he deserves.

To understand more of the Bible's grand story go to
www.storyingthescriptures.com

Discussion Guide

There are discussion guides for each of the novels at www.storytellerchristine.com.

ABOUT THE AUTHOR

Christine has worked in Taiwan, with OMF International, since 1999.

It's best not to ask Christine, "Where are you from?" She's a missionary kid who isn't sure if she should say her passport country (Australia) or her Dad's country (New Zealand) or where she's spent most of her life (Asia - Taiwan, Malaysia and the Philippines).

Christine used to be a physiotherapist, but now writes 'storyteller' on airport forms. She spends most of her time either telling Bible stories or training others to do so.

In her spare time, Christine loves all things active – hiking, cycling, swimming, snorkelling. But she also likes reading and genealogical research.

Connect with Christine
www.storytellerchristine.com/

CPSIA information can be obtained
at www.ICGtesting.com
Printed in the USA
LVHW010445211221
706819LV00010B/809